U0127779

经典英文影视派对

别怀疑，这里有人生百味

CLASSIC TV SERIES AND MOVIE SHOWS OF LIFE KALEIDOSCOPE

顾 爽◎编译

陕西师范大学出版总社有限公司
SHAANXI NORMAL UNIVERSITY GENERAL PUBLISHING HOUSE CO., LTD.

图书代号 SK10N1090

图书在版编目（CIP）数据

经典英文影视派对：别怀疑，这里有人生百味：英汉对照/顾爽编译. —西安：陕西师范大学出版总社有限公司，2012.4

ISBN 978-7-5613-5321-9

Ⅰ.①经… Ⅱ.①顾… Ⅲ.①英语—汉语—对照读物②电影—简介—世界 Ⅳ.①H319.4：J

中国版本国书馆 CIP 数据核字（2010）第 214355 号

经典英文影视派对：别怀疑，这里有人生百味

顾 爽 编译

责任编辑 曾学民
责任校对 马芳芳
封面设计 杜 帅
出版发行 陕西师范大学出版总社有限公司
社　　址 西安市长安南路 199 号 邮编 710062
网　　址 http://www.snupg.com
经　　销 新华书店
印　　刷 香河县宏润印刷有限公司
开　　本 710mm×1000mm 1/16
印　　张 17
字　　数 200 千字
版　　次 2012 年 4 月第 1 版
印　　次 2012 年 4 月第 1 次印刷
书　　号 ISBN 978-7-5613-5321-9
定　　价 32.00 元

前 言

Humanities in English

培养人文素质 成就国际通才

若想精通一门语言，没有对其文化背景的深入了解恐怕永远难登大雅之堂。在全球化日益成为国际主流的今天，英语作为西方文化头牌语言的重要性已日益凸显——今日世界，恐怕在地球上的任何角落人们都可以用英语问路、用英语聊天、用英语购物、用英语交友、用英语在跨文化间作深度交流。

正如许多西方人热切地想了解中国文化一样，中国的英语学习及爱好者对西方文化及人文的了解也处于热切的需求当中。是的，如果对西方的历史、文学、艺术、宗教、哲学没有一个最基本的了解，就连看好莱坞大片都会成为一个问题；而西方文化贡献给社会的普世价值恰恰是它深厚的人文传统及“民主、自由、博爱”等现代理念，不了解这些，则与任何稍有层次和品位的西方人的交流都将难以顺畅。

此外，国内的英语学习者如再停留在日常生活的English In General 的层次上，必将难以适应深度沟通和交流的需要，因此，对专业英语及文化背景的深入了解和学习将是提升英语能力的必由之路。有鉴于此，本套丛书为读者奉上原汁原味的人文阅读精华，其或选

自原典正文、或选自专业教材、或选自网络热贴，由精研此业者掇菁撷华，辑录成册，希望能帮助读者在学习英语的同时又能品位西方文化的独特魅力。在辑录过程中，我们力求摒弃学校教育的僵硬和枯燥，代之以更加生动、更加全面的通识阅读范本。我们写历史，致力于拨开其厚重压抑而倾向于读者感兴趣的文化、建筑、艺术、风俗等人文知识；我们写文学，力求抛开一般文学史纲目划分的束缚而代之以切合各国风情又适合读者阅读的脉络。

读万卷书行万里路，在我们无法踏上万里之路以愉耳目的时候，我们可以用阅读来滋养心灵，拓展人生版图。于某一日午后，抛开世俗的纷扰，挑一静谧之处，一杯香茗，几卷书册，品文化，长知识，学英语，在书页和文字之间触摸大千世界的真谛，在阅读中将知识内化成自己的修养，人生至乐。

文化共语言同飞，思想与阅读共舞。让我们的目光穿越时光、穿越语言，在原汁原味的英语阅读中品位人类文明共有的人文素质、人文素养、人文情怀、人文理念……并在此过程中成就自己的文化修养及完美人生。

目 录

Humanities in English

Contents

一、为信仰而战，捍卫共同的家园 ——《阿凡达》

影片简介：

未来世界中，人类为了获取潘多拉星球上的资源而启动了“阿凡达”计划，目的是要说服纳威人离开他们的家园，从而人类便可以开采那里的矿产资源。因伤而下肢瘫痪的退伍士兵杰克·萨利代替哥哥来执行这个任务，然而在与纳威人的接触中，他逐渐了解到了纳威人的生活信仰，同时也爱上了美丽的纳威公主娜蒂瑞。然而公司及军方的高层对说服的方法已经失去了耐心，他们决意以武力驱赶纳威人。在这关键的时刻，杰克该何去何从……

经典对白(一)

Encounter 偶遇

杰克在森林里迷了路，更糟的是他受到了猛兽的袭击。

这时，纳威公主娜蒂瑞出现并救了他，杰克对她充满了感激之情……

Jake: Look, I know you probably don't understand this, but thank you. Thank yo
That was pretty **impressive**[1]. I would have been **screwed**[2] if you hadn't **com
along**[3]. It was...Hey, wait a second. Hey, where're you going? **Wait up**[4]!
Just...Hey, slow down. Look, wait up, I just wanted to say thanks for killir
those things. Damn!

Neytiri: Don't thank. You don't thank for this. This is sad. Very sad only!

Jake: Okay. Okay. I'm sorry. Whatever I did, I'm sorry.

Neytiri: All this is your fault. They did not need to die.

Jake: My fault? They **attacked**[5] me, how am I the bad guy?

Neytiri: Your fault!

Jake: Hey, whoo.

Neytiri: Your fault!

Jake: Easy.

Neytiri: You're like a baby, making noise, don't know what to do.

Jake: Easy. Fine. Fine. If you love your little forest friends, why not let them jus
kill my ass? What's the thinking?

Neytiri: Why save you?

Jake: Yeah, why save me?

Neytiri: You have a strong heart. No fear. But stupid, **ignorant**[6] like a child.

Jake: Well, if I'm like a child, then eh...look, maybe you should teach me.

Neytiri: Sky people can not learn, you do not see.

1 impressive *adj.* 令人印象深刻的，令人钦佩的
2 screw *v.* 用螺丝旋拧，这里是"杀死"的意思
3 come along 出现，发生，进展
4 wait up 等候
5 attack *v.* 袭击
6 ignorant *adj.* 无知的

Jake: Teach me how to see.

Neytiri: No one can teach you to see.

Jake: Come on, can't we talk? Where did you learn to speak English? Dr. Augustine's school?

Neytiri: You're like a baby.

Jake: I need your help.

Neytiri: You should not be here.

Jake: Okay, take me with you.

Neytiri: No! Go back.

Jake: No.

Neytiri: Go back.

Jake: What...What are they?

Neytiri: Seeds of the **sacred**[7] tree. Very pure **spirits**[8].

Jake: What was that all about?

Neytiri: Come. Come.

Jake: Where are we going?

Neytiri: Come.

Jake: What's you name?

杰　克: 听着，你也许不明白我在说什么，不过，很感谢你。谢谢。刚刚你真勇猛，要不是你来帮我，我可能就死掉了。真是……嘿，等等，嘿，你要去哪儿？等一下，就一会儿……嘿，慢点儿。嘿，我只是想感谢你杀了那些怪物……啊，该死！

娜蒂瑞: 别说感谢，这事儿可不值得感谢。这事儿只会令人伤心，非常伤心！

杰　克: 好吧，对不起。我为我的所作所为感到抱歉。

7 sacred *adj.* 神圣的

8 spirit *n.* 精神，灵魂

娜蒂瑞:这都是你的错,它们本可以好好活着的。

杰　克:怎么是我的错?是它们来攻击我,为什么我却成了坏人?

娜蒂瑞:就是你的错!

杰　克:嘿,呜!

娜蒂瑞:你的错!

杰　克:别激动。

娜蒂瑞:你像个小孩儿似的乱嚷嚷,不知道该做些什么。

杰　克:冷静。好吧,好吧,如果你珍爱你那些森林里的小朋友,为什么不让它们直接杀了我呢?你是怎么想的?

娜蒂瑞:是问我为什么救你吗?

杰　克:是的,为什么救我呢?

娜蒂瑞:因为你内心坚强,无所畏惧,但你却蠢得很,像孩子一样无知。

杰　克:好吧,要是我像个小孩儿的话,那么,呃……嘿,也许你应该教教我。

娜蒂瑞:外星球来的人可学不会这些,因为你们无法感受。

杰　克:那就教我如何去感受。

娜蒂瑞:没人能教会你如何去感受。

杰　克:拜托,我们就不能聊聊吗?你在哪儿学的英语?奥古斯汀博士的学校吗?

娜蒂瑞:你真够幼稚的!

杰　克:我需要你的帮助。

娜蒂瑞:你不该留在这儿。

杰　克:好啊,那你就带我走吧。

娜蒂瑞:不!回去吧。

杰　克:不。

娜蒂瑞:回去吧。

杰　克:这……这是什么?

娜蒂瑞:圣树的种子,是非常圣洁的灵魂。

杰　克:它们代表着什么吗?

娜蒂瑞:跟我来。来啊。

杰　克：我们要去哪儿？

娜蒂瑞：跟上。

杰　克：你叫什么名字？

经典对白(二)

Love 爱情

杰克在完成加入部族的仪式之后，便正式成为了纳威部族的一员，他跟随娜蒂瑞来到了美丽的圣树下，两人互诉衷肠……

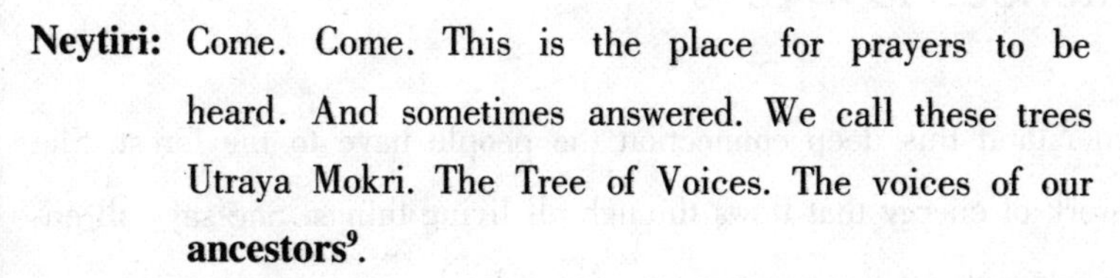

Neytiri: Come. Come. This is the place for prayers to be heard. And sometimes answered. We call these trees Utraya Mokri. The Tree of Voices. The voices of our **ancestors**[9].

Jake: I can hear them.

Neytiri: They live, Jake. Within Eywa. You are Omaticaya now. You may make your **bow**[10] from the wood of Hometree. And you may choose a woman. We have many fine women. Nenat is the best singer.

Jake: I don't want Nenat.

Neytiri: Paral is a good hunter.

Jake: Yes, she is a good hunter. I've already chosen. But this woman must also choose me.

Neytiri: She already has. I'm with you now, Jake. We are **mated**[11] for life.

9 ancestor *n.* 祖先

10 bow *n.* 弓

11 mate *v.* 交配

娜蒂瑞:过来,来啊。这里是向神灵祷告的地方。有时便会应验。我们管这些树叫"乌特拉亚莫克利",声音之树的意思。那是我们先祖的声音。

杰　克:我能听到他们。

娜蒂瑞:他们还活着,杰克,在艾娃之中。你现在是奥玛提卡雅人了。你可以用家园树的木料做一张弓。你还可以选择一个女人。这里有很多不错的女人。妮奈特是最好的歌者。

杰　克:我不想要妮奈特。

娜蒂瑞:佩拉是个很棒的猎手。

杰　克:是的,她是个很棒的猎手。我早就选好了,但是这个女人也得选择我才行。

娜蒂瑞:她早就选了你了。我们现在在一起了,杰克。我们要终身相伴。

Beautiful Sentences 妙语佳句

1. I'm trying to understand this deep connection the people have to the forest. She talks about a network of energy that flows through all living things. She says all energy is only borrowed, and one day you have to give it back.

   我试图去理解这些人与森林之间的深深的羁绊。她时常提到能量的网络,能量通过这个网络在万物之间流通。她还说所有的能量都是借来的,总有一天是要还回去的。

2. I was a stone-cold aerial hunter. Death from above. Only problem is, you're not the only one.

   我是个冷血的空中猎人,来自上天的死神。而唯一的问题是,你不是唯一的猎人。

3. Everything is backwards now. Like out there is the true world and in here is the dream. It's hard to believe it's only been 3 months. I don't even remember my old life. I don't know who I am anymore.

   如今一切都颠倒了。好像那里才是真实的世界,而这里不过是梦境。很难相信已经过了3个月的时间了。我甚至都记不得我过去的生活了,也不知道自己是谁了。

4. Na'vi say that every person is born twice. The second time is when you earn your place among the people forever.
   纳威人说,每个人都会有两次新生。第二次便是你在族人中获得永久地位之时。

5. The wealth of this world isn't in the ground. It's all around us. The Na'vi know that, and they are fighting to defend it. If you want to share this world with them, you need to understand them.
   这个世界的财富并不在地下,而是在我们的周围。纳威人知道这一点,所以他们会尽全力去捍卫它们。如果你想同他们分享这个世界,就得理解他们。

6. I was a warrior who dreamed he could bring peace. Sooner or later though, you always have to wake up.
   我曾是个梦想自己会带来和平的战士。然而迟早有一天,你必须得清醒过来。

7. Outcast...Betrayer...Alien...I was in the place the eye does not see. I needed their help, and they needed mine. But to ever face them again, I was gonna have to take it to a whole new level. Sometimes your whole life boils down to one insane move. There's something we gotta do. You're not gonna like it.
   流放者……叛徒……外星人……我所在之处, 无人可见。我需要他们的帮助,他们也需要我的帮助。但要再次面对他们的话,我必须得使情况上升到一个全新的高度。有时候真是要拼上性命的。我们得干件事儿了,估计你是不会喜欢的。

Thought about Life 人生感悟

一切事物都有其自身的存在方式。人们有时真的需要理解并尊重这种生活方式,与万事万物和谐相处,才能建造一个真正的理想家园。人们同样需要信仰。信仰真是个很奇妙的东西,很多时候,正是因为信仰,才会使人们找到奋斗的力量。爱在万物间,那才是真正强大的力量。

二、默默无闻的英雄
——《蜘蛛侠 I》

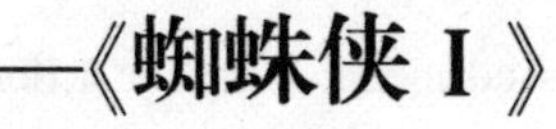

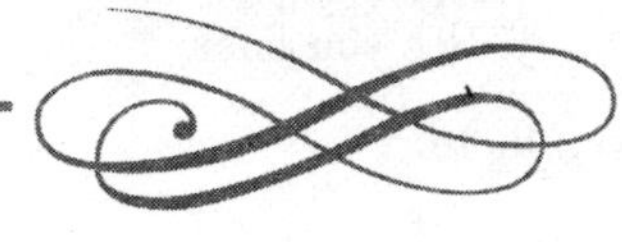

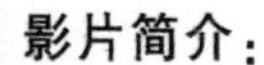

影片简介:

彼得·帕克一直是个默默无闻的学生。一次在学校组织的活动中,他被一只蜘蛛咬了一口。回家后,他却发现自己具备了一些特殊的能力——超常的视力,敏捷的反应,惊人的速度,而且还能抽丝攀爬。后来彼得便利用这种特殊的能力来帮助需要帮助的人,他被人们称作“蜘蛛侠”。彼得的好友哈里的父亲是位科学家,一日在实验的过程中,哈里的父亲把自己变成了一个绿色妖怪,他的破坏行为严重威胁到了人类的生命,而彼得为了保护民众,不得不与好友的父亲进行对战……

经典对白(一)

Change 改变

彼得的身体发生了神奇的变化,而对于这种变化,彼得却显得有些无所适从……

Aunt May: Peter! What's going on in there?

Peter: I'm exercising. I'm not dressed, Aunt May.

Aunt May: Well, you're acting so strangely, Peter.

Peter: Okay. Thanks.

Uncle Ben: Something's bothered him. Maybe he's too embarrassed to tell me what it is. Maybe I'm too embarrassed to ask him. I just don't know anymore.

Peter: I'm going to the downtown library. See you later.

Uncle Ben: Yeah, wait, Peter. I'll drive you there.

Peter: No, I'll take the train.

Uncle Ben: No, no, no, I need the exercise. Go on. Go, go.

Peter: Thanks for the ride, Uncle Ben.

Uncle Ben: No, no. Wait a moment. Wait, Peter, we eh...we need to talk.

Peter: We can talk later.

Uncle Ben: Well, we can talk now. If you let me.

Peter: What do we have to talk about? Why now?

Uncle Ben: Because we haven't talked at all for so long. May and I don't even know who you are anymore. You **shirk**[1] your **chores**[2]. You have all those **weird**[3] experiments in your room. You start fights at school. I don't know...

Peter: I didn't start that fight, I told you that.

Uncle Ben: You sure finished it.

Peter: What was I supposed to do? Run away?

Uncle Ben: No, you're not supposed to run away, but...Peter, look. You're changing. I know I went through exactly the same thing at your age.

1 shirk *v.* 逃避，规避

2 chore *n.* 家务，日常杂事

3 weird *adj.* 怪异的，奇怪的

Peter: No. Not exactly.

Uncle Ben: Peter, these are the years when a man changes into the man he's gonna become the rest of his life. Just be careful who you change into. This guy, Flash Thompson, he probably deserved what happened. But just because you can beat him up doesn't give you the right to. Remember, with great power comes great responsibility.

Peter: Are you afraid I'm gonna turn into some kind of criminal? Quit worrying about me, okay? Something's different. I'll figure it out. Stop **lecturing**[4] me, please.

Uncle Ben: I don't mean to lecture. I don't mean to **preach**[5]. And I know I'm not your father.

Peter: Then stop pretending to be!

Uncle Ben: Right. I'll pick you up here at 10.

梅婶婶：彼得，你在里面干什么呢？

彼　得：我在健身，我没穿衣服，梅婶婶。

梅婶婶：好吧，你最近的行为有点儿反常，彼得。

彼　得：好啦，谢谢了。

本叔叔：他一定有什么烦心事儿，他可能不好意思说，而我也不好意思问。真不知道该怎么办才好。

彼　得：我去市里的图书馆。再见！

本叔叔：等等，等一下，彼得。我开车送你去。

彼　得：不用了，我坐地铁。

本叔叔：不，不，没关系的。我也得去锻炼一下，走吧，走吧。

4 lecture *v.* 训诫，责备

5 preach *v.* 说教

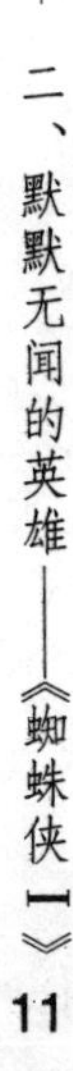

彼　得:谢谢你,本叔叔。

本叔叔:等等,等一下。彼得,我们……我们得谈谈。

彼　得:以后再谈吧。

本叔叔:如果你愿意,我们现在就可以谈谈。

彼　得:我们要谈什么?必须现在谈吗?

本叔叔:我们也好久没有谈心了,梅婶婶和我一点儿都不了解你。你不做家务,总在房间里做一些稀奇古怪的实验,甚至还在学校里打架。我不知道……

彼　得:那不是我挑起的,我告诉过你的。

本叔叔:可你确实打了。

彼　得:我能怎么做?逃跑吗?

本叔叔:不,你不该逃跑,只是……彼得,你正在改变。我了解,因为在你这个年纪,我也经历过同样的事情……

彼　得:不,太不一样。

本叔叔:彼得,你在这几年里的转变,将决定未来你是怎样一个人,千万要小心,别误入歧途。那个叫汤普森的人,或许是他活该挨打,但你有能力打他并不代表你就有权力去打他。记住:力量越大,责任也越大。

彼　得:你是怕我变成罪犯吗?别担心我了,好吗?事情不是你想的那样:我自己会想办法解决的,请别再对我说教了!

本叔叔:我不想对你说教,也没有对你说教。我知道我不是你父亲。

彼　得:那就别装作是我父亲!

本叔叔:你说得对。我十点钟来接你。

经典对白(二)

●Adoration 爱慕之情

在梅婶婶遭到“绿色恶魔”的袭击后,玛丽来探望梅婶婶,并向彼得表达了她对“蜘蛛侠”的爱慕之情……

Mary: Will she be okay?

Peter: She'll be fine. She's been sleeping all day. Thanks for coming.

Mary: Of course.

Peter: How are you? You okay about the other night?

Mary: Yeah, I'm fine. I just felt bad about leaving Aunt May.

Peter: Have you talked to Harry?

Mary: He called me. I haven't called him back. The fact is I'm in love with somebody else.

Peter: You are?

Mary: At least I think I am. It's not the right time to talk about it.

Peter: No. No. Go on. Would I know his name, this guy?

Mary: You'll think I'm a little girl with a **crush**[6].

Peter: Trust me.

Mary: It's funny. He's saved my life twice, and I've never even seen his face.

Peter: Oh, him.

Mary: You're laughing at me.

Peter: No, I understand. He is extremely cool.

Mary: But do you think it's true, all the terrible things they say about him?

Peter: No, no. Not Spider-Man, not a chance in the world. I know him a little bit. I'm **sort of**[7] his **unofficial**[8] photographer.

6 crush *n.* (口语) 迷恋

7 sort of 有点儿，有几分

8 unofficial *adj.* 非正式的，非官方的

Mary: Has he mentioned me?

Peter: Yeah.

Mary: What'd he say?

Peter: I said…he asked me what I thought about you.

Mary: And what did you say?

Peter: I said, "Spider-Man", I said, "The great thing about M.J. is when you look in her eyes and she's looking back in yours, everything feels not quite normal, because you feel stronger and weaker at the same time. You feel excited and at the same time terrified. The truth is, you don't know what you feel except you know what kind of man you want to be. It's as if you've reached the **unreachable**[9] and you weren't ready for it."

Mary: You said that?

Peter: Well, something like that.

玛丽:她还好吧?

彼得:她没事的,睡了一整天了。谢谢你来看望她。

玛丽:应该的。

彼得:你怎么样?我是说那晚,你还好吧?

玛丽:我很好,我很后悔丢下梅婶婶一走了之。

彼得:你和哈利谈过了吗?

玛丽:他给我打过电话,但我没回他。事实上,我爱上别人了。

彼得:真的?

玛丽:至少我认为是这样。现在谈这个好像不是很妥当。

彼得:不,不会的,你说吧。他叫什么?

玛丽:你一定觉得我像个小女生那样迷恋着一个人。

彼得:不会的。

玛丽:很好笑,他曾救了我两次,但我却从没见过他的脸。

9 unreachable *adj*. 不能达到的，不能实现的

彼得:原来是他。

玛丽:你在取笑我。

彼得:不,不,我明白的,他真的很酷。

玛丽:可人们说了很多关于他的坏事儿,你觉得那是真的吗?

彼得:不,不是,蜘蛛侠绝对不是坏人。我算是认识他,我怎么也是他非正式的摄影师。

玛丽:他提到过我吗?

彼得:提到过。

玛丽:他都说了什么?

彼得:我说……他问我觉得你怎么样?

玛丽:你怎么说?

彼得:我说,"蜘蛛侠,玛丽最大的优点是……当你看着她的双眼,而她也注视着你时,一切都变得不寻常了,因为你会同时感受到脆弱与坚强,也会同时感到兴奋与恐惧。其实,你并不清楚那是一种什么感觉,你只知道你想成为一个什么样的男人。就像是触到了遥不可及的梦想,可你却完全没有准备好去接受它。"

玛丽:这是你说的?

彼得:嗯,差不多是这样。

Beautiful Sentences 妙语佳句

1. Slander is spoken. In print, it's libel.
   说出来的是中伤,印出来的就是诽谤了。
2. You have a knack for getting in trouble. You have a knack for saving my life. I think I have a superhero stalker.
   你好像有惹上麻烦的习惯,而你也好像有救我的习惯。我想我有个超级英雄保镖呢。

3. I can't help thinking about the last thing I said to him. He tried to tell me something important, and I threw it in his face.
   我不由自主地想起我对他说的最后一句话，他想要告诉我一些很重要的事儿，可我却不理他。
4. You loved him and he loved you. He never doubted the man you'd grow into. How you were meant for great things. You won't disappoint him.
   你很爱他，他也很爱你。他一直都相信你会成才，会有所作为。你不会让他失望的。
5. No matter what I do, no matter how hard I try, the ones I love will always be the ones who pay.
   无论我怎么做，怎么努力，付出代价的人总是我深爱的人。

Thought about Life 人生感悟

做个真正的英雄是每个人心中的梦想，正像彼得一样，只不过他的经历的确很戏剧化。最初彼得只是随意地使用他的能力，可在本叔叔意外身亡后，彼得开始重新认识他的能力，特别是重新认识了本叔叔的话“力量越大，责任也越大”。于是彼得找到了新的生存方式——用自己的力量去保护他人，并甘愿做一个无名英雄。在他的心中，怀有一份责任感，并贯彻始终。生活中，对他人负责，即是对自己负责，这亦是我们的责任。

三、公主是怎样炼成的
——《公主日记 I》

影片简介：

15 岁的米娅只是个普通的女孩儿，她和母亲一起过着平静的生活。可是突然有一天，她却得知自己是欧洲一个叫吉诺维亚的小国的公主，并且在她 16 岁生日到来之前，她必须做出决定是要继续留在美国还是前往吉诺维亚去继承王位。她以前一直过着普通人的生活，可现在她却需要履行一个公主的职责。她那严厉的祖母——皇太后克拉莉丝对她进行了无比严格的训练，并希望她能成为一位真正的公主。米娅最终能成为真正的公主吗？她又能否找到自己的真爱……

经典对白(一)

First Meet with Grandma 初遇祖母

米娅第一次见到自己的祖母，二人很快便产生了严重的分歧……

Clarisse: Amelia, I'm so glad you could come.

Amelia: Hi! You've got a great place.

Clarisse: Thank you. Well, let me look at you. You look so...young.

Amelia: Thank you. And you look so...clean.

Clarisse: Charlotte, would you check on tea in the garden? Please, sit.

Amelia: So, my mom said you wanted...to talk to me about something. **Shoot**[1].

Clarisse: Oh, before I "shoot", I have something I want to give you. Here.

Amelia: Oh, um, thank you. Wow.

Clarisse: It's the Genovian **crest**[2]. It was mine when I was young. And that was my great-grandmother's.

Amelia: Heh, I'll keep this safe. I will take good care of it. Now, what did you want to tell me?

Clarisse: Something that I think will have a very big impact upon your life.

Amelia: I already had **braces**[3].

Clarisse: No, it's bigger than **orthodontia**[4].

Charlotte: The tea is served, ma'am.

Clarisse: Amelia, have you ever heard of Eduard Christoff Phillipe Gérard Renaldi?

Amelia: No.

Clarisse: He was the crown prince of Genovia.

Amelia: Hmm. What about him?

Clarisse: Eduard Christoff Phillipe Gérard Renaldi was your father.

Amelia: Yeah, sure. My father was the prince of Genovia. Uh-huh. You're joking.

Clarisse: Why would I joke about something like that?

1 shoot *v.* 射击，这里是“快讲”的意思

2 crest *n.* 顶饰

3 brace *n.* 支架，托架

4 orthodontia *n.* 牙齿矫正术

Amelia: No! Because if he's really a prince, then I…

Clarisse: Exactly. You're not just Amelia Thermopolis. You are Amelia Mignonette Thermopolis Renaldi, Princess of Genovia.

Amelia: Me? A princess? Shut up!

Clarisse: I beg your pardon? Shut up?

Servant: Your **Majesty**[5], in America, it doesn't always mean "Be quiet". Here it could mean, "Wow", "Gee whiz", "Golly"...

Clarisse: Oh, I understand. Thank you. Nevertheless you are the princess. And I am Queen Clarisse Renaldi.

Amelia: Why on earth would you pick me to be your princess?

Clarisse: Since your father died, you are the natural **heir**[6] to the **throne**[7] of Genovia. That's our law. I'm royal by marriage. You are royal by blood. You can rule.

Amelia: Rule? Oh, no. Oh, no. No, no, no. Now you have really got the wrong girl. I never lead anybody, not at Brownies, not at Camp Fire Girls. Queen Clarisse, my expectation in life is to be **invisible**[8] and I'm good at it.

Clarisse: Amelia, I had other expectations also. In my wildest dreams, I never expected this to happen. But you are the legal heir, the only heir to the Genovian throne. And we will accept the challenge of helping you become the princess that you are. Oh, I can give you

---

5 Majesty *n.* 陛下

6 heir *n.* 继承人

7 throne *n.* 王位

8 invisible *adj.* 看不见的，无形的

books. You will study languages, history, art, political science. I can teach you to walk, talk, sit, stand, eat, dress like a princess. And, given time, I think you'll find the place in Genovia a very pleasant place to live.

Amelia: Live in Genovia?

Clarisse: It's a wonderful country, Amelia, really.

Amelia: Whoa, whoa. Just **rewind**[7] and freeze. I'm no princess. I'm still waiting for normal body parts to arrive. I refuse to move to and rule a country. And do you want another reason? I don't want to be a princess!

Clarisse: Oh, Amelia, Amelia! Amelia, come back here!

克拉莉丝:艾米利娅,很高兴你能过来。

艾米利娅:嗨,你这儿可真漂亮!

克拉莉丝:谢谢。让我看看你,你看起来……很年轻。

艾米利娅:谢谢。你看起来……很干净。

克拉莉丝:夏洛特,你能到花园里看看茶备好了吗?请坐。

艾米利娅:因为我妈妈说你有些事儿要跟我说。讲吧!

克拉莉丝:在我"讲"之前,我要给你些东西。在这儿。

艾米利娅:哦,呃,谢谢。哇哦!

克拉莉丝:这是吉诺维亚的顶饰,是我年轻的时候用的。那个是我曾祖母的。

艾米利娅:嗯,我会好好保存的,我会小心照看它们的。你要跟我说什么?

克拉莉丝:我想跟你说的事儿,或许会严重影响到你现在的生活。

艾米利娅:我已经准备好了。

克拉莉丝:不,这件事儿可不那么简单。

夏洛特:茶已经备好了,夫人。

克拉莉丝:艾米利娅,你有听说过爱德华·克里斯托弗·菲利普·吉哈德·里纳尔迪吗?

艾米利娅:没有。

克拉莉丝:他是吉诺维亚的王子。

艾米利娅:嗯,他怎么了?

克拉莉丝:爱德华·里纳尔迪是你的父亲。

艾米利娅：是的，当然。我爸爸是吉诺维亚的王子。呃哈，你在开玩笑吧。

克拉莉丝：我为什么要拿这种事情开玩笑？

艾米利娅：哦不，因为如果他真的是王子，那我……

克拉莉丝：没错。你不仅仅是艾米利娅·瑟姆波利丝，你还是艾米利娅·米诺奈特·瑟姆波利丝·里纳尔迪，你是吉诺维亚的公主。

艾米利娅：我？还公主？闭嘴！

克拉莉丝：什么？闭嘴？

仆　　人：陛下，美语的“闭嘴”并不总是“安静”的意思，这里可能是“哦”、“天啊”、“老天”的意思。

克拉莉丝：哦，我知道了，谢谢。不管怎样，你是公主，而我是皇后克拉莉丝·里纳尔迪。

艾米利娅：你为什么非要选我做公主？

克拉莉丝：因为你的爸爸去世了，你自然而然就成了他的王位继承人，这是我国的法律规定。我因婚姻而成为王室成员，而你则是有皇室的血统。你可以统治这个国家。

艾米利娅：统治？不，不，不，你真的找错人了。我从没领导过任何人，在布兰尼斯没有，在女子篝火会上也没有。克拉莉丝女皇，我只想我的生活平平淡淡的，而我也习惯这样的生活。

克拉莉丝：艾米利娅，我也有其他的愿望。在我的梦中，也从没想过会当上皇后。但你是合法的，而且是吉诺维亚王位唯一的继承人。我们要面对挑战，帮你成为一个真正的公主。哦，我可以给你一些书，你要学习语言、历史、艺术、政治、科技，我还会教你如何像个公主一样行走、交谈、坐正、站立、用餐、打扮。给我些时间,我想你会发现吉诺维亚是个非常适宜居住的地方。

艾米利娅:还要住在吉诺维亚?

克拉莉丝:那里真的是个很好的地方,艾米利娅。

艾米利娅:哇哦,哇哦。能不能先等等,我先想想。我不是公主,我还要过正常人的生活。我不要搬去那儿,不要统治国家。你还想要其他的理由吗?我不想做公主!

克拉莉丝:哦,艾米利娅,艾米利娅!艾米利娅,回来!

经典对白(二)

A Secret Love 悄然产生的爱意

乔斯为了出名而利用米娅,媒体也拍到了他们亲吻的照片。此次风波过后,米娅发现自己竟爱上了一直在关心着自己的迈克尔……

Amelia: Oh! Uh...it's open. Come on in. Michael! Hi. How are you? What?

Michael: Little guy on your…

Amelia: Oh! Um…did Lilly tell you that I called, because I...called.

Michael: I brought your car.

Amelia: Oh, thank you. Seven times I called.

Michael: Doc. said that he fixed what he could, and if you had any problems give him a call.

Amelia: Oh, OK. Do you want the check now? I have the last payment.

Michael: Yeah. Thank you.

Amelia: Are you hungry or thirsty?

Michael: No.

Amelia: Oh! Here it is. Um...look. Thank you so much for doing this for me. It's really, really great of you.

Michael: I didn't do it for you. Doc. lets the band practice.

Amelia: Right. Of course.

Michael: I help with the cars.

Amelia: Oh, here.

Michael: Oh, thanks.

Amelia: I know you're still mad at me for blowing you off. And I'm really sorry I did. But I am going to try to make it up to you.

Michael: How?

Amelia: Well, I'm still going to the Genovian Independence Day ball. And I'm inviting you. It could be fun, you know. I'm wearing this great dress that I can't breathe in. And Lilly's got a date.

Michael: Josh looks better in a **tux**[9].

Amelia: Oh. Um...but, see, it's...I really want you to be the one I share it with. You don't have to wear a tux. You can wear **sweatpants**[10] for all I care, you know.

Michael: Don't worry about me. I just consider myself royally **flushed**[11].

艾米利娅:门没关,进来吧。麦克尔,嗨！你好吗？什么？

迈克尔:这儿有块儿小东西……

艾米利娅:哦！呃,莉莉告诉你我打过电话给你吗？我打了的。

迈克尔:我把你的车开回来了。

艾米利娅:谢谢。我打了七次电话了。

迈克尔:博士说他尽力修了,要是还有问题的话,就给他打电话。

9 tux *n.* 男士无尾的半正式晚礼服

10 sweatpants *n.* 宽松的运动裤

11 flushed *adj.* 脸红的

艾米利娅：好的。你现在要支票吗？我还有最后一张。

迈克尔：好啊，谢谢。

艾米利娅：你饿吗？渴了吗？

迈克尔：不。

艾米利娅：哦，在这儿。呃，是这样，很感谢你帮我做这些事儿，你真是太好了！

迈克尔：我没帮什么忙，博士让乐队在那儿排练。

艾米利娅：是的，当然。

迈克尔：我就帮着修车。

艾米利娅：哦，给你。

迈克尔：谢谢。

艾米利娅：我知道你还在为我毁约而生我的气，我真的很抱歉，但我会尽力补偿你的。

迈克尔：怎样补偿呢？

艾米利娅：好吧，我仍然得参加吉诺维亚独立日舞会，我会邀请你来。一定会很有趣的，知道吗，我会穿着这样的大裙子，让我透不过气来的裙子，莉莉已经有约了。

迈克尔：乔斯穿晚礼服会更好些。

艾米利娅：哦，呃，但是，我真的很想要你和我一起分享。你不必穿晚礼服，你可以穿运动裤，穿什么我都喜欢，知道吗？

迈克尔：不用担心我，我只是想到了自己穿得像皇室成员，并且脸红发烫的样子。

Beautiful Sentences 妙语佳句

1. Very well. Then I'll go meet your grandmother. But you should know that no one can make you feel inferior without your consent.
   很好。那我去见你祖母了。但你应该知道，除非你自己也这样认为，否则没有谁能让你觉得自己低人一等。

2. Your father realized that the love he could have for one person or even two could not make him forget the love he felt for his country and its people. It was the hard-

est thing he ever had to do.

你父亲认识到他爱的人只有一个,或者最多两个,可这份爱也不能使他忘记他对国家和他的子民的爱。这是他曾经做过的最艰难的决定。

3. You were awesome! You are the coolest queen ever!

你太了不起了!你是有史以来最棒的女王!

4. No one can quit being who they really are, not even a princess. Now, you can refuse the job but you are a princess by birth.

没有谁能放弃去做自己,即使是公主也不能。现在,你可以拒绝做公主的工作,但是你生来就是个公主。

5. No. I'm saying, as a grandmother, you might have been too harsh on your granddaughter.

不,我是说,作为祖母,你对孙女有点儿过于苛刻了。

6. I didn't mean it. The green monster of jealousy came out because you were Miss Popular and I thought I was losing my best friend so I got angry and upset and hurt and…I told you! I need an attitude adjustment. But the truth is, you being a princess is kind of a miracle.

我不是那个意思。我只是有些忌妒你,因为你那么受欢迎,我原以为我会失去我最好的朋友,所以我会生气,我会不安,还会很伤心,我告诉过你的!我需要调整一下我的态度,但事实是,你能做个公主,这真是个奇迹。

7. **Clarisse**: I've been thinking about it a great deal, and the truth is I think you'd make a very fine princess. You know, people think princesses are supposed to wear tiaras, marry the prince, always look pretty and live happily ever after, but it's so much more than that. It's a real job.

Amelia: You are an extraordinary person, Grandma. But I don't think I'm meant to do this. I would be so afraid that I would disappoint the people of Genovia and I couldn't bear to disappoint you again.

Clarisse: Well, as I said, I have faith in you.

克拉莉丝：我想了许久，事实上，我想你已经是个相当不错的公主了。知道吗，人们认为，公主应该佩戴王冠，嫁给王子，永远青春美丽并快乐幸福地生活，但事实上却远比这多得多。公主是份实实在在的工作。

艾米利亚：你真的很了不起，奶奶。但我想我肯定是做不到的。我很害怕，怕我会令吉诺维亚的人民失望，而且我不能再承受让你失望的痛苦了。

克拉莉丝：那正如我所说的，我信任你。

8. "My dearest daughter, today is your sixteenth birthday. Congratulations. I present you with this diary to fill the pages with your special thoughts, special thoughts of your wonderful life." "It is a custom in my family to pass on a piece of wisdom when one reaches this age. I pass it on to you as my father passed it on to me. Amelia, courage is not the absence of fear but rather the judgement that something else is more important than fear. The brave may not live forever but the cautious do not live at all. From now on, you'll be traveling the road between who you think you are and who you can be. The key is to allow yourself to make the journey. I also want you to know I loved your mother very much and still think of her often. Happy birthday, my Mia. All my love, your father."

"我最亲爱的女儿，今天是你16岁的生日，生日快乐。我把这个日记本送给你做礼物，是要你在这里记下你的想法，关于你美好生活的奇特想法。""这是我们家族的习惯，当孩子到了这个年龄时，就会把智慧传承给他。我的父亲也是这样做的，现在我也把它传给你。艾米利娅，勇气并不是不再恐惧，而是发现了还有比恐惧更重要的事物。勇气不会长存，但恐惧更不会长存。从现在开始，你将要踏上人生的旅途，在你认为你是什么样的人和你能成为什么样的人之间做出选择，但关键是要让自己踏出这一步。我也想让你知道，我很爱你的母亲，现在仍经常想起她。生日快乐，我的米娅。给你我所有的爱，你的父亲。"

Thought about Life 人生感悟

每个女孩子小时候都曾梦想做个公主，拥有幸福美妙的生活，但如果真的做了公主的话，也许就没那么简单了。公主是国家的象征，而不仅仅是个人，它的含义太复杂了。所有的公主都是凡人，或许她们都渴望过着普通人的生活，但是由于身份地位的特殊，她们总是要以履行职责、维护国家形象、服务于人民为己任。这大概就是责任重于泰山的具体体现吧。

四、救人一命即救全世界
——《辛德勒的名单》

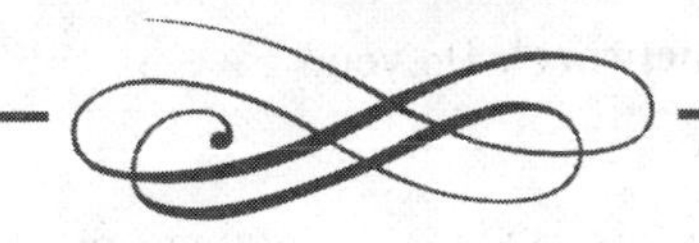

影片简介：

二战时期，德国企业家奥斯卡·辛德勒创办了一个工厂，供应军需物资，以期发战争财。由于犹太人的工资低廉，所以辛德勒便招聘了大量的犹太人作为工厂的工人。当时纳粹分子正残忍地屠杀犹太人，辛德勒的心灵也受到了极大的震撼。于是他用钱买通了德国官员，列出了一份在他的工厂工作并受保护的犹太人的名单。辛德勒的善举使得他倾家荡产，但这丝毫没有动摇他保护犹太人免遭屠杀的决心。正是因为辛德勒的努力，才使得这1100多名犹太人幸免于难……

经典对白(一)

●Urge 说服

辛德勒为其创办的工厂招募员工，他发现了伊扎克……

Schindler: Itzhak Stern! I'm looking for Itzhak Stern. Are you Itzhak Stern or not?

Itzhak: I am. Where can we talk?

Schindler: There's a company you did the books for on Lipowa Street. Made what? Pots and pans?

Itzhak: By law, I have to tell you, sir, I'm a Jew.

Schindler: Well, I'm a German. So there we are. A good company, you think?

Itzhak: Modestly successful.

Schindler: I know nothing about **enamelware**[1]. Do you?

Itzhak: I was just the accountant.

Schindler: Simple engineering though, wouldn't you think? Change the machines around, whatever you do, you could make other things, couldn't you? Field **kits**[2], mess kits. Army contracts. Once the war ends, forget it, but for now it's great. You can make a fortune, don't you think?

Itzhak: I think most people right now have other priorities.

Schindler: Like what?

Itzhak: I'm sure you'll do just fine once you get the contracts. In fact, the worse things get, the better you'll do.

Schindler: Oh, well, I can get the signatures I need. That's the easy part. Finding the money to buy the company, that's hard.

Itzhak: You don't have any money?

Schindler: Not that kind of money. You know anybody? Jews, yeah. Investors. You must have contacts in the Jewish business community working here.

Itzhak: What community? Jews can no longer own businesses. That's why this one's in **receivership**[3]. But they wouldn't own it.

1 enamelware *n.* 搪瓷，搪瓷制品

2 kit *n.* 成套的工具、元件

3 receivership *n.* 破产管理

Schindler: I'd own it. I'd pay them back in product, pots and pans. Pots and pans. Something they can use. Something they can feel in their hands. They can trade it on the black market, do whatever they want. Everybody's happy. If you want, you could run the company for me.

Itzhak: Let me understand. They'd put up all the money, I'd do all the work. What, if you don't mind my asking, would you do?

Schindler: I'd make sure it's known the company's in business. I'd see that it had a certain **panache**[4]. That's what I'm good at, not the work. Not the work. The **presentation**[5].

Itzhak: I'm sure I don't know anybody who'll be interested in this.

Schindler: Well, they should be, Itzhak Stern. Tell them they should be.

辛德勒: 伊扎克·斯特恩！我在找伊扎克·斯特恩。你是不是伊扎克·斯特恩吗？

伊扎克: 我是。咱们在哪儿谈呢？

辛德勒: 你曾在里波瓦大街的一家公司做过会计吧。那公司是做什么的？厨具吗？

伊扎克: 按照法律规定，我得先告诉你，先生，我是犹太人。

辛德勒: 哦，我是德国人，很高兴认识你。公司不错吧？

伊扎克: 还过得去。

辛德勒: 我完全不了解搪瓷制品，你怎么样？

伊扎克: 我只是个会计。

4 panache *n.* 夸耀，炫耀

5 presentation *n.* 外观

辛德勒:不过原理应该很简单,对吧？只要把机器改装一下,就能用来做别的东西,是吧？像一些大批量供给部队的军需用品。当然战争结束就不行了,不提也罢,但现在可是很火的。可以赚一笔,你觉得呢？

伊扎克:我觉得大家倒并不关注这个。

辛德勒:那他们关注什么？

伊扎克:我相信一旦你拿到军方的合同,肯定会生意兴隆的。事实上是战事越严重,对你越有利。

辛德勒:哦,当然,我能让他们在合同上签名,这很容易。难的是要凑够钱去收购那家公司。

伊扎克:你根本没钱？

辛德勒:没那么多。你这儿有熟人吗？像一些有钱的犹太人,发明家什么的。在这儿工作,这种人总会认识一些吧。

伊扎克:那你可想错了。犹太人不能再开公司了,所以这个公司才不得不卖掉,公司不会登记在犹太人的名下。

辛德勒:我可以开啊。我可以用那些锅碗瓢盆的产品来偿还他们,那些他们还用得着,也是能实在拥有的东西,甚至可以拿到黑市去换,随他们怎样用。这样不是皆大欢喜吗！如果你愿意,你可以替我打理这个公司。

伊扎克:让我想想。他们出钱,我出力,那么冒昧地问一句,你做什么呢？

辛德勒:我确保这个公司的名声。我负责公关、宣传,提高公司的知名度,这是我的专长。我可不会干活,不会。我只做做表面文章。

伊扎克:我可以肯定,我认识的人里,不会有人感兴趣的。

辛德勒:哦,会有的,伊扎克·斯特恩。告诉他们,他们应该抓住这个机会。

经典对白(二)

● Dialogue with Helen 和海伦的对话

指挥官的女仆海伦是犹太人，她认为司令迟早会杀了她，所以她对生活也不抱希望了……

Helen: I'm sure this will be better than those rags, Lisiek. Herr Direktor, I was just helping Lisiek to find something to clean the **stains**[6] from the Herr Kommandant's bathtub. Go, please.

Lisiek: Pardon me, Herr Direktor.

Schindler: You don't have to report to me, Helen. You know who I am, hmm? I'm Schindler.

Helen: Of course. I–I have heard and you have been here before.

Schindler: Here, why don't you keep this someplace? Go on, take it.

Helen: I get extra food here.

Schindler: Well, if you don't want to eat it, trade it. Or give it to Lisiek. Why not build yourself up?

Helen: My first day here, he beat me, because I threw out the bones from dinner. He came down to the basement at midnight, and he...he asked me where they were. For his dogs, you understand. I said to him, I...I don't know how I say this. I never could say it now. I said to him, "Why are you beating me?" He said, "The reason I beat you now is because you ask why I beat you."

Schindler: I know your sufferings, Helen.

Helen: It doesn't matter. I have accepted them.

Schindler: Accepted them?

6 stain *n.* 污渍

Helen: One day he will shoot me.

Schindler: No, no, no, no, he won't shoot you.

Helen: I know. I see things. We were on the roof on Monday, young Lisiek and I, and we saw the Herr Kommandant come out of the front door and down the steps by the **patio**[7] right there below us and… and there on the steps he drew his gun and he...shot a woman who was passing by. A woman carrying a **bundle**[8]. Through the throat. Just… just a woman on her way somewhere, you know. She was no fatter or thinner or slower or faster than anyone else, and I couldn't guess what had she done. The more you see of the Herr Kommandant, the more you see there is no set rules that you can live by. You can't say to yourself, "If I follow these rules, I will be safe."

Schindler: He won't shoot you because he enjoys you too much. He enjoys you so much he won't even let you wear the star. He doesn't want anyone else to know it's a Jew he's enjoying. He shot the woman from the steps, because she meant nothing to him. She was one of a series, neither offending or pleasing him. But you, Helen, it's all right. It's not that kind of a kiss.

Helen: Thank you.

海　伦: 我想这个会比抹布好用,里谢克。董事长先生,我正在帮里谢克找东西,让他去清洗指挥官的浴缸。快去吧。

里谢克: 请原谅,董事长先生。

辛德勒: 你不必向我汇报,海伦。知道我是谁吗?我是辛德勒。

海　伦: 当然,我知道您,您以前来过这儿。

辛德勒: 拿着,先藏起来。别怕,拿着。

海　伦: 我在这儿能吃饱的。

辛德勒: 你不想吃的话,也可以用来换东西,或者送给里谢克。多吃点儿没坏处!

海　伦: 我到这儿的第一天,他打了我,就因为我倒掉了晚餐吃剩的骨头。他半夜里

7 patio *n.* 庭院，平台

8 bundle *n.* 一捆，一包，一束

来到我住的地下室,他……他问我要骨头,想拿去喂他的狗。我问他,我也不知道当时怎么会说那种话,现在我肯定不会那么说的。我问他:"你为什么打我?"他说:"我打你是因为你问我为什么要打你。"

辛德勒:我知道你受了很多苦,海伦。

海　伦:这不要紧,我认命了。

辛德勒:认命?

海　伦:总有一天,他会杀了我。

辛德勒:不,不,不,他不会的。

海　伦:会的,我看见过。星期一早晨,我和小里谢克在阁楼上,我们看到指挥官从前门出去,走下院子里的台阶,就在我们下面,他站在那里,掏出手枪,朝着一个从旁经过的女人开了枪。那女人提着篮子,子弹穿透了她的喉咙。她只是个普通的过路人,你知道,她并不比别人长得胖点儿或瘦点儿,走得慢点儿或快点儿,我始终不明白她做错了什么。和指挥官相处越久,你就越觉得他做事根本没什么道理。你绝不能认为"我遵守什么规则,我就安全了",那是不行的。

辛德勒:他不会开枪打死你的,因为他非常喜欢你,所以他才不让你戴犹太人的肩章。他不想让别人知道,他喜欢一个犹太女人。他在台阶上打死的那个女人,对他来说是个无足轻重的人。她和其他人一样,既不惹他生气,也不讨他喜欢。但你就不同了,海伦。别害怕,这个吻没别的意思。

海　伦:谢谢你。

Beautiful Sentences 妙语佳句

1. I could have got more out. I could have got more.
   我本可以救出更多人的,救出更多。
2. This pin. Two people. This is gold. Two more people. He would have given me two for it, at least one. One more person. A person, Stern. For this.
   这个别针可以救两个人。它是金子做的,可以再多救两个人的。用这个,他本可以再多给我两个名额的,至少也有一个。再多一个人,斯特恩。就用这个。
3. At midnight tonight, the war is over. Tomorrow you'll begin the process of looking for survivors of your families. In most cases, you won't find them. After six long years of murder, victims are being mourned throughout the world. We've survived. Many of you have come up to me and thanked me. Thank yourselves. Thank your fearless Stern and others among you who worried about you and faced death at every moment. I'm a member of the Nazi party. I'm a munitions manufacturer. I'm a profiteer of slave labor. I am a criminal. At midnight you'll be free, and I'll be hunted. I shall remain with you until five minutes after midnight. After which time, and I hope you'll forgive me, I have to flee. I know you have received orders from our Commandant, which he has received from his superiors, to dispose of the population of this camp. Now would be the time to do it. Here they are, they're all here. This is your opportunity. Or you could leave, and return to your families as men instead of murderers. In memory of the countless victims among your people, I ask us to observe three minutes of silence.
   这个午夜,战争就结束了。明天你们就可以去寻找你们幸存的亲人了。对大多数人而言,也许并不一定找得到。经过长达 6 年的屠杀,举世都在哀悼这些受难者,但我们幸存了下来。你们当中有很多人曾当面谢我,其实你们应该感谢的是你们自己,以及你们大无畏的斯特恩,还有你们身边曾为你们担忧并时刻和你们一同面对死亡威胁的人。我是纳粹党人,也是个军火商,我是个奴役劳工的奸商,还是个战犯。午夜时分,你们将获得自由,而我将被追捕。我会和你们一起待到0时5分,届时,我希望你们能够原谅我,因为我将不得不去逃亡。我知道你们接受指挥官的命令,而你们的指挥官也一样接受他上级的命令,要你们清除这个集中营里的所有囚犯。现在正是你们动手的时候。他们在这儿,全都在这儿。这是你们的机会,或者你们可以选择离开,堂堂正正地回到家人身边,而不是以刽子手的身份回去。为纪念你们当中的无数的受害者,我希望大家来默哀三分钟。

Some may be wicked, and some may be despicable. Only when I put myself in their position did I know they are more miserable than I. So forgive all that you have met, no matter what kind of persons they are.
也许有些人很可恶,有些人很卑鄙。而当我设身为他着想的时候,我才知道:他比我还可怜。所以请原谅所有你见过的人,好人或者坏人。

Thought about Life 人生感悟

一切事物都有其自身的存在方式。人们有时真的需要理解并尊重这种生活方式,与万事万物和谐相处,才能建造一个真正的理想家园。人们同样需要信仰。信仰真是个很奇妙的东西,很多时候,正是因为信仰,才会使人们找到奋斗的力量。爱在万物间,那才是真正强大的力量。

五、为自由而战
——《勇敢的心》

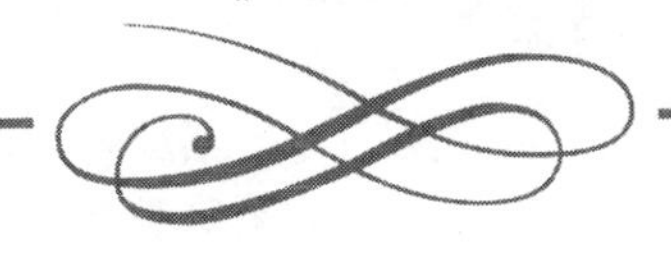

影片简介：

威廉·华莱士小的时候，他的父亲就在同英军的战斗中牺牲了。年少的他在伯父的指导下学习文化知识和格斗技能。当华莱士长大成人后，他返回家乡，然而此时的家乡却在英王的统治下，变得格外压抑。最初华莱士只想过着平静的生活，然而在他心爱的女孩儿梅伦被英国贵族抢走并杀害后，他终于忍无可忍，带领村民起义，奋力抵抗英军。但是，由于英国贵族的出尔反尔，再加上苏格兰贵族的背叛，华莱士的起义宣告失败。华莱士在临刑前，仍然高呼“自由”……

经典对白(一)

A Ride in the Rain 雨中漫步

威廉·华莱士学成归乡后，爱上了美丽的少女梅伦。在一个雨天，他约梅伦出去，二人骑着马，漫步在茂密的森林之中……

Wallace: How did you know me after so long?

Murron: Why, I didn't.

Wallace: No?

Murron: It's just that I saw you staring at me and I didn't know who you were.

Wallace: I'm sorry, I suppose I was. Are you in the habit of riding off in the rain with strangers?

Murron: It was the best way to make you leave.

Wallace: Well, if I can ever work up the courage to ask you again, I'll send you a written warning first.

Murron: It wouldn't do you much good. I can't read.

Wallace: Can you not?

Murron: No.

Wallace: Well, that's something we shall have to **remedy**[1], isn't it.

Murron: You're going to teach me to read, then?

Wallace: Aye, if you like.

Murron: Aye.

Wallace: In what language?

Murron: You're showing off now?

Wallace: That's right. Are you impressed yet?

Murron: No. Why should I be?

Wallace: Yes. Because every single day I thought about you.

Murron: Do that standing on your head, and I'll be impressed.

Wallace: My kilt'll fly up, but I'll try.

Murron: You certainly didn't learn any manners on your travels.

1 remedy *v.* 补救，治疗

Wallace: I'm afraid the Romans are far worse manners than I.

Murron: You've been to Rome?

Wallace: Aye, Uncle took me on a **pilgrimage**[2].

Murron: What was it like?

Wallace: Not nearly as beautiful as you.

Murron: What does that mean?

Wallace: Beautiful. But I belong here.

华莱士:都这么久了,你是怎么认出我的?

梅　伦:我没认出你啊。

华莱士:没有吗?

梅　伦:只是我看到你在看我,而我又不认识你。

华莱士:抱歉,我想我是在看着你。你习惯跟陌生人在雨中骑马吗?

梅　伦:可这是让你离开的最佳方法。

华莱士:好吧,要是我能再次鼓起勇气来约你,我会先写封信的。

梅　伦:写信可没什么用,我不识字。

华莱士:你不识字?

梅　伦:是啊。

华莱士:那我们就得学习识字了,对吗?

梅　伦:你打算教我识字?

华莱士:当然,只要你愿意。

梅　伦:我愿意。

华莱士:你想学哪种语言?

梅　伦:你是在炫耀吧。

华莱士:没错,令你觉得印象深刻了吧?

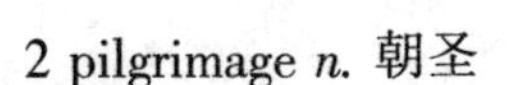

2 pilgrimage *n.* 朝圣

梅　伦：那可没有。我应该那样觉得吗？

华莱士：当然，因为我每天都会想你。

梅　伦：倒立着讲话，我会觉得印象深刻的。

华莱士：那样我的苏格兰裙会飞起来的，不过我会试试。

梅　伦：你在旅行时就没好好学学讲礼貌。

华莱士：恐怕罗马人还不如我有礼貌呢。

梅　伦：你去过罗马？

华莱士：是啊，叔叔带我去朝圣。

梅　伦：罗马怎么样？

华莱士：可不像你那么美。

梅　伦：什么意思？

华莱士：很美，但我属于这里。

经典对白(二)

A True Hero 真正的英雄

华莱士被捕入狱后，王妃殿下前来狱中看望他……

Jailer: Your Highness.

Isabelle: I will see the prisoner.

Jailer: We've got orders from the King that no one...

Isabelle: The King will be dead in a month and his son is a weakling. Who do you think will rule this kingdom? Now open the door.

Jailer: Your Majesty. Come on, **filth**[3]. Up on your feet.

Isabelle: Stop it. Leave me. I said leave me.

3 filth *n.* 肮脏的事物

Wallace: My Lady.

Isabelle: Sir... I come to beg you to **confess**[4] all and swear **allegiance**[5] to the King that he might show you mercy.

Wallace: Will he show mercy to my country?

Isabelle: Mercy is to die quickly, perhaps even live in the Tower. In time, who knows what can happen? If you can only live...

Wallace: If I swear to him, then all that I am…is dead already.

Isabelle: You will die. It will be awful.

Wallace: Every man dies. Not every man really lives.

Isabelle: Drink this. It will dull your pain.

Wallace: No. It will **numb**[6] my **wits**[7]. And I must have them all. For if I'm senseless or if I **wail**[8], then **Longshanks**[9] will have broken me.

Isabelle: I can't bear the thought of your **torture**[10]. Take it.

Wallace: All right.

狱　　卒：陛下。

伊莎贝拉：我要见犯人。

狱　　卒：国王有令，任何人都不准……

伊莎贝拉：国王不出这个月就会死，而王子又软弱无能，你认为这个国家会由谁来统治？快点儿开门。

4 confess *v.* 供认

5 allegiance *n.* 发誓效忠，忠诚

6 numb *v.* 使……变得麻木

7 wits *n.* 智力，才智

8 wail *v.* 哀号，痛哭

9 Longshanks *n.* “长腿的人”

10 torture *n.* 拷问，折磨

狱　　卒：是，陛下。起来，你这个脏东西，快站起来。

伊莎贝拉：住手。退下。我叫你退下。

华莱士：王妃殿下。

伊莎贝拉：阁下……我来是求你招认一切，并发誓效忠国王，这样或许他能饶了你呢。

华莱士：他会饶了我的国家吗？

伊莎贝拉：饶了你就能让你死得痛快点儿，或许也会把你关在塔楼里也说不定。谁知道将来会……

华莱士：可如果我向他宣誓，那样的我……跟死了也没什么两样。

伊莎贝拉：如果你死了，事情会更糟。

华莱士：每个人都会死，但并不是每个人都能真正活着。

伊莎贝拉：把这个喝了，这样就没那么痛苦了。

华莱士：不，它会让我变得麻木，我现在必须要清醒。否则，那群英国佬们就会摧毁我的。

伊莎贝拉：可我无法忍受看你受苦。喝了它。

华莱士：好吧。

Beautiful Sentences 妙语佳句

1. Your heart is free. Have the courage to follow it.
你的心是自由的，要有勇气去追寻它。

2. I'm William Wallace. And the rest of you will be spared. Go back to England. And tell them there that Scotland's daughters and her sons are yours no more. Tell them Scotland is free.
我是威廉·华莱士。我会饶了你们这些人，回英格兰去吧，并且告诉英格兰人，苏格兰的儿女不再受你们的奴役，告诉他们苏格兰是自由的。

3. I am William Wallace! And I see a whole army of my countrymen here in defiance of tyranny. You've come to fight as free men and free men you are! What will you

do without freedom? Will you fight? Against that? Aye. Fight and you may die. Run, and you'll live. At least a while. And dying in your beds, many years from now, would you be willing to trade all the days from this day to that for one chance, just one chance, to come back here and tell our enemies that they may take our lives, but they'll never take our freedom!

我就是威廉·华莱士！我看到我们的国民军在此向暴政宣战，你们是以自由人的身份来参战的，你们是自由的！如果没有自由你们会怎样？你们还愿意作战吗？愿意对抗敌人吗？是的。作战，可能会战死。而逃走，可能会活下来，至少能活上些时日，多年后便躺在床上等死。从今天起，你们是否愿意用剩下的日子来换一个机会，为了这个机会，回到这里，向我们的敌人大声宣称，他们或许会夺走我们的生命，但却夺不走我们的自由！

4. Those men who bled the ground red at Falkirk, they fought for William Wallace, and he fights for something that I've never had. And I took it from him when I betrayed him and I saw it in his face on the battlefield. And it's tearing me apart.

那些人，在福尔科克之战中抛头颅、洒热血，他们为威廉·华莱士而战，而华莱士则为我从未有过的自由而战。可我却背叛他，夺走了他的自由，在战场上我看到了他的神情，那种神情真叫我无地自容。

5. You have bled with Wallace! Now bleed with me.

你们曾与华莱士并肩作战，现在也跟我并肩作战吧。

6. You tell your King, that William Wallace will not be ruled. Nor will any Scot while I'm alive.

你告诉你的国王，就说威廉·华莱士绝不会屈服，只要我活着，苏格兰人民也绝不会屈服。

Everyone has his inherent ability(power or capacity) which is easily concealed by habbits, blured by time, and eroded by laziness(or inertia).

每个人都有潜在的能量，只是很容易被习惯所掩盖，被时间所迷离，被惰性所消磨。

7. I don't want to lose heart! I want to believe as he does. I will never be on the wrong side again.

   我不想失去信心！我想像他那样信心十足，我再也不会选择错误的一方了。

8. Peace is made in such way; slave is made in such way!

   和平是这样换来的，而奴役也是这样换来的！

Thought about Life 人生感悟

这是一部悲壮的英雄史诗，它深刻地表现出了“自由”的伟大含义。华莱士是苏格兰的民族英雄，他热爱国家，热爱人民，热爱自由，为此，他不惜牺牲自己的生命。他是“自由”的象征，正是他的精神激励着苏格兰人民不断前行，为争取民族独立而顽强斗争。华莱士最终选择了为“自由”而死，是因为他真正懂得生存的意义。可以说，他的人生才是真正完美的人生！

六、一项艰巨的救援任务
——《勇闯夺命岛》

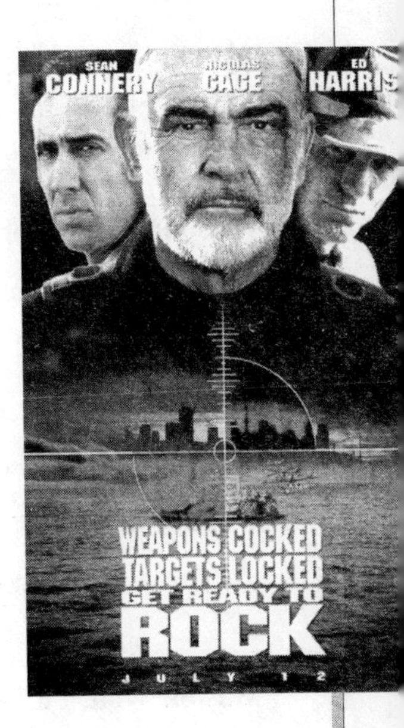

影片简介：

汉默准将为了给那些阵亡的海军陆战队员索要赔偿金，在被称作“恶魔岛”的阿卡拉岛上布置了毒气弹，并挟持了正在游览该岛的游客。为了解救人质，当局启用了一个身份特殊的人物——梅森，由他带领着一队突击队员和一位拆弹专家斯坦利去完成这个任务。然而在他们刚刚到达岛上时，就中了圈套，除了梅森和斯坦利外，其他队员全都牺牲了。他们二人将如何面对这项艰巨的任务……

经典对白(一)

A Private Talk 私人谈话

梅森在联邦调查局探员的看管下逃了出来，他的目的是……

Mason: Jade?

Stacy: No, Stacy. Jade's friend.

Mason: Were you afraid to come alone?

Jade: Yeah. It's okay.

Stacy: I'll be over here if you need me.

Mason: The last photograph I had of you, you were about ten.

Jade: Yeah? Well, I found a picture of you among my mom's things when she died.

Mason: Oh, yeah? Well, uh... Why don't we take a walk?

Stanley: I got him. Palace of Fine Arts.

Mason: Your mother, uh... Yeah, well, sh–she was very special.

Jade: Yeah, she was. But I don't think that we should **romanticize**[1] what happened between you and her. Meeting in a bar after a Led Zeppelin concert. Head out, and I was the result.

Mason: Well, I'd like to think it would've led somewhere if only...

Jade: If only what? Six federal **marshals**[2] hadn't kicked down our door and **dragged**[3] you back to prison? I'm sorry.

Mason: It's all right.

Jade: So, they let you out?

Mason: Yeah.

Jade: That's good. What did you do?

Mason: J...Jade, I don't have a great deal of time here. But I'll be coming back. And, uh...Maybe we can...

Jade: What? We can what?

Mason: You know, you're almost the only evidence that I exist.

1 romanticize *v.* 使浪漫化，传奇化

2 marshal *n.* 元帅，指挥官

3 drag *v.* 拖、拽、拉

Jade: But I don't know you.

Mason: That's what I want to change, eh? I've rehearsed this speech a thousand times on the chance that we would meet. Here we are, and I'm lost.

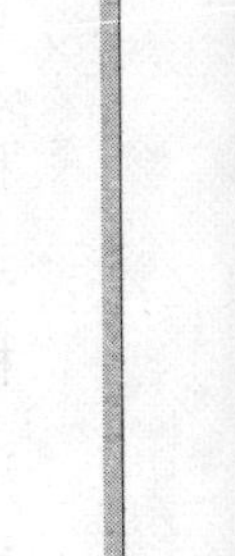

Jade: Well, I don't know how I'm supposed to be feeling either.

Mason: Jade, I'm not an evil man. If you can believe that, then it's a start.

Jade: Okay. Is this about you? You broke out of prison again, didn't you? Why did you come to me?

Stanley: FBI, ma'am. Your father's working with us. He's helping us resolve a dangerous situation.

Jade: He is?

Stanley: Yes, ma'am. Well, gee whiz, John, I guess we ought to get goin', huh?

Mason: Whatever you say, Stanley. Thank you for that. You could've handled it differently.

Stanley: What do you say we cut the chitchat, a-hole? You almost got me killed twice. And my jaw hurts like hell!

Mason: Good.

Officer: Cocksucker! If I had my way, you would be shipped back to Wolfburg in leg irons and caged like an animal for the rest of your natural fucking life! You **wrecked**[4] half the city!

梅　森：洁德？

史黛西：我是史黛西，洁德的朋友。

4 wreck *v.* 毁坏

梅　森:你害怕一个人来?

洁　德:是的。没事儿的。

史黛西:好吧,需要的话,我就在那儿。

梅　森:上次看到你的照片,你才十岁。

洁　德:是吗?妈妈去世后,我也在她的遗物里找到了你的照片。

梅　森:是吗?呃,想走走吗?

斯坦利:我发现他了。他在美术馆。

梅　森:你母亲,呃,她……她很特别。

洁　德:是的,她是很特别。但是我不太欣赏你们二人的浪漫情调。听完音乐会,在酒吧里刚刚认识,结果当晚,就有了我。

梅　森:我们本来会进展得很顺利,只是……

洁　德:只是什么?六个警察闯进我们的家把你拽到大牢里去了?很抱歉。

梅　森:没什么。

洁　德:他们放了你了?

梅　森:是的。

洁　德:很好。你犯了什么罪?

梅　森:洁德,我现在没有太多时间,但我会回来的。或许那时我们可以……

洁　德:什么?我们可以什么?

梅　森:你知道吗?或许只有你能证明我的存在。

洁　德:可我不了解你。

梅　森:那正是我想改变的!我念叨了不止一千遍见到你时我想说的话,可见面时,我还是忘记了。

洁　德:我也不知道自己心里是什么感受。

梅　森:洁德,我不是坏人。如果你相信,那就是很好的开端。

洁　德:好吧。他们是来找你的?你又逃狱了,对吗?你为什么来找我?

斯坦利:联邦探员,小姐。令尊在为我们工作,在帮我们排除一个险境。

洁　德:是吗?

斯坦利:是的,小姐。见鬼,梅森,我们该走了吧。

梅　森：听您的吩咐，斯坦利。谢谢了，你完全可以逮捕我的。

斯坦利：别跟我废话了，混蛋。你差点害死我两次，我的下巴都要疼死了！

梅　森：很好。

警　官：你这个狗杂种！要是我，一定会把你送回大牢，戴上脚镣，让你的余生都在笼子里渡过。你毁了半个城市！

Let him only see the thorns Who has eyes to see the rose.

让睁眼看着玫瑰花的人也看到它的刺。

经典对白(二)

Urge 说服

在突击队员全军覆没后，只剩下梅森和斯坦利二人了，斯坦利在试图说服梅森和他一同完成这个任务……

Stanley: Mason! Mason! There are 81 **hostages**[5] still up there.

Mason: Yeah, like me.

Stanley: All right, you wanna play tough? You wanna play tough with me? Okay. FBI! Freeze, sucker! I'll fire.

Mason: No, you won't.

Stanley: Throw down.

Mason: You're not the sort.

Stanley: Let's find out.

Mason: I could. You, no. Besides, your **safety's**[6] on.

Officer: Goodspeed, have you resolved the situation?

Stanley: Not yet. He's got all the guns now, sir.

Officer: Shit!

5 hostage *n.* 人质

6 safety *n.* 保险栓

Stanley: You're right, I don't use guns and I don't kick down doors. This is what I do.

Mason: I haven't got my glasses.

Stanley: What it says is Chemical Weapons Specialist. That's right. I got a **lunatic**[7] up there, man with 15 missiles armed with some really **funky**[8] stuff.

Mason: That lying Womack. You could've told my daughter.

Stanley: It was **classified**[9]. Look, I'm in the same situation. They've got my girlfriend in the city with a baby on the way. Look, I can **defuse**[10] the rockets. I really can. But I'm gonna need your help, and I'm gonna need it right now.

斯坦利:梅森！梅森！上面还有81名人质呢。

梅　森:对,像我一样。

斯坦利:好啊,你还真不领情？想来硬的？好！联邦探员,站着别动,浑蛋！我会开枪的。

梅　森:不,你不会。

斯坦利:放下武器。

梅　森:你不是那种人。

斯坦利:试试看啊！

梅　森:我行,可你不行。你连保险栓都没打开。

警　官:古德斯比,问题解决了吗？

斯坦利:还没有。他把我的枪也给缴了。

警　官:该死！

斯坦利:你说得没错,我不使枪,也不会踹门。这才是我做的事儿。

梅　森:我没戴眼镜。

斯坦利:上面写着化学武器专家。听着,上面有个疯子,他有十五枚有致命的毒气导弹。

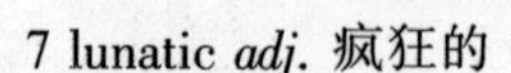

7 lunatic *adj.* 疯狂的

8 funky *adj.* 畏缩的，怯懦的

9 classified *adj.* 机密的

10 defuse *v.* 拆除

梅　森:沃马克这个骗子。你该告诉我女儿的。

斯坦利:那是高度机密。我的情况跟你一样,我的女朋友也在城里,而且还怀了孩子。听着,我能拆除导弹,我真的能,不过我现在需要你的帮助。

Beautiful Sentences 妙语佳句

1. Sir, we know why you're out here. God knows I agree with you. But like you, I swore to defend this country against all enemies, foreign, sir, and domestic. General, we've spilled the same blood in the same mud. You know goddamn well I can't give that order.
   将军,我们知道你的意图。其实我也赞同你。但我跟你一样,也发誓要保卫祖国,消灭一切敌人,不论他们是国外的,还是国内的。将军,我们都为这个国家洒过热血,你知道我是不会下这命令的。
2. Men following the general, you're under oath as United States Marines! Have you forgotten that? We all have shipmates we remember. Some of them were shit on and pissed on by the Pentagon. But that doesn't give you the right to mutiny!
   跟随将军的战士们,你们曾誓言效忠国家。你们忘了吗?我们都有战友命丧战场,有些人甚至是被五角大楼给耍了。但这不能成为你们叛变的理由啊!
3. Oh, I was trained by the best. British Intelligence. Come on. But in retrospect, I'd rather have been a poet or a farmer.
   我受过世界顶级的训练,在英国情报局。来吧。老实说,我更愿意当个诗人或是农夫。
4. Uh, nurtured the hope that there was hope. That one day I'd

Be sure that you have never had any regrets in your life which only lasts for a few decades. Laugh or cry as you like, and it's meaningless to oppress yourself.

人生短短几十年,不要给自己留下什么遗憾,想笑就笑,想哭就哭,该爱的时候就去爱,无须压抑自己。

breathe free air. Perhaps meet my daughter. Modest hopes, but, uh, they kept a man alive.

我在心里怀有希望,希望有一天能再次呼吸新鲜空气,或许还能见到我的女儿。虽说希望很渺茫,却能让人活下去。

5. Hummel won't do it. He's a soldier, not a murderer. I read it in his eyes.

汉默不会那么做的,他是个军人,不是屠夫,从他的眼里我看得出来。

Thought about Life 人生感悟

人们有时候要忍受各种不公正的待遇。有时我们甚至觉得这种不公正会使我们抑郁、沮丧,甚至对未来失去信心。然而转念想一想,像梅森那样,心中怀有美好的希望,无论怎样绝望,都相信前方会有一丝希望,那样也许境遇就会不同了。也许豁然开朗的桃花源就是怀有希望的人能够找到的吧。

七、我愿用生命来守护这个秘密
——《风语者》

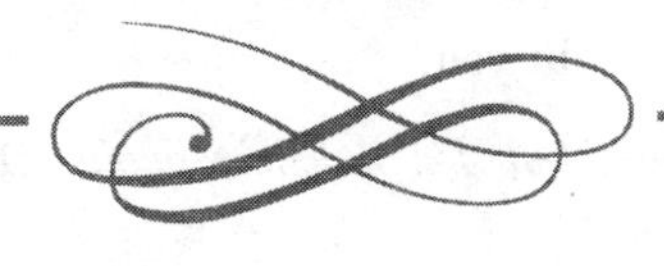

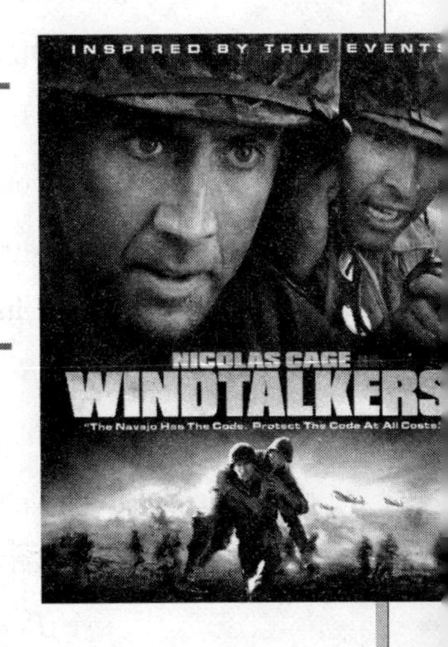

影片简介:

二战初期,美国海军召集了几百名印第安纳瓦霍族人作为他们独有的“密码战士”来传递情报,人称他们为“风语者”。由于“风语者”肩负着美军机密,因此军方也为每个“风语者”配备了一名海军士兵来贴身保护他们。海军陆战队员乔·安德斯的任务就是保护“风语者”本。然而,他的任务并不是保护“风语者”,而是保护“密码”,在“风语者”被俘时,他就要无情地杀掉“风语者”。在战友情谊和军人职责面前,乔该如何选择……

经典对白(一)

Choice 抉择

在激烈的战斗中,“风语者”查理不幸被日本士兵俘虏,就在这关键的时刻,乔痛苦地选择了杀掉他以保护密码。在本得知此事后，便怒斥乔，甚至要杀了他……

Ben: Enders! I can't find Ox or Whitehorse. Have you seen them?

Joe: He's over there.

Ben: Oh, shit... This was supposed to be a secured area! What happened?

Joe: I killed him.

Ben: You...you what?

Joe: I took my **grenade**[1] and... and I threw it and I **blew** him **up**[2].

Ben: What the hell is wrong with you?

(*Ben starts to beat Joe, but Joe doesn't avoid. Others try to stop Ben.*)

Another Soldier: Yahzee! Yahzee! Yahzee, no!

Ben: Get up!

(*Ben uses a gun pointing Joe.*)

Joe: Come on. You can do it.

Another Soldier: Yahzee. Let him go. Yahzee, no.

Joe: Go on. Why can't? Come on. Do it. Do it!

Another Soldier: No.

本:安德斯！我没找到小欧或怀特豪斯。你看见他们了吗？

乔:他在那儿呢。

本:老天,妈的……这里不是挺安全的吗！发生了什么？

乔:我杀了他。

本:你……你说什么？

乔:我把手榴弹拿出来,然后……然后我扔了过去,把他给炸死了。

本:你他妈的有什么毛病？

(本开始打乔,但是乔并不躲闪。其他人试图阻拦本。)

1 grenade *n.* 手榴弹

2 blow up 爆炸，炸死某人

另一名士兵：亚吉！亚吉！亚吉，住手！

本：你给我起来！

（本用枪指着乔。）

乔：来啊，开枪吧。你可以做到的。

另一名士兵：亚吉！饶了他吧。亚吉，住手吧。

乔：来啊。为什么不开枪？来啊，开枪。开枪啊！

另一名士兵：不。

While our dream is confronted with the reality, you always feel painful. Just trample on the pain, or you'll be beat down by it.

当幻想和现实面对时，总是很痛苦的。要么你被痛苦击倒，要么你把痛苦踩在脚下。

经典对白(二)

Friendship 友情

失去了同胞的本十分难过，他不顾乔的警告擅自跑去杀敌，而使自己陷入险境。乔为了救本，献出了自己的生命……

Joe: All right, let's go. We're gonna make it outta here.

Ben: Damn it, Joe. Just **get it over with**[3].

Joe: Shut up, Ben.

Ben: Do it, Joe. Do it!

Joe: No one else is gonna die, Ben. No one else is dying.

(*Joe carries Ben on his shoulder in the rain of shots, then drags him back to their trench.*)

Ben: Joe, we did it. God. God! Oh, my God...Oh, Joe... We saved a lot of **marines**[4] today.

Joe: Yeah, we did, Ben. Charlie...You know I didn't want to. Right?

3 get sth. over with 做完某事，把某事完成

4 marine *n.* 海军陆战队队员

Joe: Hail...Hail Mary... full of grace... our... our Lord is with thee... Holy Mary, mother of God... pray for us...

Another Soldier: I got the last of 'em, Joe.

(*The war is over. Ben takes his son to Joe's grave.*)

Ben: His name was Joe Enders...from South Philadelphia. He was a fierce **warrior**[5], a good marine. If you ever tell a story about him, George... say he was my friend.

乔:好了,快走吧。我们得离开这儿。

本:可恶,乔。你杀了我吧。

乔:闭嘴,本。

本:动手吧,乔。快动手!

乔:没人会死的,本。再没人会死了!

(乔冒着枪林弹雨背着本,拖着本向着壕沟跑去。)

本:乔,我们做到了。天啊。天!我的天啊……哦,乔……我们今天救了很多陆战队员。

乔:是啊,我们做到了,本。查理……你知道我不想的……对吗?

乔:神……神非常……伟大……我们的……我们的上帝与您同在……圣洁的玛丽,您是圣母……请为我们祈祷……

另一名士兵:我们消灭敌人了,乔。

(战争结束了,本带着他的儿子来到乔的墓地。)

本:他的名字叫乔·安德斯……来自费城南部。他是一名英勇的战士,一名优秀的陆战队队员。乔治,以后你若是讲起关于他的事迹时……请记得说他是我的朋友。

5 warrior *n.* 勇士

Beautiful Sentences 妙语佳句

1. Under no circumstances can you allow your codetalker to fall into enemy hands. Your mission…is to protect the code...at all costs.
   无论发生什么情况,都绝不能让电码破译员落入敌人手中。你的任务……就是保护密码……不惜一切代价。
2. You mean what am I doing in this uniform? It's my war too, Sergeant. I'm fighting for my country, for my land, for my people.
   你是问我为什么来参军吗?这也是我的战争,中士。我为我们的国家、我们的土地和我们的同胞而战。
3. I got orders, Gunny. He's my responsibility.
   甘尼,我受命保护他。这是我的责任。
4. To honor them. Their memory. You know, it wasn't your fault, Joe. You were just followin' orders.
   只是想去悼念他们和他们的精神。要知道,这不是你的错,乔。你只不过是奉命行事罢了。
5. This detail. My duty. I can't do it.
   有关于我的职责,这里写得很详细。我做不到。
6. I was following orders, Ben. My orders were to protect the code. If one of you got caught, talked, the code would be useless. I was following orders, Ben.
   我只是在执行任务,本。我的任务是保护密码。如果你们当中有人被捕,若是他讲出实情,那密码也就没有用了。我只是在执行任务,本。

Penitence is something that enervates our spirit, causing a greater loss than loss itself and making a bigger mistake than mistake itself, so never regret.

后悔是一种耗费精神的情绪,后悔是比损失更大的损失,比错误更大的错误,所以不要后悔。

Thought about Life 人生感悟

友情与责任,二者都是人生中最重要的事物,它们对人生的重要意义也根本不具备可比性。然而让人无奈的是,人生有时就是要面临着这种艰难的抉择,人们不得不选择其一而舍弃另一个。当抉择之时来临之际,有人选择逃避,也有人选择勇敢面对,关键在于你要如何把握你自己的人生了。

八、电影业的里程碑——《雨中曲》

影片简介：

好莱坞的一个明星之夜，影视巨星唐阴差阳错地与青年女子凯西相遇。凯西对唐的表演方式很不以为然，然而唐却对聪慧的凯西萌生了爱意。当时，好莱坞电影业正经历着由无声影片向有声影片过渡的巨变，由于技术上的不成熟，唐和他的老搭档女演员莱蒙共同主演的有声电影《决斗骑士》也以惨败收场。就在唐的事业陷入低谷时，凯西却在幕后帮助了他……

经典对白(一)

First Meet with Kathy 初遇凯西

唐在路上被一群热情的影迷团团围住，幸好被凯西小姐所救，不过两人在车上聊得可并不投机……

Don: I'd very much like to know whose **hospitality**[1] I'm enjoying.

Kathy: Selden Kathy Selden.

Don: **Enchanted**[2], Miss Selden. I'm sorry I frightened you. I was getting a little too much love from my **adoring**[3] fans.

Kathy: Oh, that's what you were running away from. They did that to you? That's terrible!

Don: Yes. Yes, it is, isn't it? It is terrible. Well, we movie stars get the glory. I guess we have to take the little heartaches that go with it. People think we lead lives of **glamour**[4] and romance, but we're really lonely—terribly lonely.

Kathy: Oh, Mr. Lockwood, I really can't tell you how sorry I am about taking you for a criminal before. But it was understandable, under the circumstances. I knew I'd seen you.

Don: Which of my pictures have you seen?

Kathy: I don't remember. I saw one once.

Don: You saw one once?

Kathy: Yes, I think you were **dueling**[5] and there was a girl—Lina Lamont. But I don't go to the movies much. If you've seen one you've seen them all.

Don: Thank you.

Kathy: Oh, **no offense**[6]. Movies are entertaining enough for the **masses**[7] but the **personalities**[8] on the screen just don't **impress**[9] me. I mean they don't talk,

1 hospitality *n.* 热情
2 enchanted *adj.* 令人陶醉的，入迷的
3 adoring *adj.* 崇拜的，爱慕的
4 glamour *n.* 魅力
5 duel *v.* 决斗
6 no offense 无意冒犯
7 mass *n.* 大众
8 personality *n.* 个性
9 impress *v.* 给人留下深刻印象

they don't act, they just make a lot of **dumb**[10] show. Well, you know…like that.

Don: You mean like what I do?

Kathy: Well, yes! Here we are, Sunset and Camden.

Don: Wait a minute, you mean I'm not an actor? **Pantomime**[11] on the screen isn't acting?

Kathy: Of course not. Acting means great parts, wonderful lines, speaking the glorious words. Shakespeare. Ibsen.

Don: Words... Tell me what's your **lofty**[12] **mission**[13] in life that let's you **sneer**[14] at my **humble**[15] **profession**[16]?

Kathy: I'm an actress...

Don: Oh...

Kathy: ...on the stage.

Don: Oh, on the stage. Well, I'd like to see you act, what are you in right now? I could brush up on my English, or bring along an **interpreter**[17], that is if they'd let in a "movie" actor.

Kathy: Well, I'm not in a play right now, but I will be. I'm going to New York...

Don: Oh, you're going to New York and then some day we'll

You know some birds are not meant to be caged, their feathers are just too bright.

你知道,有些鸟儿是注定不会被关在牢笼里的,它们的每一片羽毛都闪耀着自由的光辉。

10 dumb *adj.* 沉默的，无声的，愚笨的
11 pantomime *n.* 哑剧
12 lofty *adj.* 崇高的
13 mission *n.* 任务，使命
14 sneer *v.* 嘲笑，讥笑
15 humble *adj.* 卑微的，低下的
16 profession *n.* 职业
17 interpreter *n.* 翻译，译员

all hear of you, won't we? Kathy Selden as Juliet, as Lady Macbeth, as King Lear. You'll have to wear a beard for that one of course.

Kathy: Oh, you can laugh if you want, but at least the stage is a **dignified**[18] profession.

Don: Dignified profession.

Kathy: What do you have to be so **conceited**[19] about? You're nothing but a shadow on film... a shadow. You're not flesh and blood.

Don: Oh, no?

Kathy: Stop!

Don: What can I do to you? I'm only a shadow.

Kathy: You keep away from me! Just because you're a big movie star, wild parties, swimming pools, you expect every girl to fall in a dead faint at your feet. Well, don't you touch me!

Don: Fear not, sweet lady! I will not **molest**[20] you. I am but a humble **jester**[21], and you?You are too far above me! Farewell, Ethel Barrymore! I must tear myself from your side!

唐:这位女士,你对我如此热情,我能知道您的名字吗?

凯西:塞尔顿。凯西·塞尔顿。

唐:哦,真迷人,塞尔顿小姐。实在抱歉,刚刚吓到你了。我的影迷实在是太崇拜我了。

凯西:啊,你逃跑就是为了这个。他们就是这样崇拜你的?太恐怖了!

唐:是啊,是啊,可不是吗?很吓人吧。我们这些影星既然得到了荣誉,就不得不去承受那些随之而来的麻烦事儿。人们都认为我们生活在魅力和浪漫之中,但事实上我们很孤独——非常地孤独。

凯西:哦,洛克伍德先生,刚刚把你当成罪犯,我实在无法表达我有多么的抱歉。不

18 dignified *adj.* 有尊严的，体面的
19 conceited *adj.* 自负的
20 molest *v.* 骚扰，调戏
21 jester *n.* 小丑，爱开玩笑的人

过出于那种情况,也是可以理解的。我就知道我见过你。

唐:你看过我演的哪部片子?

凯西:我记不得了。我曾经看过一部。

唐:你只看过一部?

凯西:是的,我想那时你正与人决斗,还有个女孩儿——叫莉娜·莱蒙。但是我不常去看电影,看过一部也就等于都看过了。

唐:哦,谢谢。

凯西:哦,我无意冒犯。电影具有很强的大众娱乐性,但是银幕上的人物个性并没有给我留下很深刻的印象。我是说他们既不说话,也不做动作,只不过摆出几个呆子似的造型。哦,你知道的吧……像这样。

There is something inside, that they can't get to, that they can't touch. That's yours.
那是一种内在的东西,他们到达不了,也无法触及的,那是你的。

唐:你指的是我做的那些动作吗?

凯西:哦,是的。哦,我们到了。尚塞特和卡姆登。

唐:请等一下,你是说我不是个演员?银幕上的哑剧表演也不算是表演?

凯西:当然不是了。表演指的是伟大的部分,美妙的台词,讲一些华丽的辞藻,像莎士比亚,易卜生那样的。

唐:还辞藻呢……请问您是做什么崇高职业的,能让您如此嘲笑我这种职业卑微的人呢?

凯西:我是一名女演员……

唐:哦……

凯西:……在舞台上表演的。

唐:哦,在舞台上表演的。好啊,我倒很想看看你的表演呢,那最近您在上演什么剧目呢?或许我可以修炼下自己的英语,或是和您学学台词,要是他们也能允许我这个"电影"演员来表演的话。

凯西:我现在还没有演剧呢,但我将要演的。我打算去纽约……

唐:哦,你打算去纽约啊,那总有一天大家会听说你啦,对吧?凯西·塞尔顿饰演朱丽叶,饰演麦克白夫人,饰演李尔王。哦,当然,演这个角色的时候你得挂上胡子。

凯西:哦,你尽管嘲笑我好了,但是至少舞台剧演员是个神圣的职业。

唐:神圣的职业。

凯西:你有什么了不起的,让你这么自命不凡?你不过是胶片中的一个影子而已……一个影子,无血无肉。

唐:哦,是吗?

凯西:嘿,停下来!

唐:我不过是个影子,我能把你怎么样?

凯西:你离我远点儿!就因为你是个大电影明星吗?狂热的舞会,游泳池,你指望每个女孩子都拜倒在你脚下吗?你别碰我!

唐:别担心,小美人!我可不会欺负你。我不过是个谦卑的小丑,而你呢?你可是远高于我之上呢!再见了,埃塞尔·巴里摩尔!我必须得和您分别了!

经典对白(二)

A Fantastic Idea 绝妙的主意

在影片《决斗骑士》惨败后,唐与凯西及好友科兹莫在一起商讨今后的出路,此时凯西想到了一个绝妙的主意……

Don: Well, take a last look at it. It'll be up for **auction**[22] in the morning.

Cosmo: Oh, you're out of your mind. It's Saturday. No bank is going to **foreclose**[23] until Monday.

Kathy: It wasn't so bad.

22 auction *n.* 拍卖

23 foreclose *v.* 取消抵押品的赎回权

Cosmo: Oh, that's what I've been trying to tell him.

Don: No. There's no use kidding myself. Once they **release**[24] *The Dueling* ***Cavalier***[25], Lockwood and Lamont are through. The picture's a museum piece. I'm a museum piece.

Kathy: Things went wrong with the sound. If you'd just get the technical end **straightened out**[26]...

Don: No, it wasn't that. Now, look, this is sweet of both of you, but I... Something happened to me tonight. I...I... Everything you said about me is true, Kathy. I'm no actor. I never was. Just a lot of dumb show. I know that now.

Remember what should be remembered, and forget what should be forgotten.Alter what is changeable, and accept what is mutable.
记住该记住的，忘记该忘记的。改变能改变的，接受不能改变的。

Cosmo: Well, at least you're **taking it lying down**[27].

Don: No kidding, Cosmo. Did you ever see anything as **idiotic**[28] as me on that screen tonight?

Cosmo: Yeah. How about Lina?

Don: All right, I ran her a close second. Maybe it was a photo finish. Anyway, I'm through, fellas.

Kathy: Don, you're not through.

Cosmo: Of course not. Why? With your looks, your figure, you could drive an ice **wagon**[29] or shine shoes.

Kathy: Block hats.

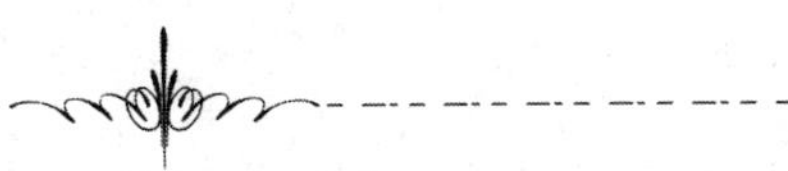

24 release *v.* 发行

25 cavalier *n.* 骑士

26 straighten out 解决，改正

27 take it lying down 甘愿接受某事

28 idiotic *adj.* 愚蠢的，傻的

29 wagon *n.* 货车，四轮马车

Cosmo: Sell pencils.

Kathy: Dig **ditches**[30].

Cosmo: Or worse still, go back into **vaudeville**[31]. (*sings*) "**Fit as a fiddle**[32] and ready for love. I could jump over the moon up above. Fit as a fiddle and ready for love."

Don: Too bad I didn't do that in *The Dueling Cavalier*. They might've liked it.

Kathy: Why don't you?

Don: What?

Kathy: Make a musical.

Don: A musical?

Cosmo: Sure. Make a musical. The new Don Lockwood. He **yodels**[33], he jumps about to music.

Don: Oh, the only trouble is that after they release *The Dueling Cavalier*, nobody'd come to see me jump off the Woolworth Building into a damp **rag**[34].

Cosmo: Then why don't you turn *The Dueling Cavalier* into a musical?

Don: *Dueling Cavalier*?

Cosmo: Sure. They've got six weeks before it's released.

Kathy: Yeah, add some songs and dances, trim the bad scenes, add a couple of new ones.

Cosmo: And you got it.

Don: Hey, I think it'll work.

Kathy: Of course!

Cosmo: It's a **cinch**[35].

30 ditch *n.* 沟，渠

31 vaudeville *n.* 通俗滑稽喜剧

32 fit as a fiddle 身体健康

33 yodel *v.* 用岳得尔唱法演唱

34 rag *n.* (常用复数) 破旧衣服

35 cinch *n.* 容易做的事

Don: You know it may be crazy, but we're gonna do it. *The Dueling Cavalier* is now a musical.

Cosmo: Hot dog!

Kathy: Hallelujah!

Don: Whoopee! Fellas, I feel this is my lucky day, March 23rd.

Cosmo: Oh, no, your lucky day's the 24th.

Don: What do you mean the 24th?

Cosmo: It's 1:30 already. It's morning!

Don: Yes. And what a lovely morning!

唐:好吧,再看它最后一眼了。明早它就该拍卖了。

科兹莫:哦,你疯了吧?再说今天是周六,周一之前这里还是属于你的。

凯　西:没那么糟糕。

科兹莫:哦,那正是我想告诉他的。

唐:不,欺骗自己是没有用的。一旦《决斗骑士》发行了,洛克伍德和莱蒙就全完了。这部电影也就成为历史了,而我也一样成为历史了。

凯　西:问题就出在声音上。如果你掌握了发音技术的话,那……

唐:不,不完全是这样。你们俩的好意我心领了,但是我……今晚我出了点儿问题。我……我……你们以前对我的评价是对的,凯西。我不是个演员,从来都不是。我只不过演过几部哑剧。现在我知道了。

科兹莫:好了,至少你还认识到了这一点。

唐:别开我玩笑了,科兹莫。你还见过比我今晚在银幕上的表演更愚蠢的事儿吗?

科兹莫:是的。琳娜怎么样?

唐:啊,她怎么也比我强啊。也许那不过是洗印照片。反正

Apart from tears, only time could wear everything away. While feeling is being processed by time, conflicts would be reconciled as time goes by, just like a cup of tea that is being continuously diluted.

能冲刷一切的除了眼泪,就是时间,以时间来推移感情,时间越长,冲突越淡,仿佛不断稀释的茶。

我是完了,伙计们。

凯　西:唐,你没有完。

科兹莫:当然你没有完。为什么呢?凭你的长相,你的身材,你还可以卖冰糕或是擦鞋。

凯　西:做帽子。

科兹莫:卖铅笔。

凯　西:挖沟。

科兹莫:还有更糟的呢,重返喜剧舞台。(唱)"身体健康恋爱忙。我要飞到月球上。身体健康恋爱忙。"

唐:真糟糕,我没在《决斗骑士》里那样做。他们很可能会喜欢的。

凯　西:为什么不那么做呢?

唐:什么?

凯　西:拍一部音乐片啊。

唐:音乐片?

科兹莫:对啊,拍一部音乐片。全新的唐·洛克伍德。用岳得尔唱法去唱,投身于音乐片。

唐:唯一麻烦的就是当《决斗骑士》发行后,就没人会来看我脱下马褂换上烂衣了。

科兹莫:那为什么不把《决斗骑士》改成歌舞片呢?

唐:《决斗骑士》?

科兹莫:是啊。在它发行前,我们还有六个星期的时间。

凯　西:对啊,加上一些歌舞,润色一下不太好的场景,再加上几个新的场景。

科兹莫:说到点子上了。

唐:嘿,我觉得这样能行。

凯　西:当然了!

科兹莫:这很简单。

唐:知道吗,这可能很疯狂,但是我们也要做。现在《决斗骑士》是一部音乐片了。

科兹莫:好极了!

凯　西:哈利路亚!

唐:哦耶!伙计们,我觉得今天真是我的幸运日啊,3月23日。

科兹莫:哦不,你的幸运日是24号。

唐:你怎么说是24号?

科兹莫:现在早就1:30了。到早晨了!

唐:是啊。多美妙的早晨啊!

Hope is a good thing and maybe the best of things. And no good thing ever dies.
希望是一个好东西,也许是最好的,好东西是不会消亡的。

Beautiful Sentences 妙语佳句

1. Well, Dora, I've had one motto which I've always lived by, "Dignity. Always dignity."
   是的,朵拉,我有一句生活格言,那就是"尊严,永远都要有尊严。"
2. The price of fame, Don. Now, you've got the glory. You're gonna take the little heartaches going with it. Now, look at me. I got no glory. I got no fame. I got no big mansions. I got no money. But I've got...What have I got? I gotta get out of here.
   名声的代价,唐。现在你已经得到了荣誉,那你就得接受荣誉带给你的麻烦事儿。你看我,既没得到荣誉,也没有出名,没房没地又没钱的。但是我得到了……我得到什么了?哦,我得离开这儿了。
3. But what's the first thing an actor to learn? "The show must go on, come rain, come shine, come snow, come sleet! The show must go on!"
   一名演员最初要学习的事情是什么?那就是:"表演必须要

进行下去。不管是刮风下雨,还是烈日当空,也不管是冰天雪地,还是雨雪交加!表演必须要进行下去!”

4. A beautiful girl is like a great work of art. She's stylish, she's chic, and she also is smart.

美女就像是一件艺术品。着装入时,打扮时髦,而且聪明伶俐。

Thought about Life 人生感悟

变革是需要勇气的。在变革的过程中,总会遇到很多挫折、失败与痛苦,但它们都是最终成功的绝佳伴侣。人们应当感谢那些为了变革而做出牺牲的幕后英雄们,因为他们承担了大多数人的痛苦与孤独。最终,当人们习惯了新生事物的时候,处在变革前沿的领导者们又将向着新的方向前进了。

九、为你设下的圈套
——《偷天陷阱》

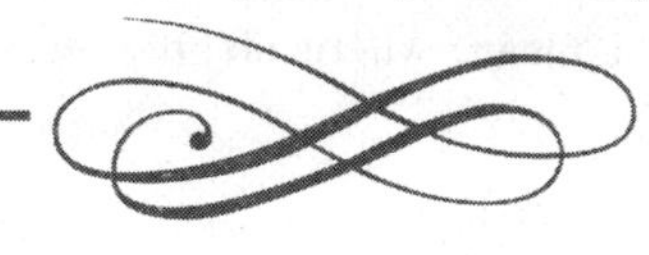

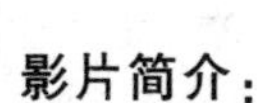

影片简介：

麦克是位有名的艺术品大盗。一日，伦勃朗的一幅名画被盗，人们怀疑是麦克所为。保险公司调查员弗吉尼亚受命调查麦克，可事实上那幅名画却是她偷走的，她的目的是要与麦克合作，准备偷窃更大的目标。而麦克则答应与她合作，可他的目的却是要帮警方诱捕这位女盗贼。然而更为意外的是，两位盗贼在互相为对方设计的陷阱中相爱了……

经典对白(一)

Beginning of Cooperation 合作的开始

麦克带着珍来到他的私人宅邸，珍对这里的一切都充满了好奇……

Gin: No lock? No security?

Mac: You're not **casing the joint**[1] already, are you? This way.

Gin: Oh, wow!

Mac: Shall we?

Gin: Oh, my God. This is quite a **collection**[2].

Mac: Thank you.

Gin: Only **contemporary**[3] art?

Mac: You sound surprised.

Gin: No, it's just not what I expected. I mean, where are the suits of **armor**[4] and crossed **swords**[5]?

Mac: Up in the **attic**[6]. Whiskey?

Gin: Sure. I'd love one. Wow! Is all this paid for?

Mac: With blood. Cheers.

Gin: To the mask.

Mac: I'll show you to your room.

Gin: Who else do you bring here?

Mac: No one.

Gin: That's sad.

Mac: Why?

Gin: Well, to have something like this and not share it with anyone.

Mac: I don't need to share it with anyone. Most people buy art just to **show** it **off**[7]. I collect art for me. Your room's this way. Good night, then.

1 case the joint slang. (行窃前) 探察地形，打探

2 collection *n.* 收藏，收藏品

3 contemporary *adj.* 当代的；同一时代的

4 armor *n.* 盔甲

5 sword *n.* 刀，剑

6 attic *n.* 阁楼

7 show off 炫耀

Gin: But it's still early.

Mac: Yes, we have an early start.

Gin: But I'm not tired! Where do you sleep?

Mac: Why?

Gin: Just in case I need anything.

Mac: May I ask you something?

Gin: Sure.

Mac: Has there ever been anyone you couldn't **manipulate**[8], **beguile**[9], or **seduce**[10]?

Gin: No. Why, do I make you uneasy, Mac?

Mac: No. No, not at all. In fact, I think now might be a good time for you and I to, uh... discuss something.

Gin: Well, what do you have in mind?

Mac: The rules.

Gin: Oh! OK.

Mac: In order for there to be complete trust between thieves, there can be nothing personal. A job is a job. You do your part, I do mine. If one of us is thinking about something other than the task at hand, we'll either both get caught, or both get dead. Good night again.

珍: 没锁？也没个保安？

麦克: 你不是想打这儿的主意吧？这边请。

珍: 哦，哇哦！

麦克: 来吧？

珍: 哦，天啊！这么多收藏品！

Men talk of killing time, while time quietly kills them.
人们在谈论消磨时间，与此同时，时间也在不声不想地销蚀人们的生命。

8 manipulate *v*. 操纵，控制

9 beguile *v*. 诱骗，使着迷

10 seduce *v*. 引诱，诱惑

麦克:谢谢。

珍:只有当代艺术作品吗?

麦克:你感到很惊奇。

珍:不,我只是感到有点儿意外。我是说,整套的盔甲和十字剑放在哪儿?

麦克:在楼上的阁楼里。喝威士忌吗?

珍:好啊,来一杯吧。哇,这些都是用钱买的?

麦克:靠玩命。干杯。

珍:为面具。

麦克:我带你去你的房间。

珍:还有谁来吗?

麦克:没有了。

珍:真可惜。

麦克:怎么这么说?

珍:嗯,这么好的艺术品但却无人分享。

麦克:我并不需要与人分享。大多数人收藏艺术品只是为了炫耀,而我是为我自己收藏。你的房间在这边。好了,晚安。

珍:可是现在还早啊?

麦克:是啊,我们得尽早开工。

珍:可我还不累呢。你睡哪里?

麦克:干嘛?

珍:要是有事我可以找你啊。

麦克:能问你个问题吗?

珍:当然。

麦克:你没有碰到过不接受你的操控,或是不受你迷惑的人吗?

珍:没有。怎么,我令你觉得不自在?

麦克:不,完全不会。事实上,我觉得现在倒是个好机会让我们,呃……来谈一谈。

珍:嗯,你想要谈什么?

麦克:规则。

珍：哦，好啊！

麦克：若要小偷完全信任对方，就不能把个人感情牵扯进去。工作就是工作，你干你的，我干我的。若是有人想着别的事情而不是手边的工作，我们就会因此而被捕或是送命。那晚安了。

Thought feeds itself with its own words and grows.
思想以他自己的语言喂养它自己而成长起来了。

经典对白(二)

Another Trap 另一个陷阱

珍独自一人在车站等待麦克，可她等来的却是……

Gin: Oh! My God! Mac! Oh, I'm sorry! I'm sorry.

Mac: Both all right.

Gin: So what's wrong?

Mac: Wrong? Nothing's wrong. Everything is the... way it has to be.

Gin: What?

FBI: Virginia Baker? Special Agent Aaron Thibadeaux, FBI.

Gin: Come on!

FBI: You're under arrest for grand **larceny**[11]. You have the right to remain silent...

Gin: Mac? Mac!

FBI: Anything you say can be used against you in a court of law. Thanks, Mac. You got your one minute.

Gin: You're a cop.

Mac: No. Well, not exactly. Thibadeaux, believe it or not, is

11 larceny *n.* 盗窃

FBI. And two years ago he caught me and, uh, cut a deal. The deal was that... I had to deliver you. They've been onto you for quite a while.

Gin: And Cruz knew, too?

Mac: No, he's just found out.

Gin: I don't get it. Why didn't you pick me up before? What were you waiting for?

Mac: Well, at first I, uh... well, I wanted to see if you could do it.

Gin: Bullshit! Come on!

Mac: And I wanted to see if I could do it.

Gin: Weren't we partners? I can't believe you'd do this to me.

Mac: Well, you'd better believe it! It's all over. I gave them Greene, the Rembrandt, the mask, and the full seven billion.

Gin: What do you mean, seven?

Mac: So you'll just have to make do with one, hm?

Cruz: I thought you said one minute.

FBI: Relax, Hector. He knows what he's doin'.

Mac: Now, plan C. In your pocket, you'll find an envelope. A passport, visa, money. Where you go from here is up to you. And you'll still hold the record...alone.

FBI: Mac!

Gin: I don't understand. Why are you doing this?

Mac: Well, believe me, I was prepared for everything, except you.

FBI: Mac! Time's up!

Gin: Come with me.

Mac: Gin, your life, it's all ahead of you. Mine...this is all I've got.

Gin: No. You've got me. You got me.

Mac: Listen carefully. In your other pocket...

FBI: Let's do it.

(*Gin uses a gun pointing Mac's head.*)

Gin: Move and I blow his head off!

FBI: Everybody, just be cool.

Gin: Nobody move! No one moves, OK?

FBI: Fellas, put your weapons down.

Gin: You, too, Hector! I swear I'm gonna kill him if you move!

FBI: We'll get her at the next stop.

Gin: Bye, Mac.

FBI: She's headed toward the next station. Move! Go! Go! Move it now! No guns! Get out of here now!

Cruz: You know, I don't know what just went down here, but I'm gonna see that you're **busted**[12] **outta**[13] the Bureau for it. It **ain't**[14] over, Mac.

Mac: I believe you.

FBI: Well, Mac, this looks like the end of a terrible friendship. But you still owe me for today.

Mac: I always pay my debts. Four **prototype**[15] super **chips**[16]. Value five million dollars each.

FBI: Hope she was worth it.

Mac: Oh, she was.

FBI: I'll be seein' you, Mac.

Mac: I don't think so.

FBI: OK, Bob, let the people back on the platform. Bring me a damn car.

(Now, Gin appears on the platform, again.)

Mac: How did you do it?

Life was like a box of chocolates, you never know what you're gonna get.
生命就像一盒巧克力，你永远无法得知下一块是什么味道。

12 bust *v.* 起诉，降级

13 outta=out of slang. 在……之外

14 ain't=isn't slang. 不是

15 prototype *n.* 原型

16 chip *n.* 芯片

Gin: I jumped trains mid-station. When the train slowed down, I just... It was perfect.

Mac: Was it now?

Gin: You know what, Mac? I don't wanna hold the record alone.

Mac: No?

Gin: I need your help on another job.

Mac: Wow, the Crown Jewels or something?

Gin: No! Come on, too easy! I was thinking of... Well... I know this guy in South Africa. Diamonds, diamonds, diamonds! The biggest diamonds you'll ever see in your life! Have I told you how much I love diamonds? Mac? Mac? Mac!

Mac: What!

Gin: So, what do you think?

Mac: About what?

Gin: About my idea.

Mac: It's doable.

Gin: Ohh! Oh, I'm sorry! I'm sorry!

珍:哦,天啊!麦克!哦,抱歉!抱歉!

麦克:看来我们两个都没事儿了。

珍:是啊,怎么了?

麦克:怎么了?没事儿。一切……都很正常。

珍:什么?

探员:弗吉尼亚·贝克?我是联邦调查局特工阿伦·堤贝多。

珍:别逗了!

探员:你因巨额窃盗罪被捕。你有权保持沉默……

珍:麦克?麦克!

探员:你所说的将作为呈堂证供。谢了,麦克。你们有一分钟的时间。

珍:你是警察?

麦克:不。呃,不完全是。信不信由你,堤贝多是联邦调查员。两年前,他逮到了我,呃，我们达成了协议。协议就是……我得帮他们诱捕你。他们早就盯上你了。

珍：库斯也知道这件事？

麦克：不。他才知道。

珍：我不明白。为什么你们先前不抓我？你们在等什么？

麦克：这个嘛，起初……我，呃……我想看看你有多大能耐。

珍：胡扯！别蒙我了！

麦克：我也想知道我自己的本事。

珍：我们不是搭档吗？真不敢相信你会这样对我。

麦克：那你最好还是相信吧！都结束了。我供出了格林，还把伦勃朗的那幅画和面具都给他们了，还有那70亿美元。

珍：你说70亿，什么意思？

麦克：也就是说，只留给你10亿过日子了，明白？

库斯：不是说一分钟嘛。

探员：别紧张，海特。他自有分寸。

麦克：现在，用C方案。你的口袋里有只信封。里面有护照、签证和钱。想去哪儿随你。而且你还保持着纪录……独自保持的。

探员：麦克！

珍：我不明白。你为什么要这样做？

麦克：相信我，我最放心的就是你了。

探员：麦克！时间到了！

珍：跟我一起走。

麦克：珍，你有大好前程，而我……也只能这样了。

珍：不，你有我。你有我呢。

麦克：听好了，在你的另一个口袋里……

探员：行动吧。

（珍用枪指着麦克的头。）

Miracles happen every day.

奇迹每天都在发生。

珍:谁动我就打死他。

探员:大家要保持冷静。

珍:谁都不许动!谁都不许动!

探员:把枪放下。

珍:还有你,海特!你要是动,我就打死他!

探员:我们到下一站逮捕她。

珍:再见,麦克。

探员:她去下一站了。行动!快点!快!不要带抢!快离开这里!快!快追!

库斯:老实说……我不知道你们怎么把事情搞成这样,像你这种人一定不能呆在局里。麦克,也饶不了你。

麦克:我相信。

探员:麦克,看来我们的交情到此结束了。可今天的事儿,你还欠着我呢。

麦克:我不会欠你人情的。四块超级电脑芯片原型,每块值500万美元。

探员:希望她值得你这样。

麦克:她值得。

探员:后会有期。

麦克:不可能了。

探员:鲍勃,放人进来吧。再给我弄辆车。

(这时,珍又出现在月台上。)

麦克:怎么回事儿?

珍:我半站地就跳车了。火车减速时,我就……太完美了。

麦克:现在呢?

珍:知道吗,麦克?我可不想一个人保持着纪录。

麦克:不。

珍:下个任务我需要你的帮助。

麦克:哇哦,你要偷王冠珠宝什么的吗?

珍:不!得了吧,那太简单了!我刚才在想……好吧……我知道南非有个人。钻石啊,钻石!那会是你一生中见过的最大的钻石!我告诉过你我有多爱钻石吗?

麦克？麦克？麦克！

麦克：干嘛！

珍：你看怎么样？

麦克：什么怎么样？

珍：我的主意。

麦克：我看可行。

珍：哦！抱歉！抱歉！

It's hard to stay mad when there's so much beauty in the world.

世界充满美丽，我又怎能忿忿不休。

Beautiful Sentences 妙语佳句

1. Rule No. 1, never carry a gun, or you might be tempted to use it. Rule No. 2, never trust a naked woman.
   规则之一，一定不要带枪，带着它就会想要用它。规则之二，一定不要相信没穿衣服的女人。
2. In order for there to be complete trust between thieves, there can be nothing personal. A job is a job. You do your part, I do mine. If one of us is thinking about something other than the task at hand, we'll either both get caught, or both get dead.
   若要小偷完全信任对方，就不能把个人感情牵扯进去。工作就是工作，你干你的，我干我的。若是有人想着别的事情而不是手边的工作，我们就会因此而被捕或是送命。
3. Like the wise man said, first we try, then we trust.
   正如那位聪明人说的，考验过后才是信任。
4. It's impossible, but doable.
   那不可能，但是可行。
5. Now, you change partners, you change the rules. And the rules are...Mac does the job, I watch Mac's back. You don't call off

nothing unless I say so.

要是更换搭档，就得改变游戏规则。而我们的规则是……麦克操刀，我做掩护。如果我不同意取消行动，你就不能取消。

6. If you can't feel alive now, you never will.

要是你现在都觉得没活路了，那就永远都不会有了。

7. Believe me, I was prepared for everything, except you.

相信我，我最放心的就是你了。

Thought about Life 人生感悟

人类总是生活在一个极为复杂的圈子中，很多事情表面看似如此，但实际上也许是另一番景象。而且很多事情也不是我们能够掌控的，事态的发展我们也无法预料。就像麦克和珍一样，分别保留着各自的想法，虽说二人合作之初的目的并不相同，但事情最终的发展结果还是会让他们都感到意外的吧。

十、埃及第一女王的传奇人生
——《埃及艳后》

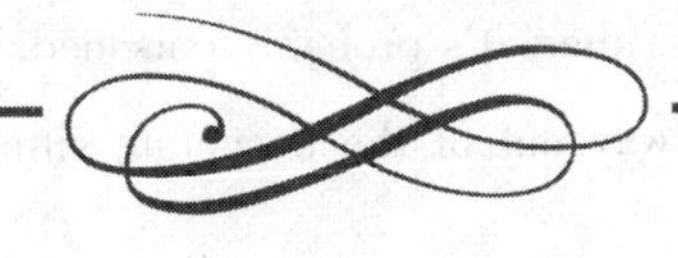

影片简介：

古罗马帝国时期，凯撒打败庞培后，又远征埃及。埃及女皇克莉奥帕特拉为了其政治目的，利用这个机会与凯撒联姻，稳固了她在埃及的皇权，从而建立起一个横跨欧亚非三大洲的强大帝国。女王与凯撒惊天动地的爱情也由此拉开了序幕。在凯撒遇刺身亡后，她又与罗马大将安东尼开始了一段暴风骤雨般的恋情……

经典对白(一)

A Secret Talk 秘密会谈

克莉奥帕特拉藏身于地毯之中，得以见到凯撒，她同凯撒进行了一次秘密会谈……

Caesar: Well, I'm pleased that you received my **summons**[1] after all and were able to...

Cleopatra: Summons? I'm pleased to say I received nothing of the kind. I'm surprised that you thought I would answer one.

Caesar: Young lady, the voyage in your non-magic carpet has **apparently**[2] not tired you, but I've had an exhausting day.

Cleopatra: Caesar, it is **essential**[3] that we understand each other. Only through me can you hope to escape from the desperate situation in which you find yourself. I wouldn't bite into that if I were you. Did you bring it with you? Have you had it tasted? If neither, it's probably poisoned.

Caesar: Well, at least it's another way out of the desperate situation in which I find myself.

Cleopatra: You're being **tolerant**[4] of me, aren't you? Is it because you're so much older? Your maps are **inferior**[5], out of date, compared to mine.

Caesar: They and I have aged together.

Cleopatra: The lakes to the west are poorly marked. Certain important hill positions not even noted.

Caesar: I must arrange for you to address my map makers and general staff.

Cleopatra: We've gotten off to a bad start, haven't we? I've done nothing but **rub**[6] you the wrong way.

Caesar: I'm not sure I want to be rubbed by you at all, young lady. It is permissible for me to sit, is it not?

Cleopatra: Caesar, as quickly as possible, you must set me alone on the **throne**[7] of Egypt.

1 summon *n.* 召见

2 apparently *adv.* 明显地，显而易见地

3 essential *adj.* 必要的，重要的

4 tolerant *adj.* 容忍的，宽容的

5 inferior *adj.* 劣等的，质量差的

6 rub *v.* 惹恼某人

7 throne *n.* 宝座，王位

Caesar: My **mission**[8] here is to put to an end the tire some **squabbling**[9] between your brother and you.

Cleopatra: You're not a fool. Or are you?

Caesar: **Immodestly**[10], perhaps, no.

Cleopatra: You've seen my brother and listened to him and that truly evil man to whom he belongs?

Caesar: Yes.

Cleopatra: Shall we agree, you and I, upon what Rome really wants, has always wanted of Egypt? Corn, grain, treasure–it's the old story. Roman greatness built upon Egyptian riches. You shall have them. You shall have them all–and in peace. But there is only one way, my way. Make me queen.

Caesar: That sounds very much like an **ultimatum**[11].

Cleopatra: There is no other way.

Caesar: From one whose total assets, up to a few moments ago, was a devoted slave and a rolled-up carpet.

Cleopatra: But I have you now, Caesar. Besides, there are my armies and the simple fact that no **mortal**[12] hand can destroy me.

Caesar: Ah, yes. I seem to recall some mention of an **obsession**[13] you have about your **divinity**[14]. Isis, is it not?

8 mission *n.* 任务
9 squabble *n.* 争论，口角
10 immodestly *adv.* 毫不谦虚地
11 ultimatum *n.* 最后通牒
12 mortal *n.* 凡人，世人
13 obsession *n.* 沉迷，妄想
14 divinity *n.* 神性

Cleopatra: I shall have to insist that you mind what you say. I am Isis. I am **worshipped**[15] by millions who believe it. You are not to confuse what I am with the so-called divine origin that every Roman general seems to acquire together with his **shield**[16]. It was Venus you chose to be **descended**[17] from, wasn't it?

Caesar: I must now do a little insisting of my own. First, your journey has tired you after all, and you wish to **retire**[18].

Cleopatra: I am not your servant, Caesar. Do not **dismiss**[19] me.

Caesar: Secondly, you have no armies, young lady. Such as they were, they are gone because you could not pay them. The riches of Egypt are not available, even for your own use, much less to give away. Perhaps in a day or two, we can speak again.

Cleopatra: That may be too late for both of us.

Caesar: Your safety will be my responsibility.

Cleopatra: And what about your own?

Caesar: I am prepared, I believe, for the time being.

Cleopatra: I hope so. I hope you are as wise, as brilliant, the god they say you are. You Roman generals become divine so quickly. A few victories, a few **massacres**[20]. Only yesterday, Pompey was a god. They murdered him, didn't they?

Caesar: Yes.

Cleopatra: Because they thought it would please you. It didn't, did it?

Caesar: No. Today I found myself remembering how much my daughter loved him. She died trying to bear him a son. Gave him this ring.

15 worship *v.* 崇拜，膜拜

16 shield *n.* 盾牌

17 descend *v.* 世代相传，传给

18 retire *v.* 就寝，休息

19 dismiss *v.* 将某人打发走

20 massacre *n.* 屠杀

Cleopatra: Sleep well tonight, Caesar. These next days may be difficult for you. Good night.

凯撒:既然您接受了我的召见,而且还能……

女王:召见?我根本没被召见过。奇怪的是,你认为我会答应吗?

凯撒:小姐,看来你的"魔毯"之旅并不累啊,但我今天可是累坏了。

女王:凯撒,我们得相互了解。你现在的情形很危险,只有我才能帮你逃离这个险境。要是我的话,我决不会吃的。是你带过来的?尝过吗?否则,很可能有毒的。

凯撒:至少它也是一种逃离危险状况的方式。

女王:你在容忍我,对吧?或许是因为你年龄太大了?你的地图可比我的差多了,还很落后。

凯撒:它们已经伴我多年了。

女王:西边的湖泊标记不清,有些重要的山区甚至没有注明。

凯撒:这些就请你跟我的绘图师和参谋长说吧。

女王:我们初次见面可不太融洽,对吗?我除了不讨好你外,也没做什么吧。

凯撒:我也并不希望你来讨好我,小姐。我可以坐下吧,嗯?

女王:凯撒,你一定要尽快帮我登上埃及的王位。

凯撒:我到这儿来,只是为了平息你们姐弟之间的纷争。

女王:你不是傻瓜,对吧?

凯撒:当然不是了。

女王:你见过我弟弟?你听信他和他身边那个恶毒的人?我的弟弟竟受他摆布。

凯撒:是的。

女王:我们都同意,罗马一直很想要埃及吧?玉米、谷物和宝藏,这些都是老生常谈了。罗马的伟大是建立在埃及的富足之上的。你会得到这些的,得到全部,用和平的方式。但方法只有一个,让我当女王。

凯撒:这听起来像是最后通牒。

女王:没别的方法了。

凯撒:可这个人几分钟前,仅有个忠仆和一张地毯。

女王:现在我有你了,凯撒。而且我有军队,无人能够摧毁的军队。

凯撒:对了,我好像听说你具有神性。艾希斯女神,对吗?

女王:我提醒你说话得小心一点儿。我就是艾希斯女神,受到众人的膜拜。我不允许你把我和罗马将军崇拜的神混淆在一起。你们选择的是维纳斯女神,是吗?

凯撒:我得坚持我的意见了。第一,你旅途劳累,需要休息了。

女王:我不是你的仆人,凯撒,你别打发我。

凯撒:第二,你没有军队,小姐。因为你发不出军饷,士兵都跑了。埃及的财富连你都用不上,更别提要赠与他人了。过几天,我们再谈吧。

女王:那对你我来说,就太迟了。

凯撒:你的安全就是我的责任。

女王:那你自己呢?

凯撒:目前,我已做好了准备。

女王:但愿如此。希望你如传闻中一样明智、聪慧。人们很快就会把罗马的将军当成神,这只需几场胜利,几场屠杀。昨天庞培还是个神。是罗马人杀了他吗?

凯撒:是的。

女王:因为他们认为这样会讨好你。但是没有,对吗?

凯撒:是的。我今天才发觉,我的女儿有多么爱他。她因想为他怀个孩子而死,还给了他这枚戒指。

女王:今晚好好睡吧,凯撒。明天对你来说或许更为难过。晚安。

经典对白(二)

The Night of a Dance Party 酒会之夜

安东尼应邀来到克莉奥帕特拉女王的船上，那晚船上举行了一场盛大的舞会……

Death is just a part of life, something we're all destined to do.
死亡是生命的一部分，是我们注定要去做的一件事。

Cleopatra: Marc Antony, how **prompt**[21] you are.

Antony: If I had not been, it would be **unforgivable**[22] of me.

Cleopatra: I had hoped to be here to welcome you as you came aboard.

Antony: If you had been, it would be unforgivable of me.

Cleopatra: Be more tolerant. Forgive yourself now and then.

Antony: Almost three years. Is it possible that you've become even more beautiful?

Cleopatra: Almost three? That long? The time has passed so quickly.

Antony: Your necklace. It seems to be made of gold coins. Coins of Caesar.

Cleopatra: Do you find it **attractive**[23]?

Antony: Very.

Cleopatra: And I find what you're wearing most **becoming**[24]. Greek, isn't it?

21 prompt *adj.* 迅速的

22 unforgivable *adj.* 不可原谅的

23 attractive *adj.* 有吸引力的，有魅力的

24 becoming *adj.* 合适的，适当的

Antony: I have a fondness for almost all Greek things.

Cleopatra: As an almost all-Greek thing, I'm **flattered**[25].

Antony: An unusual necklace. Nothing but gold coins of Caesar. How did you come by it?

Cleopatra: I had it made. I wear it always.

Antony: A **fabulous**[26] **feast**[27].

Cleopatra: One is so limited when one travels by ship.

Antony: This fabulous ship, together with its queen, the fabulous Cleopatra.

Cleopatra: The name of Marc Antony is not exactly unknown to the world. Why, in the last year or so since we met...

Antony: Almost three.

Cleopatra: By now you have become one-third the master of Rome.

Antony: You don't permit yourself to forget him, is that it?

Cleopatra: That's an odd way of putting it. Don't permit myself?

Antony: You find it necessary to wear him around your neck?

Cleopatra: You forget, Antony, in these almost three years, how full your own life has been.

Antony: These can't have been uneventful years for you. You rule Egypt alone.

Cleopatra: Oh, they have been busy, but not full. There's a difference. There cannot be enough hours in the days of a queen, and her nights have too many. So I fill them with memories.

Antony: Of Caesar?

Cleopatra: And of a dream that almost came true. You may remember.

Antony: I remembered that night in Rome, saying it could still come true.

Cleopatra: You said so much that night to so many.

25 flatter *v.* 阿谀奉迎，谄媚

26 fabulous *adj.* 极好的，极为盛大的

27 feast *n.* 筵席，盛宴

Antony: Let me get rid of them all.

Cleopatra: Why? I have arranged an entertainment, a dance in the Greek fashion to welcome the god Bacchus.

Antony: If I make a great show of going, they'll have to leave too. Then I can return and we can, uh...we can talk alone, you and I.

Cleopatra: When would you return?

Antony: In an hour, no more than two.

Cleopatra: How long would you stay?

Antony: Until we had nothing more to say.

Cleopatra: Are you a strong swimmer? We sail at sunrise.

Antony: I don't understand.

Cleopatra: Home to Alexandria, to Egypt.

Antony: Then you've come all this way for just this one night? All this way to make a fool of me.

Cleopatra: Perhaps you would feel less of a fool, if you stayed the night with me, is that it?

Antony: I've told you before. With you, words do not come easily to me. There is too much unsaid within me that I cannot say.

Cleopatra: Then I cannot know it.

Antony: There is much unsaid within you too.

Cleopatra: That is probably true of everybody.

Antony: Stay for a while. I have known you so long but so little. Give me time.

Cleopatra: Not I, not Egypt and Rome together. Not even the gods have time to give you. But Antony, use what you have. Don't waste it by playing at god here in Tarsus while Octavian in Rome becomes a god.

I happen to believe you make your own destiny. You have to do the best with what God gave you.
我相信命运在你自己的手里，你要凭着上帝给你的一切尽力而为。

女　王:马克·安东尼,你动作可真快啊!

安东尼:不这样就太不可原谅了。

女　王:我本想在我的船上欢迎你的。

安东尼:果真如此,我可真是不可原谅了。

女　王:那就对自己宽容点儿,偶尔也要原谅自己的。

安东尼:都快三年了,你竟比昔日还要美艳!

女　王:三年了?有那么久吗?时间过得可真快!

安东尼:你的项链,好像是金币做的。是凯撒的金币。

女　王:漂亮吗?

安东尼:非常漂亮。

女　王:我觉得你的穿着也十分得体。希腊造的,对吗?

安东尼:我一向都很喜欢希腊的东西。

女　王:我也有希腊血统,你这样说真让我受宠若惊。

安东尼:真是条不寻常的项链,全由凯撒金币制成。你怎么弄到的?

女　王:我订做的,一直戴在身上。

安东尼:真是豪华的宴会!

女　王:在船上,能力有限。

安东尼:豪华的船,以及它的女王,富有的克莉奥帕特拉女王。

女　王:马克·安东尼这个名字也是世人熟知的。你看,我们自去年见过面后……

安东尼:几乎快三年了。

女　王:如今你也成了三分之一个罗马的主人了。

安东尼:你还是不让自己忘了他,对吗?

女　王:这话听来有些怪异。为何是“不让自己”?

安东尼:有必要把他戴在脖子上吗?

女　王:你忘了,安东尼,这三年来,你的生活是多么充实。

安东尼:你的生活也不会那么平淡的,你得单独统治埃及。

女　王:是很忙,但并不充实。这是有差别的。女王的工作时间总嫌不够,而在漫漫长夜里，我只能沉溺于回忆之中。

安东尼：回忆凯撒？

女　王：和一个几乎要实现的梦。你可能还记得那个梦吧。

安东尼：我记得在罗马的那个夜晚，说这个梦仍能实现。

女　王：那晚你说了很多，很多。

安东尼：我把他们全都打发走吧。

女　王：为什么？我已经安排了娱乐节目和希腊式的舞蹈，来欢迎酒神巴克科斯。

安东尼：要是我离开的话，他们也都会离开。然后我再回来，我们可以，呃……我们可以私下谈谈，只有你和我。

女　王：你何时回来？

安东尼：一小时以后，不超过两小时。

女　王：你打算呆多久？

安东尼：直到无话可说为止。

女　王：你的游泳技术好吗？我们天亮就起航。

安东尼：我不明白。

女　王：回亚历山大的家，回埃及。

安东尼：你大老远来就只呆这一晚？只为了让我出洋相！

女　王：如果你留下来陪我过夜，就比较有面子了，对吗？

安东尼：我说过，和你在一起，我便不善言辞。我心里有很多话，但却说不出来。

女　王：你不说我便什么都不知道。

安东尼：你也有很多话没有说吧。

女　王：大概每个人都是这样的吧。

安东尼：多呆几天吧。我们相识虽久，但相知不多。给我点儿时间。

女　王：我不行，埃及和罗马也不行，即使是神也没有时间能

If you are ever in trouble, don't try to be brave, just run, just run away.

你若遇上麻烦，不要逞强，你要跑，远远跑开。

够给你。不过安东尼,你得利用你现有的一切条件,别把它浪费在塔希斯的身上,而屋大维都已成为罗马的神了。

Beautiful Sentences 妙语佳句

1. Trust, the word has always made me apprehensive. Like wine, whenever I've tried it, the after effects have not been good. So I've given up wine and trusting.
   信任,这个词总是令我疑惑。就像酒一样,饮酒后的副作用一直是难受。所以我戒了酒,也不再信任他人。
2. A woman, too, must make the barren land fruitful. She must make life grow where there was no life. Just as the Mother Nile feeds and replenishes the earth. I am the Nile.
   女人应该让贫瘠的土地硕果累累,应该让生命无中生有,正像尼罗河哺育并滋养着大地一样。我就是尼罗河。
3. Make his dream yours, Caesar. His grand design. Pick it up where he left off. Out of the patchwork of conquests, one world. And out of one world, one nation. One people on Earth living in peace.
   让他的梦想变成你的,凯撒。他那恢宏的计划啊。重拾他的旧业,继续征服,去征服整个世界。让整个世界成为一个国家,一个民族,让这个国家的每一个人都生活在和平之中。
4. A good thing to remember, my son, what you will not let go, no one will take from you.
   好好记住一件事儿,儿子,你不肯放手的东西,任何人都抢不走。
5. From the first instant I saw you entering Rome on that monstrous stone beast, shining in the sun like a...like a little gold toy, how I envied Caesar. I went suddenly sick with it. Not his conquests or his triumphs. Not his titles or the roaring of the mob. I envied him you.
   我第一次见你时,你坐在狮身人面像上来到罗马,在阳光下闪闪发光,如同黄金一般。从那一刻起，我便十分羡慕凯撒。我突然变得很狂躁，不是因为他的胜利、名衔和人民的拥戴，而是你，我因你而羡慕他。

6. How wrong...how wrong I was. Antony, the love, you followed is here. Without you, Antony, this is not a world I want to live in, much less conquer. Because for me, there would be no love anywhere. Do you want me to die with you? I will. Or do you want me to live with you? Whatever you choose.

   我错了，大错特错。安东尼，你追随的爱就在这里。没有你，安东尼，这便不是我想象中的世界，更别提去征服了。因为对我来说，到处都没有爱了。你要我跟你一起死，我会的。或者你要我跟你一起活着，不管你选择哪一种。

It made me look like a duck in water.
它让我如鱼得水。

7. All kings and especially queens are afraid. They just manage not to show it, something ordinary people cannot do.

   天下的国王，特别是女王都会害怕。他们只是克制着不表现出来而已，这可不是普通人能做到的。

8. The taste of these, they say, is sharp and swiftly over. How strangely awake I feel, as if living had been just a long dream. Someone else's dream now finished at last. But now, will begin a dream of my own which will never end. Antony. Antony, wait.

   据说这东西味道浓烈，还会快速解决问题。奇怪的是，我竟如此清醒，好像生命就是一场长久的梦。现在，他人的梦终于结束了，此刻，就要开始我个人的梦了，一场永无止境的梦。安东尼，安东尼，等等我。

Thought about Life 人生感悟

女王的一生是不平凡的，或许在外人看来，她的地位、她的财富以及她至高无上的权利都是我们追逐一生都难以实现的梦。可就是这样一个女人，却也有着常人无法想象的无奈，她需要掩饰她的痛苦、她的恐惧，还有她的爱情。也许正是因为她的位高权重，她便只能以国家的利益为重。为了她的国家和她的孩子，她又只能去爱强大的男人。这大概就是不平凡的代价吧。

十一、保有秘密的夫妇 ——《史密斯夫妇》

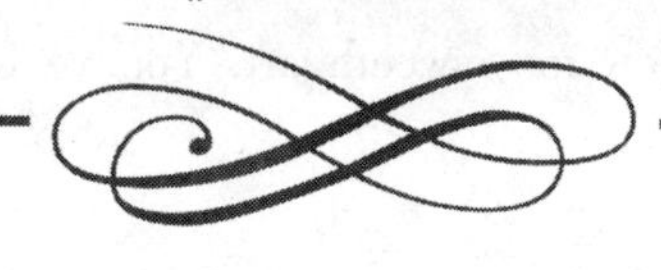

影片简介:

约翰·史密斯和珍·史密斯是一对普通的夫妇,二人婚后便一直过着平静的生活。然而虽然平静,二人却总觉得似乎缺少了些什么。或许是因为相互不了解和不信任,他们的感情产生了危机。很快史密斯夫妇便发现了对方的秘密,原来这夫妇二人都是职业杀手,并分别为两家杀手组织工作。在二人发现对方的身份后,还能继续生活下去吗?还是他们会续写一个皆大欢喜的结尾呢……

经典对白(一)

A Dinner 晚餐

珍和约翰发现了对方的身份,但是他们却没有道破,而是如往常一样坐在一块儿吃晚餐……

Jane: Perfect timing.

John: As always. This is a nice surprise.

Jane: I hope so. You're home early.

John: I missed you.

Jane: Mm. I missed you, too. Shall we?

John: Yes. Thought you only broke these out for special occasions.

Jane: This is a special occasion. Mm!

John: Mm! Pot roast. My favorite. Allow me, sweetheart. You've been on your feet all day.

Jane: Thank you.

John: Sure. So, how's work?

Jane: Actually, we had a...a little trouble with a commission.

John: Is that right?

Jane: Yeah. Double booking with another firm.

John: Huh.

Jane: Green beans?

John: No, thank you.

Jane: You'll have some.

John: I hope everything works out okay

Jane: It hasn't yet, but it will.

John: Pot roast is my favorite. Sweetheart, could you pass the salt? Ha-ha. Did you try something new?

Jane: Mm-hmm. So, how was Atlanta?

John: Had a few problems ourselves. Some figures didn't add up.

Jane: Big deal?

John: Life or death. Wine?

Jane: Yeah.

John: I got it.

Jane: I got it. I'll get a towel.

John: Janey? Honey? Jane! Jane!

Jane: How could I be so stupid?

John: Jane! Jane! God. Oh, dear God.

Jane: Oh.

John: Wait. No, no, no, no. Accident. Honey? Accident. Jane, stop the car! Now! Jane. You've **overreacting**[1]! Let's not get carried away. We don't want to go to sleep angry.

Jane: God!

John: Pull over. Pull over! Pull over! Now, look! We need to talk!

I don't know if we each have a destiny, or if we're all just floating around accidentally like on a breeze.

我不懂我们是否有着各自的命运，还是只是到处随风飘荡。

珍：来得正好。

约翰：向来如此。好一个惊喜。

珍：但愿如此呢。你提前回来了。

约翰：我想你啊。

珍：嗯，我也想你。开饭？

约翰：好啊。你只在特别时刻才会准备这些的吧。

珍：现在就是特别的时刻。嗯！

约翰：嗯，炖肉，我的最爱。让我来，宝贝儿。你已经累了一天了。

珍：谢谢。

约翰：不用客气。工作怎么样？

珍：老实说，我们有份订单出了点小问题。

约翰：是吗？

珍：嗯，跟另一家公司撞车了。

约翰：嗯。

珍：来点青豆？

1. overreact *v.* 过度反应

约翰:不用,谢谢。

珍:吃点儿吧。

约翰:但愿问题能圆满解决。

珍:还没解决,不过会的。

约翰:炖肉,我的最爱。宝贝儿,能把盐递过来吗?哈哈。你加了新配料?

珍:嗯哼。亚特兰大怎么样了?

约翰:也有点儿问题。有些账目对不上。

珍:严重吗?

约翰:性命攸关。来点儿葡萄酒?

珍:好啊。

约翰:我来。

珍:我来。我去拿毛巾。

约翰:珍妮?老婆?珍!珍!

珍:我怎么会这么蠢?

约翰:珍!珍!天哪!哦,天啊!

珍:哦!

约翰:嘿,等等。不,不,不,不!这是个意外。宝贝儿?是个意外!珍!停车!快停车!珍,别发这么大火!别太激动了。生气睡觉可不爽。

珍:天哪!

约翰:快停车!快停车!我们得谈谈!

经典对白(二)

Talks over the Phone 电话交谈

珍发现了约翰是个杀手,她决意要杀掉他……

Jane: Jane Smith.

John: That's the second time you tried to kill me.

Jane: Oh, come on. It was just a little **bomb**[2].

John: I want you to know. I'm going home, and I'm gonna burn everything I ever bought you.

Jane: I'll **race**[3] you there, baby. You there yet?

John: The first time we met, what was your first thought?

Jane: You tell me.

John: I thought...I thought you looked like Christmas morning. I don't know how else to say it.

Jane: And why are you telling me this now?

John: I guess, in the end, you start thinking about the beginning. So there it is. I thought you should know. So how about it, Jane? Hmm?

Jane: I thought...I thought that you were the most beautiful mark I'd ever seen.

John: So it was all business, yeah?

Jane: All business.

John: From the go.

Jane: Cold, hard math.

John: Thank you. That's what I needed to know. Okay.

Jane: Okay.

Everything you see exists together in a delicate balance.
世界上所有的生命都在微妙的平衡中生存。

珍:珍·史密斯。

约翰:这是你第二次想要杀死我了。

珍:拜托,只是一枚小炸弹而已。

约翰:我要让你知道,我要回家,把我为你买的所有东西都烧

2. bomb *n.* 炸弹
3. race *v.* 追赶

掉。

珍：那比比谁先到吧，宝贝儿。你到了吗？

约翰：初次见面时，你的感觉怎么样？

珍：你先说。

约翰：我觉得……你看起来像是圣诞节的清晨。我不知道还能用什么词儿了。

珍：你为什么现在跟我说这个？

约翰：我想到了最后，总会怀念最初。我想我应该告诉你。那你呢，珍？嗯？

珍：我觉得……我倒是觉得你是我见过的最帅的目标。

约翰：这只是工作需要？

珍：工作需要。

约翰：从一开始就是？

珍：是的，冷静的计划。

约翰：谢谢。我需要知道这些。就这样。

珍：就这样。

Beautiful Sentences 妙语佳句

1. Happy endings are just stories that haven't finished yet.
   只有那些还没完结的故事才让人觉得皆大欢喜。
2. Why is it you think we failed? Because we were leading separate lives? Or was it all the lying that did us in?
   我们为什么过不下去了？因为我们各过各的生活？还是因为互相欺骗呢？
3. You approached our marriage like a job, something to be reckoned, planned and executed. And you avoided it.
   你把我们的婚姻当成了工作，先侦查、再计划，然后执行。而你却在逃避。
4. You know, there will always be challenges, threats out there. But you can handle it together.
   你们知道，生活中总会有挑战，总会有威胁，但你们可以一起面对。

Thought about Life 人生感悟

人说婚姻是爱情的坟墓，当然这座围城总会让外面的人想进来，让里面的人想出去。大多数人都向往平淡的生活，然而像史密斯夫妇这样特殊的伴侣还真是少见，只有挑战、威胁、冒险、刺激才能给他们的生活带来新的乐趣。这大概和工作性质有关吧。总之，婚姻的真谛便是相互了解，相互信任，共同面对困难和挑战，这才是两个人真正沟通的开始。

Complaints are the greatest offerings that God obtains from human beings, as well as the most faithful prayers human beings might utter to God.

怨言是上天得至人类最大的供物，也是人类祷告中最真诚的部分。

十二、用情感编织的交响曲
——《音乐之声》

影片简介：

冯·特拉普上校是位有着七个孩子的鳏夫，在他妻子去世后，他先后请了十二名家庭教师来帮他照看孩子，而女家庭教师玛丽亚就是这第十二位。上校对家庭成员要求十分严格，但是玛丽亚却用她那颗温柔善良的心赢得了上校和孩子们的喜爱。在与冯·特拉普一家相处的过程中，玛丽亚和上校渐渐相爱并共结连理。可在他们蜜月的过程中，德军占领了奥地利。上校一家迫于德军的追捕，在萨尔茨堡音乐节上用歌声深情地表达了他们对祖国的热爱，此后，他们便逃离了祖国……

经典对白(一)

The New Governess 新来的家庭教师

家庭教师玛丽亚刚刚来到上校家，她好奇地在房间里走着，这时她遇见了上校……

Captain: In the future, you'll kindly remember there are certain rooms in this house which are not to be **disturbed**[1].

Maria: Yes, Captain, sir.

Captain: Why do you **stare**[2] at me that way?

Maria: Well, you don't look at all like a sea captain, sir.

Captain: I'm afraid you don't look very much like a **governess**[3]. Turn around, please.

Maria: What?

Captain: Turn. Hat off. You'll have to put on another dress before you meet the children.

Maria: But I don't have another one. When we entered the **abbey**[4], our **worldly**[5] clothes are given to the poor.

Captain: What about this one?

Maria: The poor didn't want this one.

Captain: Hmm.

Maria: I would have made myself a new dress but there wasn't time. I can make my own clothes.

Captain: Well, I'll see that you get some material. Today, if possible. Now, **Fraulein**[6]...eh...

Maria: Maria.

Captain: Fraulein Maria, I don't know how much the **Mother**[7] has told you?

Maria: Not much.

1 disturb *v.* 打扰，妨碍，这里是拟人化的用法

2 stare *v.* 注视，盯着看

3 governess *n.* 女家庭教师

4 abbey *n.* 修道院

5 worldly *adj.* 世俗的，世间的

6 fraulein *n.* 小姐（德语）

7 Mother *n.* 女修道院院长

Captain: You're the twelfth in a long line of governesses, who have come to look after my children since their mother died. I trust that you will be an **improvement**[8] on the last one. She stayed only two hours.

Maria: What's wrong with the children, sir?

Captain: There was nothing wrong with the children, only the governesses. They were completely unable to maintain **discipline**[9]. Without it, the house cannot be properly run. Please remember that, Fraulein.

Maria: Yes, sir.

Captain: Every morning you will **drill**[10] the children in their studies. I will not permit them to **dream away**[11] their summer holidays. Each afternoon they will **march**[12] about the ground, breathing deeply. Bedtime is to be strictly **observed**[13]. No exceptions.

Maria: Excuse me, sir. When do they play?

Captain: You'll see to that they conduct themselves at all time with the **utmost**[14] **orderliness**[15] and **decorum**[16]. I'm placing you **in command**[17].

I'm only brave when I have to be. Being brave doesn't mean you go looking for trouble.
我只是在必要的时候才会勇敢，勇敢并不代表你要到处闯祸。

8 improvement *n.* 改善，进步
9 discipline *n.* 纪律
10 drill *v.* 反复练习
11 dream away 虚度时光
12 march *v.* 行军，这里指对孩子们进行常规的军事训练
13 observe *v.* 遵守
14 utmost adj. 极度的，最大的
15 orderliness *n.* 整齐有序，有条不紊
16 decorum *n.* 礼节，礼貌
17 in command 领导

Maria: Yes, sir.

(*Captain blows his whistle, and the children walk down the stairs one by one.*)

Captain: Now, this is your new governess, Fraulein Maria. As I sound your signals, you will **step forward**[18] and give your name. You, Fraulein, will listen carefully. Learn their signal so you can call them when you want them.

上校:以后要记住,在这个家里有几间屋子是不能进去的。

玛丽亚:是,上校先生。

上校:为什么这样看着我?

玛丽亚:啊,您看上去可不像个海军上校,先生。

上校:我看你也不像个家庭教师。请转过身。

玛丽亚:什么?

上校:转身。脱帽。看你这身衣服,见我的孩子们前,你得再换一套。

玛丽亚:但我没有可换的。我们一进修道院,就把平时穿的衣服送给穷人了。

上校:那这一件呢?

玛丽亚:这件穷人不要。

上校:嗯。

玛丽亚:我本来想做件新衣服,可是来不及了。我自己会做衣服。

上校:那我去买些衣料吧。也许今天就去,你叫……呃……

玛丽亚:玛丽亚。

上校:玛丽亚小姐,院长嬷嬷跟你交待了多少?

玛丽亚:不多。

上校:我的妻子死后,在我聘请的一连串家庭教师中,你是第十二个。我相信你会比上一个好些,她只待了两小时。

玛丽亚:孩子们怎么了?

上校:孩子完全没错,责任在家庭教师。她们不能维持纪律,没有纪律,这个家就很难得到恰当的管理,请你记住这一点,小姐。

18 step forward 向前迈步

玛丽亚：是，先生。

上校：每天早上要给孩子们温习功课。我绝不允许他们把暑假时间白白荒废掉。每天下午要带他们到院子里进行操练，做深呼吸。到晚上要严格遵守睡觉时间。无一例外。

玛丽亚：可是，他们游戏的时间呢？

上校：你务必要使他们的行为举止在任何时候都要规规矩矩，彬彬有礼。由你全权指挥。

玛丽亚：是，先生。

（上校吹起了哨子，孩子们一个接一个地从楼梯上走了下来。）

上校：好，这位是你们新的家庭教师，玛丽亚小姐。听到你们各自的信号，就出列报名。玛丽亚小姐，你要仔细听，记住信号，在叫他们的时候你才能照着样子吹。

经典对白(二)

● Express His Love 表达爱意

玛丽亚因爱上了上校而惆怅不已，而上校也意识到自己爱上了玛丽亚，夜晚二人在院子里相遇……

Captain: Hello. I thought I just might find you here.

Maria: Was there something you wanted?

Captain: No, no, no, sit down please. Please, eh... May I? You know I was thinking and I was wondering two things. Why did you run away to the abbey, and what was it that made you come back.

Maria: Well, I had an **obligation**[19] to **fulfill**[20] and I came back to fulfill it.

Captain: Is that all?

Maria: And I missed the children.

Captain: Yes. Only the children?

Maria: No. Yes! Isn't it right I should have missed them?

Captain: Oh, yes, yes of course. I was only hoping that perhaps you... perhaps you might... er...

Maria: Yes?

Captain: Well...eh...nothing was the same when you were away. And it'll be all-wrong again after you leave. And I just thought that perhaps you might...eh...change your mind?

Maria: I'm sure the **baroness**[21] will be able to make things fine for you.

Captain: Maria, there isn't going to be any baroness.

Maria: There isn't?

Captain: No.

Maria: I don't understand.

Captain: Well, we've...eh...called off our **engagement**[22], you see and...eh...

Maria: Oh, I'm sorry.

Captain: Yes...You are?

Maria: You did?

Captain: Yes. Well, you can't marry someone when you're...in love with someone else...can you?

Maria: The Reverend Mother always says "When the Lord closes a door, somewhere he opens a window".

Captain: What else does the **Reverend**[23] Mother say?

19 obligation *n.* 义务

20 fulfill *v.* 履行

21 baroness *n.* 男爵夫人

22 engagement *n.* 婚约

23 reverend *adj.* 受人尊敬的，可敬的

Maria: That you have to look for your life.

Captain: Is that why you came back? And have you found it... Maria?

Maria: I think I have. I know I have.

Captain: I love you.

Maria: Oh, can this be happening to me?

上校:你好,我想我在这儿准能找到你。

玛丽亚:您有什么事儿吗?

上校:不,不,不,不是。请坐,坐啊。呃……可以吗?我一直在思考两件事儿,可却想不出来。为什么你会逃回到修道院去?还有又是什么使得你又回来了呢?

玛丽亚:我还没做完我应该做的,所以我回来做完它。

上校:就为这个?

玛丽亚:我还很想念孩子们。

上校:对,就想孩子吗?

玛丽亚:不。对,难道我不应该想他们吗?

上校:不,不,当然应该想他们的。我只是在想,也许你……也许你会……

玛丽亚:什么?

上校:呃,你不在的时候一切都变了。你要是再走了,还会变成这样。所以我在想,你是不是……会改变主意?

玛丽亚:我相信男爵夫人会为您安排好一切的。

上校:玛丽亚,没有什么男爵夫人了。

玛丽亚:没有了?

上校:是的。

玛丽亚:我不明白。

上校:我们……呃……已经解除了婚约,你知道的,所以……

玛丽亚:那真遗憾。

Yes, the past can hurt. But I think you can either run from it or learn from it.

对,过去是痛楚的,但我认为你要么可以逃避,要么可以向它学习。

上校:你觉得遗憾?

玛丽亚:你真的解除了婚约?

上校:是啊。一个人不能跟另一个人结婚的同时爱的……是别人……对吗?

玛丽亚:院长嬷嬷总是说"天主关上了门,却又在别处开了扇窗"。

上校:院长嬷嬷还说了些什么?

玛丽亚:生活要靠自己去寻找。

上校:所以你回来了?那你找到了吗,玛丽亚?

玛丽亚:我想是的。不,我找到了。

上校:我爱你。

玛丽亚:哦,这种事儿真的降临到我头上了吗?

Beautiful Sentences 妙语佳句

一提起《音乐之声》这部影片,人们马上就能联想到那脍炙人口的歌曲《哆来咪》。是的,这部影片除了有细腻的情节,精彩的对白,给人印象最深刻的就是那美妙的音乐了。下文节选了其中几段经典的唱词,与大家共同分享。

1. ***My Favorite Things***

Raindrops on roses and whiskers on kittens,
Bright copper kettles and warm woolen mittens,
Brown paper packages tied up with strings—
These are a few of my favorite things.
Cream-colored ponies and crisp apple strudels,
Doorbells and sleigh bells and schnitzel with noodles,
Wild geese that fly with the moon on their wings—
These are a few of my favorite things.
Girls in white dresses with blue satin sashes,
Snowflakers that stay on my nose and eyelashes,
Silver-white winters that melt into springs—

These are few of my favorite things.

When the dog bites,

When the bee stings,

When I'm feeling sad,

I simply remember my favorite things.

And then I don't feel so bad!

《我最喜爱的事物》

玫瑰花上的雨滴,小猫咪的胡须,

亮闪闪的铜壶,暖暖的毛绒手套,

系着丝带的棕色纸盒,

这些都是我喜爱的事物。

乳白色的小马驹,脆脆的苹果馅卷饼,

门铃、雪橇铃铛,油炸肉排加面条,

野鹅在飞舞,月光撒在它们的翅膀上,

这些都是我喜爱的事物。

女孩子们穿着白裙,系着蓝色的丝缎腰带,

雪花片片落在我的笔尖和睫毛上,

冬天的冰雪融化,迎来了春天,

这些都是我喜爱的事物。

当小狗咬我,

蜜蜂蜇我,

当我觉得不快乐时,

就会想起我喜爱的事物,

然后我就不再悲伤了。

(注：这段唱词表达了玛丽亚的乐观天性和豁达的处事哲学，她将这种人生观用美妙的歌声交给孩子们，和孩子们共同表达对生活的热爱。)

2. ***Climb Every Mountain***

Climb every mountain, Search high and low.

Follow every byway, every path you know.

Climb every mountain, Ford every stream.

Follow every rainbow, till you find your dream.

A dream that will need all the love you can give.

Every day of your life for as long as you live.

《攀越群山》

攀越每座高山,上下而求索,

穿越每条小路,你所知道的所有的路。

攀越每座高山,跋涉每条溪流,

追寻每条彩虹,直至寻到梦想。

这个梦想需要你倾注所有的爱,

在你有生之年里的每一天。

(注:这段唱词表达了上校一家不畏艰难,勇于面对生活中任何困苦的决心。孩子们在经历了许多生活的艰辛后,也渐渐理解了面对人生困境的生活态度。他们一家幸福地生活在一起。)

Thought about Life 人生感悟

情感是人与人之间沟通的桥梁,每一个人都处在情感的包围之中。亲情、友情乃至爱情,都是人们生活中不可或缺的情感。上校一直隐藏着他对孩子们和亡妻的感情,所以他一直是压抑的、苦闷的,而玛丽亚的出现把快乐又带回到了他身边。当他敞开心扉时,就能与孩子们,与玛丽亚相互理解和关爱,那将是一件多么快乐的事啊!

十三、暮年的幸福
——《金色池塘》(1981)

影片简介：

年近七旬的老妇人埃塞尔和他的老伴儿诺曼离开了城市的喧嚣,回到了以前生活的故居,一座位于池塘边的小木屋中。埃塞尔对新生活充满了期待，可她的老伴儿诺曼却恰恰相反，他意志消沉,脾气古怪。原来诺曼一直对年岁渐长而感到恐慌，也为即将到来的死亡而感到恐惧。再加上诺曼和女儿之间一直存在代沟,更不要提照看外孙了。然而一次意外却让诺曼重新审视了自己的生活,他将如何面对三代人的情感问题,又将如何摆脱年长带给他的心理恐惧呢……？

经典对白(一)

Return to the Old House 重返故居

埃塞尔和诺曼重返故居，埃塞尔对这里的一切都充满了好奇，而诺曼却有些意志消沉……

Norman: Someone's at the door.

Ethel: It's me, you old **poop**[1]!

Norman: Well, look at you.

Ethel: Yeah, look at me? Quite a sight, aren't I? Oh, Norman! It's so beautiful. Everything's just waking up. Little, tiny birds. Little, tiny leaves. I saw a **patch**[2] of little, tiny flowers over by the old cellar hole. I forget what they're called. Little, tiny, yellow things. Well, want to help me with the dust covers?

Norman: I don't have anything else to do.

Ethel: Come on.

Norman: What were you doin' out in the woods?

Ethel: Norman, what do you think I was doing? I was getting wood. Hey, I met the nicest couple.

Norman: Yeah? Where?

Ethel: In the woods.

Norman: Couple of people?

Ethel: No, a couple of **antelope**[3]. Of course a couple of people. Their name is Migliori, I believe.

Norman: Migliori? What sort of a name is that?

Ethel: I don't know, darling. Italian, I suppose. They're up from Boston.

Norman: They speak English?

Ethel: Well, of course they speak English. They're a nice middle-aged couple, just like us.

---

1 poop *n.* (俚) 傻子，傻瓜

2 patch *n.* 一小块儿地

3 antelope *n.* 羚羊

Norman: If they're just like us, they're not middle-aged.

Ethel: Of course they are.

Norman: Middle-aged means the middle, Ethel. Middle of life. People don't live to be 150!

Ethel: Well, we're at the far edge of middle age. That's all.

Norman: We're not, you know. We're not middle-aged. You're old, and I'm ancient.

Ethel: Oh, pooh! You're in your 70s, and I'm in my 60s.

Norman: Just barely on both counts.

Ethel: Would you like to spend the rest of the afternoon **quibbling**[4] about this?

Norman: We can, If you like.

Ethel: Oh, for the Lord's sake. The Miglioris, whatever their age group, have invited us to have dinner sometime. Wouldn't that be nice?

Norman: I don't know. I'm not sure my stomach's ready for **rigatoni**[5], that sort of thing.

Ethel: Oh, no! Poor Elmer! He's had a terrible fall. Poor little Elmer. The life you've led. He was my first true love, you know.

Norman: Known all along I wasn't the first in line.

Ethel: No, you were a rather cheap **substitute**[6] for Elmer. And now he's had a fall.

Norman: Maybe he wanted to kill himself. Maybe he wanted to be **cremated**[7]. Probably got cancer or **termites**[8] or

This is my kingdom. If I don't fight for it, who will?

这是我的国土,我不为她而战斗,谁为呢?

4 quibble *v.* 吹毛求疵，诡辩

5 rigatoni *n.* 意大利通心粉

6 substitute *n.* 替代物，替代品

7 cremate *v.* 火葬

8 termite *n.* 白蚁

something.

Ethel: Shut up, Norman!

Norman: Not a bad way to go, huh? Quick front **flip**[9] off the **mantle**[10], end up in the fire. Nothin' to it.

Ethel: Norman, will you shut up?

Norman: When my number's up, do that for me, will you. **Prop**[11] me up on the mantle, point out which way is down. Might even try for a full gainer with a half twist.

Ethel: Norman Thayer Jr., your **fascination**[12] with dying is beginning to **frazzle**[13] my good humor.

Norman: Not fascination. Just crosses my mind now and then.

Ethel: Every five minutes. Don't you have anything else to think about?

Norman: Nothing quite as interesting.

Ethel: Well, what's stopping you? Why don't you take your dive and get it over with?

Norman: And leave you alone with Elmer? You must be mad!

Ethel: Oh, for pity's sake. Come on and help me get the **canoe**[14] off the **porch**[15].

诺　曼:有人敲门。

埃塞尔:是我,你个老糊涂!

诺　曼:你看看你。

埃塞尔:是,看看我?很滑稽,是吧?哦,诺曼!真是美极啦。万物刚刚复苏,那些可爱的小鸟,鲜嫩的叶子。我还看见了一片可爱的小野花,就在地窖的洞口那

9 flip *v.* 翻转

10 mantle *n.* 壁炉架

11 prop *v.* 支持,支撑

12 fascination *n.* 幻想中的事物

13 frazzle *v.* 磨损,使疲惫不堪

14 canoe *n.* 独木舟

15 porch *n.* 门廊

儿。我忘了叫什么啦！黄色的小花。来吧，能帮我掸掸屋里的灰尘吗？

诺　曼：反正我也没别的事情可做。

埃塞尔：来吧。

诺　曼：你刚刚在树林里干什么呢？

埃塞尔：诺曼，你觉得我去树林能干什么呢？我是去捡柴。嗨，我还遇见了完美的一对儿。

诺　曼：是吗？在哪？

埃塞尔：在树林里。

诺　曼：一对夫妇？

埃塞尔：不，是一对羚羊。哈，当然是一对夫妇啦。我记得他们是姓密哥利奥里。

诺　曼：密哥利奥里？这是什么名字？

埃塞尔：谁知道呢？我想是意大利人吧。他们是从波士顿搬来的。

诺　曼：说英语吗？

埃塞尔：他们当然说英语，是一对儿甜蜜的中年夫妇，和我们一样。

诺　曼：要是他们和我们一样，那就不算是中年啦。

埃塞尔：怎么就不是啦？

诺　曼：中年是指人年龄的一半，埃塞尔。人可活不到150岁！

埃塞尔：那么我们正处在中年的晚期，这行了吧！

诺　曼：还是不对，我们可不是中年。你老了，而我更老。

埃塞尔：哦，算了吧！你是70多岁，而我不过是60多岁。

诺　曼：这都不能算是中年。

埃塞尔：你又想为这事耗费一下午和我斗嘴吗？

诺　曼：你想的话，我愿意奉陪。

埃塞尔：老天啊！别管他们夫妇是什么年龄段的人了，他们邀

Land is the only thing in the world worth working for, worth fighting for, worth dying for. Because it's the only thing that lasts.

土地是世界上唯一值得你去为之工作，为之战斗，为之牺牲的东西，因为它是唯一永恒的东西。

请我们有空去吃饭。这个不错吧?

诺　曼:不知道,我可能消化不了像通心粉之类的意大利菜。

埃塞尔:哦不!我的埃尔莫!他摔得可不轻。可怜的埃尔莫,你可真不幸。知道吗,他是我的初恋情人。

诺　曼:我一直都知道我不是你的初恋。

埃塞尔:当然,你还真是个不合格的替代者。他这次可真是摔坏了!

诺　曼:或许它想自杀吧,要么就是想把自己火葬了,再有就是得了癌症,被白蚁咬了。

埃塞尔:闭嘴,诺曼!

诺　曼:这方法还不赖,嗯?从壁炉上往下一跳,寻求点刺激,在烈火之中结束生命。

埃塞尔:诺曼,你给我闭嘴行吗?

诺　曼:当我大限将至的时候,你来帮我做这件事儿,好吗?扶我上去,指着我应该跳下去的方向,或许我很容易就能跳出个满分来。

埃塞尔:诺曼·塞伊,你这套对死亡津津乐道的论述,已经破坏了我原本很好的情绪。

诺　曼:这可不是津津乐道,而是忍不住就想到了它。

埃塞尔:每5分钟就想一次。你没有别的事好想了吗?

诺　曼:都没这个有趣。

埃塞尔:那好,没人拦着你。你现在就去跳吧,好把这事儿了了。

诺　曼:把你和埃尔莫单独留下?你真是疯了!

埃塞尔:哦,你行行好吧。来吧,帮我把木舟拿下来。

经典对白(二)

Understanding 理解

在诺曼和比利钓鱼回来后,切尔西决定和父亲诺曼好好谈谈,她想试着去理解父亲……

Billy: Hey! Look at you!

Chelsea: Hi, kid.

Billy: Where's the dentist?

Chelsea: He had to get back. He'll call you tonight.

Billy: Okay.

Chelsea: Hello, Norman.

Norman: Well, well.

Billy: Oh, Chelsea! We caught Walter. Do you know who Walter is?

Chelsea: Well, I have a feeling he's a fish.

Billy: Yes. A **humongous**[16] fish! And we caught him today, didn't we, Norman?

Chelsea: Well, let me see him.

Norman: We let him go.

Billy: Yeah. We let him go.

Chelsea: I think I've heard this story before.

Billy: No! No, it's true. Norman and I thought that if Walter's lived this long, we should let him keep on living. I'm gonna go tell Ethel. Hey, Norman! We caught the son of a bitch! We caught him! Good job! Whoo!

Chelsea: You got yourself a friend, huh?

Norman: Yeah, he's all right. Hasn't been too difficult.

Chelsea: How's your forehead?

Norman: Huh? Oh, this. It's all right. Lot of pain. Nothing to worry about.

Now I find myself in a world which for me is worse than death. A world in which there is no place for me.

现在我发现自己活在一个比死还要痛苦的世界，一个无我容身之处的世界。

16 humongous *adj*. 极大的

Chelsea: Norman, I want to talk to you.

Norman: What seems to be the problem?

Chelsea: There's no problem. I just...I want to talk to you. I think that...maybe you and I should have the kind of relationship that we're supposed to have.

Norman: What kind of relationship is that?

Chelsea: Well, you know...like a father and a daughter.

Norman: Oh, just in the nick of time, huh? Worried about the will, are you? I'm leaving everything to you except what I'm taking with me.

Chelsea: Just stop it. I don't want anything. It seems that you and me have been mad at each other for so long.

Norman: I didn't know we were mad. I thought we just didn't like each other.

Chelsea: I want to be your friend.

Norman: Oh. This mean you'll come around more often? Mean a lot to your mother.

Chelsea: I'll come around more often.

Norman: Well.

Chelsea: Yep. Oh! I got married in Brussels.

Norman: You did? In Brussels?

Chelsea: He makes me very happy.

Norman: Well, good. Does he speak English?

Chelsea: Bill, I married Bill.

Norman: Bill? Oh, Bill! I'm glad, Chelsea. That's "so frantastic."

Chelsea: What?

Norman: Is Billy gonna be living with you?

Chelsea: Uh-huh.

Norman: Well, good. Isn't that something? Good for you. You know something? I got him doing the back flip just like a pro.

Chelsea: Oh, yeah? That's great.

Norman: Want me to get him down and show you?

Chelsea: No. Not right now.

Norman: Okay. Oh, that's right. You never were a great back flipper, were you?

Chelsea: I was always too fat, remember?

Norman: Yeah, I do remember that now. Well, probably a lot easier for a boy.

Chelsea: I beg your pardon. Do you want to see me do a back flip?

Norman: Huh?

Chelsea: I am gonna do a goddamn back flip.

Norman: Chelsea, you don't have to.

Chelsea: I want to!

Norman: Make sure you go up, not just back. Up and back.

Chelsea: Oh, I'm scared.

Norman: Nothing to be scared of. The back flip is one of the easiest dives of all.

Chelsea: I'm scared anyway.

Norman: Don't do it. It doesn't matter if you don't do the stupid dive. It's not important.

Chelsea: I did it!

Norman: She did it! Chelsea did a back flip!

Chelsea: I went over! It was lousy, but I did it!

Ethel: Good for you!

Norman: Yea!

比　利：嘿！瞧你！

切尔西：嘿，孩子！

比　利：牙医呢？

切尔西：他得先回去的。晚上他会打电话来的。

Home. I'll go home. And I'll think of some way to get him back. After all, tomorrow is another day.

家，我要回家。我要想办法让他回来。不管怎样，明天又是全新的一天。

比　利：好啊。

切尔西：你好，诺曼。

诺　曼：好，好……

比　利：哦，切尔西！我们逮到沃尔特了。你知道沃尔特是谁吗？

切尔西：我猜是条鱼吧。

比　利：没错，是条超大的鱼！我们今天终于把它逮到了，对吧，诺曼？

切尔西：好啊，让我看看。

诺　曼：我们把它放了。

比　利：是的，把它放了。

切尔西：我以前好像听人编过这个故事。

比　利：不！不，是真的。我们想沃尔特都活了这么久了，就该让它继续活下去。我去告诉埃塞尔。嘿，诺曼！我们抓住了那个老混蛋！抓住了！这太棒了！哦哦！

切尔西：你交上了个朋友，嗯？

诺　曼：是啊，他很好，我们挺投缘的。

切尔西：你的额头怎么样了？

诺　曼：嗯？哦，这个？没事。挺疼，可没事了。

切尔西：诺曼，我想跟你谈谈。

诺　曼：有什么问题吗？

切尔西：没有什么问题，我只是……想跟你谈谈。我想也许……我们之间应该有种正常一点儿的关系。

诺　曼：什么样的关系？

切尔西：你知道的，就是……父女间的那种关系。

诺　曼：噢，谈得可真是时候啊？关心遗嘱了是吧？除了我要带走的，其余的全都留给你。

切尔西：别那么说，我什么也不要。我只是觉得我们之间的积怨太久了。

诺　曼：我觉得倒是谈不上什么积怨。我以为我们对彼此没有好感。

切尔西：我想成为你的朋友。

若　曼:哦。这就是说你会经常来了?你妈妈会很高兴的。

刀尔西:我会经常来的。

若　曼:好。

刀尔西:行了。噢!我在布鲁塞尔结婚了。

若　曼:真的?在布鲁塞尔?

刀尔西:他使我感到幸福。

若　曼:很好。他讲英语吗?

刀尔西:比尔,我嫁给了比尔。

若　曼:比尔?噢,比尔!真替你高兴,切尔西。真是"太绝了"。

刀尔西:什么?

若　曼:比利和你们住在一起吗?

刀尔西:嗯。

若　曼:那太好了。这对你来说真是一件大好事啊!知道吗?我教会了他后空翻入水。

刀尔西:真的?太棒了!

若　曼:想要他跳给你看看吗?

刀尔西:不,以后吧。

若　曼:好吧,噢,想起来了,你小的时候总是跳不好,对吧?

刀尔西:我那时候太胖,记得吗?

若　曼:当然还记得呢。可能男孩子学那个会容易点儿。

刀尔西:你说什么?你想看我做个后空翻入水吗?

若　曼:哈?

刀尔西:我现在就要做个该死的后空翻入水。

若　曼:切尔西,你不必那么做。

刀尔西:我要做!

若　曼:记住要往高了跳,不仅仅是向后。要高,再向后仰。

刀尔西:噢,我很害怕。

若　曼:别害怕。后空翻是所有跳水姿势中最容易的。

Wisdom appears in contradiction to itself, which is a trick life plays on philosophy of life.

智慧的代价是矛盾。这是人生对人生观开的玩笑。

切尔西:可我还是很怕。

诺　曼:那就算了。你会不会做这愚蠢的后空翻都不要紧的。没什么大不了的。

切尔西:我成功了!

诺　曼:她成功了!切尔西成功了!

切尔西:我成功了!虽然姿势不佳,可我成功了!

埃塞尔:好样的!

诺　曼:耶!

Beautiful Sentences 妙语佳句

1. You want to know why I came back so fast? I got to the end of our lane, I couldn't remember where the old town road was. I wandered a way in the woods. There was nothing familiar. Not one damn tree. Scared me half to death. That's why I came running back here to you. See your pretty face, I could feel safe. I was still me.
你想知道我为什么这么快就回来了吗?我走到那条小路的尽头,却记不起去老镇的路了。我走到了树林里,一切都是那么陌生,连棵认识的树都没有。我吓得要命,所以我才跑回来见你。看见你那漂亮的脸,我才觉得安全,踏实。

2. Listen to me, mister. You're my knight in shining armor. Don't you forget it. You're gonna get back on that horse and I'm gonna be right behind you, holding on tight and away we're gonna go, go, go!
听我说,亲爱的。你永远是我潇洒的白马王子。千万记着我的话,有一天你还会骑上那匹马,我还会坐在你的身后,紧紧地抱着你,我们一起向前跑啊,跑啊!

3. I suppose you expect me to sing something now. Well, I'm not about to. I've been trying all day to draw some profound conclusions about living fourscore years. Haven't thought of anything. Surprised it got here so fast. But I'm glad I got to spend so much time with this beautiful woman. What's your name again? I want to thank all of you for coming all the way here from Disneyland to witness this historic event. Now that I'm out of hot air, I'm gonna need a little assistance to get these

candles out.

你们大概也希望我唱几句吧,当然我也不会唱。我想了一整天,想总结出一些人生哲理,毕竟我活了近80年了。可我还什么都没想出来呢,就一下子变得这么老了。令我感到开心的是,这么多年来能和这位美丽的女子和我一起共度生活。我能否再此请教您的芳名?还要感谢你们大老远的从迪斯尼乐园赶到这里来,做这个历史时刻的见证人。好了,废话说完了,请诸位帮我把蜡烛吹灭吧。

All life is a game of luck.
生活本来就全靠运气。

4. You stay away for years at a time. You never come home unless I beg you to, and then when you do, all you can do is be disagreeable about the past. What's the point? Don't you think that everyone looks back on their childhood with a certain amount of bitterness and regret about something? It doesn't have to ruin your life, darling. You're a big girl now. Aren't you tired of it all? Bore, bore. Life marches by, Chels. I suggest you get on with it.

记得有一段时间,你有几年都远离这里,不肯回家。每次都是我请求你,你才会回来。而每次你回家后,又总是对过去发生的事耿耿于怀。这是为什么呢?你不觉得每个人在回忆童年的时候,都会有些事情让人觉得痛苦和遗憾吗?但你不能让这些事情毁了你一辈子,亲爱的。你是个大孩子了,难道你对这些还不感到厌倦吗?无聊啊,无聊。生活总是在前进的,切尔西,希望你能跟上它的脚步。

5. That's right. He cleans the stupid ones, and I clean the smart ones. Fortunately, the smart ones are too smart to get caught. That's why they're in schools.

是这样的,他收拾笨的,我收拾聪明的。幸好聪明的鱼都不上钩,这也是它们生存下来的原因啊。

6. Billy, sometimes, you have to look hard at a person and remember that he's doing the best he can. He's just trying to find his way, that's all. Just like you.
比利,有时候,你要非常用心地去观察一个人,而且你得记住,他正尽力而为,只是他要找到他自己的方式,仅此而已。和你是一样的。
7. I'm sorry too. But, darling, you're wrong about your dad. He does care. He cares deeply. It's just that he's an absolute mutt about telling anyone. I know he'd walk through fire for me, and he'd walk through fire for you too. And if you don't understand that, you're not looking closely enough.
我也很抱歉!可是孩子,你误解你爸爸了。他很在意你,非常非常地在意你,可是这个傻子他从来都不愿把话说出来。我知道他会为我而牺牲自己,同样,他也会为你而牺牲自己。如果你还不理解他的话,是因为你没有深入地去体会。

Thought about Life 人生感悟

人到暮年时往往会产生孤独和恐惧的感觉,那种感觉是真实存在的,它会时刻萦绕在我们的心头,挥之不去。正如老年的诺曼一样,他无意和儿女们作对,他只是在以自己的方式来反抗生活的压力,来面对死亡的恐惧。老年时,我们会变得无法和周围的人沟通,会觉得生活的圈子越来越小,最后竟只剩下回忆。也许我们应该对年长者更加关爱,贴近他们,了解他们内心的渴求。因为当我们自己年老时,也会希望他人这样来帮助我们的。

十四、顽童的克星
——《魔法保姆 I》(2005)

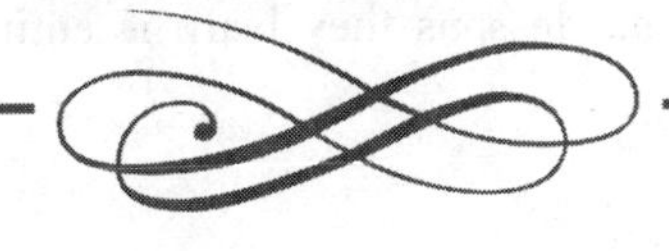

影片简介：

布朗先生刚刚丧偶，他家中还有 7 个顽皮的孩子需要他来照管。他之前聘请的几位保姆都被孩子们气走了。他在无奈之下，请来了一位名叫麦克菲的保姆来照看孩子。麦克菲长相丑陋，最初孩子们仍像以前那样，设计刁难她，可是无论孩子们使用何种方法，保姆麦克菲都有应对的方法。为了解决家里的债务问题，布朗先生不得不再娶一位妻子，只有这样，严厉的姑妈才能继续资助他们。然而孩子们却不喜欢这位新娘，他们便向保姆麦克菲求助……

经典对白(一)

Express His Thanks 表达谢意

在保姆麦克菲的帮助下，塞蒙想到了个好主意，既帮助了伊万吉玲，也阻止了阿德莱德姑妈带走克里斯蒂安娜，布朗先生为此向她表示感谢……

Brown: Thank you, Nanny McPhee. You were a **tremendous**[1] help.

McPhee: Not at all. I think you will find that lesson three, to get dressed when they're told, is complete.

Brown: Just to get dressed when they're told? They've learned a great deal more than that.

McPhee: I have five lessons to teach. What lessons they learn is entirely up to them. Goodnight, Mr. Brown.

Brown: Nanny McPhee...

McPhee: Yes, Mr. Brown?

Brown: She will be all right, won't she? Evangeline, I mean. Sorry, I can't help being concerned. Aunt Adelaide can be so, eh...well, you saw.

McPhee: She will certainly be all right.

Brown: Good. I suppose she volunteered to go, did she? Couldn't wait to be shot of us, I imagine.

McPhee: Not quite. It was Simon's idea. He knew Evangeline might like to educate herself and that her going would save Christianna. He's a very clever boy.

Brown: Good heavens. Simon, eh? Well, good for him. Quick...quick thinking.

McPhee: Goodnight, Mr. Brown.

布　朗:谢谢你,保姆麦克菲。你帮了我们大忙。

麦克菲:不用谢。我想你该发现第三课——听话穿衣,已经上完了。

布　朗:只是听话地穿衣吗?我看他们学到的可远不止这些呢。

麦克菲:我有五课要教给他们,他们要学什么,完全是由他们自己决定的。晚安,布朗先生。

1 tremendous *adj.* 极大的，了不起的

布　朗：保姆麦克菲……

麦克菲：还有什么事吗，布朗先生？

布　朗：她会没事的，是吧？我是说，伊万吉玲。抱歉，我实在没法不去担心她。阿德莱德姑妈实在是有些……噢，你也看到了吧。

麦克菲：放心吧，她会很好的。

布　朗：那就好。我猜她是自己要去的吧，是吗？我想她大概是不愿看着我们被分开吧。

麦克菲：不完全是这样。那是塞蒙的主意，他知道伊万吉玲想得到良好的教育，而她去的话同时也帮了克里斯蒂安娜。他是个非常聪明的孩子。

布　朗：天啊，是塞蒙的主意，嗯？噢，真有他的。反应还真快，真快。

麦克菲：晚安，布朗先生。

Seize this day! Begin now! Each day is a new life. Seize it. For in today already walks tomorrow.

把握住今天！现在就开始！每天是一种新的生活。抓住它。因为今天已经走到了明天。

经典对白(二)

A Happy Ending 幸福的结局

就在布朗先生的婚礼以失败告终之时，塞蒙留住了阿德莱德姑妈，并要父亲娶伊万吉玲……

Simon: Wait, Aunt Adelaide! Wait! You agreed. You gave your word that if our father remarried this month, you'd support us.

Adelaide: I did.

Simon: So if he marries today, you'll have to keep your word.

Adelaide: Oh, you're wasting my time!

Simon: No. No. No, I'm not. He will marry today.

Brown: What?

Adelaide: What?

…

Lily: He'll marry Evangeline.

Adelaide: Incest?

Tora: No! No! Aunt Adelaide. Evangeline isn't our sister.

Adelaide: Not your sister?

Tora: Of course she's not our sister.

Adelaide: Well, who is she, then?

Evangeline: I'm his **scullery**[2] maid.

Adelaide: What?

Lily: Evangeline, do you love Papa?

Evangeline: Of course not. I know my place. That wouldn't be right. I mean...Yes.

Lily: Papa, do you love Evangeline?

Brown: What're you saying? That would be totally improper. A thing like that could...could never happen. I mean, obviously...Yes.

Adelaide: He's marrying the scullery maid? Oh!

Quickly: It's snowing! Well, I never! Snow! Snow in August!

Vicar: I take it, then, Mr. Brown, that the young lady is not in fact the fruit of your **loins**[3]? Because the Church would have to take a rather dim view of it if she were.

Brown: No. What happened was my son Simon is a very clever boy.

Sebastian: Evangeline...for the record, whatever I may have said about stepmothers, that whole "evil breed" moment, most **emphatically**[4] does not apply

2 scullery *n.* 碗碟洗涤处

3 loins *n.* 腰；生殖器官

4 emphatically *adv.* 强调地

·to you.

McPhee: This way.

Vicar: Jolly good. If I may then invite you all to join us once more. Hallelujah.

Evangeline: Oh, Nanny McPhee...I'm so nervous.

McPhee: Deep breaths.

Evangeline: I don't look much like a bride, do I?

McPhee: You will. How's the reading coming along?

Evangeline: It's much better. But I still haven't got to the end of that story.

McPhee: No need. You are the end of the story.

Experience is the best of school-masters, only the school-fees are heavy.

经验是最好的老师，就是学费比较昂贵。

塞　　蒙：等一下，阿德莱德姑妈！等等！你答应过的，你承诺过如果我们的父亲这个月再婚的话，你就资助我们。

阿德莱德：是这样的。

塞　　蒙：所以如果他今天结婚的话，你就要履行你的诺言。

阿德莱德：哦，你这是在浪费时间！

塞　　蒙：不，不，不是的，我没有。他今天会结婚的。

布　　朗：什么？

阿德莱德：什么？

……

莉　　莉：他会娶伊万吉玲。

阿德莱德：这不是乱伦了？

朵　　拉：不！不是的，阿德莱德姑妈。伊万吉玲不是我们的姐姐。

阿德莱德：不是你们的姐姐？

朵　　拉：她当然不是。

阿德莱德：那她是谁？

伊万吉玲：我是他的侍女。

阿德莱德：什么？

莉　　莉：伊万吉玲，你爱爸爸吗？

伊万吉玲：当然不爱。我知道我的地位，那样是不对的。我是说……是的，我爱他。

莉　　莉：爸爸，你爱伊万吉玲吗？

布　　朗：你说什么？那样太不合适了。像那样的事……是永远不会发生的。我是说，很明显……是的，我爱她。

阿德莱德：他要娶个女佣？噢！

奎 克 丽：下雪了！噢，我从没见过八月里下雪！

牧　　师：我想，布朗先生，那位年轻的女士事实上并不是您的孩子了？因为如果她是您孩子的话，教会可是会非常鄙夷的。

布　　朗：她当然不是了。这一切都是塞蒙计划的，他是个非常聪明的孩子。

塞巴蒂安：伊万吉玲，我很正式地对你说，对于我先前所说过的关于继母的言论，也就是那些"魔种"之类的话，很明显是不适合你的。

麦 克 菲：这边来。

牧　　师：这是个令人高兴的时刻，我想再次邀请大家来参加我们的仪式。哈利路亚！

伊万吉玲：哦，保姆麦克菲，我……好紧张。

麦 克 菲：深呼吸。

伊万吉玲：我看起来不太像新娘，是吗？

麦 克 菲：你看上去美极了。书读得怎么样了？

伊万吉玲：读得差不多了，只是我还是没有读到故事的结局。

麦 克 菲：没必要了，你就是故事的结局。

Beautiful Sentences 妙语佳句

1. There is something you should understand about the way I work. When you need me but do not want me, then I must stay. When you want me but no longer need me, then I have to go. It's rather sad, really, but there it is.

你们应该了解我的做事方式。当你们需要我,但却并不想让我留下的时候,我一定会留下来;而当你们想让我留下来,但却不再需要我的时候,我也不得不离开。这的确很让人难过,真的,但事实就是这样。

2. You do not understand the adult world. You know, there are certain things that...certain things...You will leave me this instant. Go home! You never listen!

你不会理解大人的事儿的。要知道,有些事情……有些事情……你让我静一下。快回家去!你从不听我们的意见!

3. When the money stops, the house will be taken. Some of you will perhaps be put into the workhouse. Some will be put into the care into the care of others. I don't know how many of you will be allowed to stay together. I'm sorry to have failed you, children. You deserve so much better.

如果资助没有了,房子就会被收走,而你们中或许也会有人被送进劳教所,还有的会被送给他人来抚养。我不知道你们会有几个人能生活在一起。对不起,孩子们,我让你们失望了。你们应该过得更好的。

4. Wait. Father wasn't being rude. No one on earth could be less rude. He was protecting you from the naughty things we were doing.

等一下。爸爸不是那样粗鲁的人。世上不会有人比他还温柔的,他只是想保护你不被我们那些顽皮的把戏所伤。

5. At least this way, we'll all be together. That's what matters most, isn't it, Hum? I promise I'll never hide anything that affects us from you again. I see you're more than capable of understanding it.

至少这样我们就可以待在一起了,那才是最重要的,对吧,

It can be inferred that you lack confidence in a victory over your rivals from the fact that you're irritable against them.

如果敌人让你生气,那说明你还没有胜他的把握。

嗯？我向你们保证以后我再也不会隐瞒任何关于我们的事情了，我知道你们完全能理解我的。

Thought about Life 人生感悟

这是一部轻松的家庭喜剧。布朗先生很爱他的孩子们，所以他宁愿自己来背负沉重的家庭债务，也要让孩子们过上快乐的生活。可是天真的孩子们并不能理解父亲这样做的用意，他们单纯地以为父亲只是想再娶个妻子，而不顾他们的感受。大人和孩子们都在用他们自己的方式来表达情感，虽然他们都深爱着对方，但是他们的情感太缺乏沟通了。或许有时候孩子们需要的往往不是大人的呵护，而是他们的理解。

十五、疯狂的寻宝历险记
——《盗墓迷城 I》

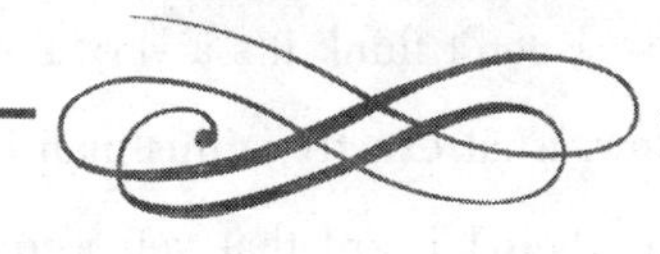

影片简介：

相传在古埃及时代，法老的妻子和邪恶的祭司伊莫顿的奸情曝光后，祭司伊莫顿的灵魂便受到了诅咒，被深深地埋藏在地底。3000年后，军人欧康诺在一次战役中曾到过埋藏伊莫顿的地方，据说那里还埋藏着数不尽的珍宝。几年后，欧康诺在面临死刑之时，幸被一位图书馆员伊芙琳所救。于是知晓珍宝埋藏地的欧康诺便加入了寻宝者伊芙琳和她哥哥乔纳森的疯狂寻宝之旅……

经典对白(一)

A New Member of the Team 团队的新成员

为了寻找宝藏，乔纳森带着伊芙琳到狱中找欧康诺，可是欧康诺即将被执行绞刑……

Evelyn: You told me that you got it on a dig down in Thebes.

Jonathan: Well, I made a mistake.

Evelyn: You lied to me.

Jonathan: I lie to everybody. What makes you so special?

Evelyn: I am your sister.

Jonathan: That just makes you more **gullible**[1].

Evelyn: Jonathan, you stole it from a drunk at the local **casbah**[2]...

Jonathan: Picked his pocket, actually, so I don't think it's a very good top...

Evelyn: Stop being so **ridiculous**[3]. Now, what exactly is this man in prison for?

Guard: Oh, this I do not know. But when I heard that you were coming I asked him that myself.

Evelyn: And what did he say?

Guard: He said he was just looking for a good time.

Evelyn: This is the man that you stole it from?

Jonathan: Yes, exactly. So why don't we just go **sniff**[4] out a spot of Tiffin...

O'Connell: Who are you? And who's the **broad**[5]?

Evelyn: "Broad"?

Jonathan: I-I'm just a local sort of **missionary**[6] **chap**[7] spreading the good word. But this is my sister Evy.

Evelyn: How do you do?

O'Connell: Oh, well. Guess she's not a total loss.

1 gullible *adj.* 易受骗的

2 casbah *n.* 北非的一些旧城

3 ridiculous *adj.* 可笑的，荒唐的

4 sniff *v.* 嗅，闻

5 broad *n.* (俚) 女人

6 missionary *n.* 传教士

7 chap *n.* 小伙子，家伙

Evelyn: I beg your pardon.

Guard: I'll be back in a moment.

Jonathan: Ask him about the box.

Evelyn: Um, we have found uh, hello, excuse me. We both found your puzzle box, and we've come to ask you about it.

O'Connell: No.

Evelyn: No?

O'Connell: No. You came to ask me about Hamunaptra.

Jonathan: Shh. Shh.

Evelyn: H–how do you know the box **pertains**[8] to Hamunaptra?

O'Connell: Because that's where I was when I found it. I was there.

Jonathan: But how do we know that's not a load of pig's wallow?

O'Connell: Do I know you?

Jonathan: No, no. I've just got one of those faces.

Evelyn: You were actually at Hamunaptra?

O'Connell: Yeah, I was there.

Evelyn: You swear?

O'Connell: Every damn day.

Evelyn: No, I didn't mean that…

O'Connell: I know what you mean. I was there. Seti's place, city of the dead.

Evelyn: Could you tell me how to get there? I mean the exact location.

O'Connell: You want to know?

8 pertain *v.* 从属，有关

Evelyn: W-well, yes.

O'Connell: Do you really want to know?

Evelyn: Yes.

O'Connell: Then get me the hell out of here! Do it, lady!

Evelyn: Where are they taking him?

Guard: To be hanged. Apparently he had a very good time.

Evelyn: I will give you 100 pounds to save this man's life.

Guard: Madame I would pay 100 pounds just to see him hang.

Evelyn: Two hundred pounds!

Guard: Proceed!

Evelyn: Three hundred pounds!

Executioner: Any last requests, pig?

O'Connell: Yeah. Loosen the knot and let me go.

Guard: Of course we don't let him go!

Evelyn: Five hundred pounds!

Guard: And what else? I'm a very lonely man. Yalla tlak!

Evelyn: No!

Guard: Ha ha! His neck did not break! Oh, I'm so sorry. Now we must watch him strangle to death.

Evelyn: He knows the location to Hamunaptra.

Guard: You lie.

Evelyn: I would never!

Guard: Are you telling me this **filthy**[9] godless son of a pig knows where to find the city of the dead?

Evelyn: Yes!

Guard: Truly?

---

9 filthy *adj*. 肮脏的，下流的

Evelyn: Yes! And if you cut him down, we will give you ten percent.

Guard: Fifty percent.

Evelyn: Twenty.

Guard: Forty.

Evelyn: Thirty!

Guard: Twenty-five.

Evelyn: Ah! Deal.

Guard: Ahh! Cut him down!

伊芙琳: 你说你是在底比斯挖出来的。

乔纳森: 好吧,我弄错了。

伊芙琳: 你骗我。

乔纳森: 我谁都骗。难道你就该特殊吗?

伊芙琳: 可我是你妹妹。

乔纳森: 所以你更好骗。

伊芙琳: 乔纳森,你说你从当地旧城区里的一个醉鬼身上偷来的……

乔纳森: 事实上是顺手牵羊,所以我不认为它是……

伊芙琳: 别开玩笑了。这家伙为什么坐牢?

警　卫: 这我就不清楚了。不过听说你要来,我就亲自问了他。

伊芙琳: 那他怎么说?

警　卫: 他说,他只是在找乐子。

伊芙琳: 你就是从他身上偷来的?

乔纳森: 是的,我看我们不如找个地方去吃点儿东西……

欧康诺: 你是谁?这娘们儿又是谁?

伊芙琳: 娘们儿?

乔纳森: 我是本地的传教士,来传福音的。这是我妹妹伊芙琳。

伊芙琳: 您好!

I love waking up in the morning and not knowing what's going to happen, or who I'm going to meet, where I'm going to wind up.

我喜欢早上起来时一切都是未知的,不知会遇见什么人,会有什么样的结局。

欧康诺:嗯,还行,还不算难看。

伊芙琳:你说什么?

警　卫:我失陪一下。

乔纳森:问他盒子的事。

伊芙琳:呃,我们找到了,呃,嘿,打扰一下。我们找到了你的魔盒,来这儿是想请教你一些问题。

欧康诺:不。

伊芙琳:不?

欧康诺:不,你是来问我有关哈姆纳塔的事儿的。

乔纳森:嘘,嘘。

伊芙琳:你怎么知道盒子和哈姆纳塔有关?

欧康诺:因为我就是在那里找到这个盒子的。就在那儿。

乔纳森:我们怎么知道你不是在吹牛?

欧康诺:我认识你吗?

乔纳森:不认识,我长了张大众脸。

伊芙琳:你真的到过哈姆纳塔?

欧康诺:是的,去过。

伊芙琳:你发誓?

欧康诺:我发誓。

伊芙琳:不,我不是那个意思……

欧康诺:我知道你什么意思。我去过那儿。塞提的地盘,死亡之城。

伊芙琳:你能告诉我要怎么去吗?我是说,确切的位置。

欧康诺:你想知道?

伊芙琳:是的。

欧康诺:你真的想知道?

伊芙琳:是。

欧康诺:那就把我从这儿弄出去!快点,小姐!

伊芙琳:他们要带他去哪儿?

警　卫:绞刑台。看样子他找到乐子了。

伊芙琳:我给你一百镑,放了他。

警　卫:女士,我给你一百镑看他被吊死。

伊芙琳:两百镑!

警　卫:行刑!

伊芙琳:三百镑!

刽子手:你还有什么遗言吗?

欧康诺:有,把绳子松了,放我走。

警　卫:我们当然不会放他走。

伊芙琳:五百镑!

警　卫:还有呢?我是个寂寞的男人。行刑!

伊芙琳:不要!

警　卫:哈!他的脖子还没断呢。很抱歉,现在我们得看着他被勒死。

伊芙琳:他知道哈姆纳塔在哪儿。

警　卫:你说谎。

伊芙琳:我从不说谎。

警　卫:你是说这只令人恶心的死猪知道死亡之城在哪儿?

伊芙琳:是的!

警　卫:真的?

伊芙琳:真的!如果你放他下来,我们就分你一成。

警　卫:五成。

伊芙琳:两成。

警　卫:四成。

伊芙琳:三成!

警　卫:两成半。

伊芙琳:好,成交!

警　卫:啊!放他下来!

I figure life is a gift and I don't intend on wasting it. You never know what hand you're going to get dealt next. You learn to take life as it comes at you.

我觉得生命是一份礼物,我不想浪费它,你不会知道下一手牌会是什么,要学会接受生活。

经典对白(二)

A Dialogue on the Ship 船上的对话

在船上，伊芙琳对欧康诺说起自己此行的目的所在……

O'Connell: Sorry. Didn't mean to scare ya.

Evelyn: The only thing that scares me, Mr. O'Connell, are your manners.

O'Connell: Still angry about that kiss, huh?

Evelyn: Well, if you call that a kiss. Um, did I miss something? Are we going into battle?

O'Connell: Lady, there's something out there. Something underneath that sand.

Evelyn: Yes, well, I'm hoping to find a certain **artifact**[10]. A book, actually. My brother thinks there's treasure. What do you think's out there?

O'Connell: In a word? Evil. The Bedouin and the Tuaregs believe that Hamunaptra is cursed.

Evelyn: Ooh, look, I don't believe in fairy tales and **hokum**[11], Mr. O'Connell, but I do believe one of the most famous books in history is buried there, *The book of Amun-ra*. It contains within it all the secret **incantations**[12] of the old kingdom. It's what first interested me in Egypt when I was a child. It's why I came here sort of a life's pursuit.

O'Connell: And the fact that they say it's made out of pure gold makes no never mind to you? Right?

Evelyn: You know your history.

10 artifact *n.* 人工制品

11 hokum *n.* 废话

12 incantation *n.* 咒语

O'Connell: I know my treasure.

Evelyn: Um...by the way, why did you kiss me?

O'Connell: I was about to be hanged it seemed like a good idea at the time.

Evelyn: Oh!

O'Connell: What? What'd I say?

欧康诺: 抱歉,不是故意要吓你的。

伊芙琳: 唯一会吓到我的,欧康诺先生,是你的举止行为。

欧康诺: 还在为那个吻而生气,嗯?

伊芙琳: 如果那也能称得上是个吻?呃,我是不是误会了?我们……是要去打仗吗?

欧康诺: 小姐,那个地方有些东西,埋在沙地下面。

伊芙琳: 哦,当然,我希望能找到一件古代文物,事实上它是本书。我哥哥认为那里有宝藏。你觉得那里会有什么?

欧康诺: 简单的说,魔鬼。贝都因人和柏柏尔人都相信哈姆纳塔受到了诅咒。

伊芙琳: 我才不相信那些毫无根据的传说,欧康诺先生,但是我相信那里埋藏着一本史上最有名的古书《太阳金经》。这本书里记载了所有古埃及王国的神秘咒语,它也是第一本让我迷上埃及的书,那会儿我还是个孩子呢。我来这儿就是为了找寻我毕生的追求。

欧康诺: 所以你根本不在意那本书是不是用黄金打造的,对吧?

伊芙琳: 你也是来探寻历史的吧。

欧康诺: 我是来寻宝的。

伊芙琳: 呃……顺便问一下,你为什么吻我?

欧康诺: 我都快被吊死了,这么做似乎还不错。

伊芙琳: 哦!

欧康诺: 怎么了?我说错什么了?

God shall wipe away all the tears from their eyes, and there shall be no more death. Neither shall there be sorrow or dying, neither shall there be any more pain, for the former world has passed away.

上帝擦去他们所有的眼泪。死亡不再有,也不再有悲伤和生死离别,不再有痛苦,因往事已矣。

Beautiful Sentences 妙语佳句

1. Let's be nice, children. If we're going to play together we must learn to share. There are other places to dig.
   大家不要吵,孩子们。如果我们要一起玩,就得学会分享。我们去挖别的地方。
2. I believe if I can see it and I can touch it, then it's real. That's what I believe.
   要是看得到摸得着的东西,那就是真实存在的,这才是我所相信的。
3. It is better to be the right hand of the devil than in his path. As long as I serve him, I am immune.
   帮他做事总比跟他作对要好。只要我伺候他,他就不会杀我。
4. You know, nasty little fellows such as yourself always get their comeuppance.
   知道吗,像你这种卑鄙小人,最终都会得到报应的。
5. Mister O'Connell, can you look me in the eye, and guarantee me that this isn't all some kind of a flimflam?
   欧康诺先生,你能看着我的眼睛并向我保证,你绝对没有对我说谎?
6. Oh, my god. It's a...it's a sarcophagus buried at the base of Anubis. He must have been someone of great importance or he did something very naughty.
   天啊,这是……是具石棺,埋在阿努比斯死神的脚下。他要么是身世显赫之人,要么就是犯了滔天大罪。

Thought about Life 人生感悟

埃及是个神秘的国度,它留给我们太多未解的谜题和未知的宝藏,难怪会有无数的探险家到那里去探秘。人们对神秘的事物总是有着莫名的喜好,总想探个究竟,甚至不惜为此而牺牲性命。也许为了科学研究去探险,会是件有意义的事儿。不过我们得知道探险背后的初衷是什么,如果单纯是为了好奇或贪心,那样或许就有些得不偿失了。

十六、惊险的空中之旅
——《空中监狱》

影片简介：

突击队队员卡梅伦·坡为保护刚刚怀孕的妻子免受流氓恶棍的骚扰而失手杀了人，被判入狱8年。在狱中，他表现良好，并在女儿8岁生日那天获释。归心似箭的他想早点儿回到家中，便向典狱长请求搭乘飞机回去。然而警方正准备用这架飞机将一批残暴的罪犯运送到其他监狱去，而且不巧的是，在飞行途中，这群罪犯又劫持了飞机。联邦探员认为，这些罪犯死有余辜，便决定将飞机炸毁。卡梅伦能否脱离险境？他又能否赶回去庆祝女儿的生日……

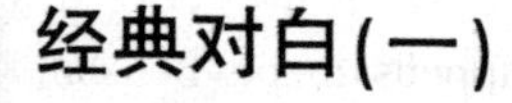

经典对白(一)

●Control the Situation 控制局势

缉毒探员威利掏出枪试图控制局势，但却害死了自己，塞洛斯对坡的表现大加赞赏……

Poe: I think you should just stop.

Willie: Stay back, man. Stay back!

Poe: Just stop, right? Before somebody gets killed.

Willie: Back!

Poe: All right, cowboy, I'm back.

Willie: Stay back.

Poe: You know you're in a situation you can't control, right?

Willie: I can't control it? I can't control it?

Black Man: You're a dead man.

Willie: Shut the fuck up! Ah!

Cyrus: What's your name convict?

Poe: My name?

Cyrus: Yeah.

Poe: Poe.

Cyrus: Nice work, Poe. Truly nice work.

Mike: Nice goin', son. Not only did you not save this dude's life, you done made best friends with Cyrus the damn Virus.

Black Man: Hey, Cyrus, I, uh, I got some good news and I got some bad news.

Cyrus: Yeah, what's the good news?

Black Man: Well, the goods news is I found Benson, Carls and Popovitch.

Cyrus: What's the bad news?

Black Man: The bad news is this dead fellow right here happens to be Benson. This Aryan fellow with the bullet hole in his forehead is, is Carls. And, and this **honky**[1] he's draggin' in is Popovitch. I don't know

1 honky *n.* (俚) 对白人的轻蔑称呼

how to tell you this, Cyrus, but we are three white guys short. Or as they say in **Ebonics**[2], "We be fucked." Look man, I just wanna know. All right, you didn't...you didn't mean that dirty-nigger crack head shit, did you?

Cyrus: Gimme that gun. Hell, yes, I meant it. Listen, Carson City is expecting six men to get off this plane. And we're gonna give'em exactly what they expect. So I need three volunteers.

Mike: Come on, let's go, son.

Billy: Don't look at me, pal.

Poe: What about her?

Billy: I'm servin' eight **consecutive**[3] life sentences. I am not getting off this plane.

Mike: I got my **insulin**[4], all right, but they broke all the damn needles. If I don't get my shot in the next couple of hours, somebody gonna be sending flowers to my mother.

Another Man: Hey, I'll go. I'm too old for his shit.

Mike: I mean, no offense.

Sally: I can take care of myself.

Poe: I can see that.

Cyrus: Go ahead, go to the back. Anybody else?

Mike: Hey, right here, man. Us two.

Cyrus: Great, go ahead. Go to the back. Hey, whoa,

Work hard! Work will save you. Work is the only thing that will see you through this.

努力工作吧!工作能拯救你。埋头苦干可令你忘记痛楚。

2 Ebonics *n.* 黑人英语

3 consecutive *adj.* 连续的，连贯的

4 insulin *n.* 胰岛素

stop. The guys they're expecting are white. That puts you shit out of luck.

Mike: Hey, come on, man.

Cyrus: I'll tell you what. Sit down. One of my **associates**[5] will bring you a phone book, and you call the Affirmative Action office. You, go ahead.

Mike: Yeah, that's it. I'm gone, man. I'm dead in two hours.

Poe: No. I'll get off scream to high heaven. This plane won't leave Carson City.

Nathan: We need another white boy to volunteer.

Cyrus: Pilot's white.

Billy: Wait, wait, wait. The pilot? Who's gonna fly the plane?

Cyrus: Relax, Billy. Welcome to the machine.

坡:你最好停手。

威利:退后！你给我退后！

坡:住手好吗？你会害死人的。

威利:退后！

坡:好吧，我退后。

威利:退后！

坡:这件事儿你搞不定。

威利:我搞不定？我搞不定？

黑人:你死定了！

威利:给我闭嘴！啊！

塞洛斯:你叫什么，兄弟？

坡:我吗？

塞洛斯:对。

5 associate *n.* 同伴，伙伴

坡:我姓坡。

塞洛斯:干得漂亮,坡!真的很漂亮!

麦克:这下好了,你非但没能救他一命,反倒和"致命病毒"塞洛斯结为好友。

黑人:嘿,塞洛斯,我有个好消息,还有个坏消息。

塞洛斯:嗯,什么好消息?

黑人:好消息是我找到了本森、卡尔斯和波普维特斯了。

塞洛斯:那坏消息呢?

黑人:坏消息是这个死人刚好是本森,这个头部中枪的白人是卡尔斯,他正拖着的这个白人家伙就是波普维特斯了。我不知道怎么跟你说,塞洛斯,不过我们少了三个白人。用我们黑人的话来说就是"我们死定了"。听着,我只想知道一件事!好吧,你真的……真的觉得我是个死不足惜的黑人?

塞洛斯:把枪给我。告诉你,我就是这个意思。听着,到了卡森市,得有6个人下机,我们得凑够这个数,现在我们需要三名志愿者。

麦克:来吧,我们去吧。

比利:别看我,伙计。

坡:那她怎么办?

比利:我八次被判终身监禁,我可不要下机。

麦克:虽然我有胰岛素,好吧,可是针筒都被他们弄碎了。我要是再不打针,再过几小时,我就挂了。

另一个人:嘿,我去。我也活得够本儿了。

麦克:我是说,别怪我。

萨莉:我能照顾自己。

坡:看得出来。

塞洛斯:好的,到后面去,还有吗?

You make millions of decisions that mean nothing and then one day your order takes out and it changes your life.

你每天都在做很多看起来毫无意义的决定,但某天你的某个决定就能改变你的一生。

坡:嘿,这儿,我们两个。

塞洛斯:很好,走吧,到后面去。嘿,慢着,他们要的是白人,你只能自认倒霉了。

麦克:嘿,别这样,老兄。

塞洛斯:听着,坐下。我的帮手会把电话簿拿给你的,你大可以去投诉我种族歧视。你,继续走。

麦克:完了,我死定了。再过两个小时我就死定了。

坡:不会的。我下了飞机会大喊大叫的,飞机绝对无法离开卡森市的。

内森:还差一个白人。

塞洛斯:飞行员是个白人。

比利:等等,等等,你说飞行员?那飞机谁开?

塞洛斯:别紧张,比利。欢迎来到空中监狱。

经典对白(二)

Get to Know Cameron 了解卡梅伦

坡明明有机会下飞机,可他却没有下,对此,探员文斯感到不甚理解。他想进一步了解坡,便约坡的妻子翠茜娅谈话……

Vince: Hello. I'm...I'm Vince Larkin.

Tricia: Hello. Tricia Poe.

Vince: Nice to meet ya. This, this must be Casey. Hello, Casey.

Casey: Hello, Mr. Larkin.

Vince: Nice to meet ya. So how are you doin'? I'm sorry. That's, uh...**scratch**[6] that Dumb question. You...You wanted to see your husband today, and then thi whole thing happened.

6 scratch *v*. 抓,搔,刮

ricia: Maybe you could just tell me exactly what's going on here and...

Vince: We're doing everything we can to get the plane down. Actually, that's w–why I wanted to talk to you.

...

Vince: It seems that your husband, Cameron...had an opportunity to get off the plane and he didn't do it. And I was hoping you could...maybe help me figure out why.

Tricia: That would make two of us. I don't know.

Vince: I mean, it's possible, it's...it's not uncommon...that some parolees actually fear their **release**[7] date. A certain degree of **institutionalization**[8] sets in. Fear of coming home. Fear of living in society. Any of this make sense?

Tricia: No, no. That's not Cameron. I mean, if you, if you knew him, if you read his letters, or if you talked to him on the phone, you'd know that...I mean, he's been waitin' for this day for eight years. He's not gonna...I mean, look, he's got this little, this little girl to come home to. Wouldn't you...do the same thing?

Vince: There'd have to be a pretty strong reason to keep me on that plane.

Tricia: Well, knowing Cameron, I'm sure there is a good reason. Uh, maybe, if you, if you do see him or if you talk to him...maybe you could just tell him to come home, all right? Be kinda nice to have him around.

Vince: You got it.

Mistakes live in the neighborhood of truth and therefore delude us.

谬误是真理的近邻，因此谬误常使我们迷惑。

7 release *n.* 释放

8 institutionalization *n.* 寄居机构

文　斯：你好。我是文斯·赖肯。

翠茜娅：你好。翠茜娅·坡。

文　斯：幸会，幸会。这一定就是凯西了吧。你好，凯西。

凯　西：你好，赖肯先生。

文　斯：很高兴认识你。你们好吗？抱歉，不用理会这个问题了，这么问很蠢吧。本来今天你会见到你丈夫的，结果却出了这种事。

翠茜娅：你能不能告诉我到底出了什么事，还有……

文　斯：我们正在用一切可能的方法逼迫这架飞机降落。事实上，这正是我想和你谈的。

……

文　斯：看起来，你的丈夫卡梅伦……有机会下机但却不下，我在想也许你能帮我解决这个问题。

翠茜娅：或许吧，我也不知道。

文　斯：我是说，有没有可能……当然，也不是很常见了，许多假释犯会害怕被释放出狱。他们关在牢里呆得太久了，害怕回家，怕重返社会。你觉得有没有道理？

翠茜娅：不，不会，卡梅伦不会的。我是说，如果你认识他，看过他的信，或是跟他讲过电话，你就会知道……我是说，他等这一天已经等了八年了，他不会……我是说，看，他的小女儿在等他回家。换作是你，你也会这么做的吧？

文　斯：那一定是有十足的理由要他留在飞机上。

翠茜娅：是的，我了解卡梅伦，他一定有很充分的理由。呃，要是你看到他或者能和他说上话，你能叫他赶快回家吗？有他在家挺幸福的。

文　斯：没问题。

Beautiful Sentences 妙语佳句

1. The tape's just a little precaution in case any of you are rocked by the sudden impulse to squeal like a pig. Not that we don't trust you. But let's face it, you're

criminals.

用胶带封住你们的嘴只是为了防止你们像头猪那样突然乱叫,并不是我们不信任你们,但是你们毕竟是罪犯,并不值得信任。

Fact one. We got a plane up there filled with killers, rapists and thieves and we got this guy Cameron Poe, in on an involuntary manslaughter beef. Non-gang affiliated. He's a parolee hitchin' a ride home. Fact two. Poe has a chance to get off the plane. Doesn't do it. Why? Fact three. Our guard, Falzon, said a convict named Cameron Poe planted Sims's tape recorder on him. These are interesting facts. You do the math on this, and we got an ally on that plane.

第一点,飞机上全是杀手和强暴犯,姓坡的却只是过失杀人,他获得假释准备回家。第二点,他有机会却不下机,为什么?第三点,费警卫说姓坡的犯人把录音机塞给他,很有意思。仔细想想,他是我们的盟友呢。

Who are you to decide the value of a man's life? There are innocent people up there!

你有什么权利来决定他人的生死?那上面还有无辜的人呢!

Sorry, boss, but there's only two men I trust. One of them's me. The other's not you.

抱歉,长官,我只相信两个人。一个是我自己,而另一个可不是你。

If this thing goes bad, Larkin, I'm afraid my daughter won't understand. If you talk to my wife again, you tell her, I love her. She's my hummingbird. But I couldn't leave a fallen man behind. You'll do that for me, won't you, Larkin?

如果这次行动失败了,赖肯,我想我女儿是不会了解了。要是你有机会再和我妻子谈话，请你告诉她，我很爱她，她是我的小心肝儿。但我不能抛弃朋友。你会帮我的忙吗，赖肯？

6. Don't fire. Malloy, listen to him! He's a friend! He's just trying to get home to see his wife and kid! Don't fire!

别开火！梅洛伊，听他的话！他是我们的盟友！他只想回家，回到他妻儿的身边！别开火！

7. Just so's you know, Marshal Larkin, there's now three men I trust.

我要你知道，赖肯警官，我现在相信三个人了。

Thought about Life 人生感悟

主人公卡梅伦有着幸福的家庭，有个信任他并深爱他的妻子，还有个可爱的小女儿。所以他能为了帮助朋友而放弃与家人团聚的机会，这实在是很难得的。在卡梅伦的内心深处，他也一定会担心自己会永远地失去见到妻儿的机会，但是他觉得自己有责任不让这群罪大恶极的罪犯逃脱。在亲情、友情、责任三者之间，我们是否有这样的勇气来做出选择呢？

十七、旧梦重游
——《爱丽丝梦游仙境》(2010)

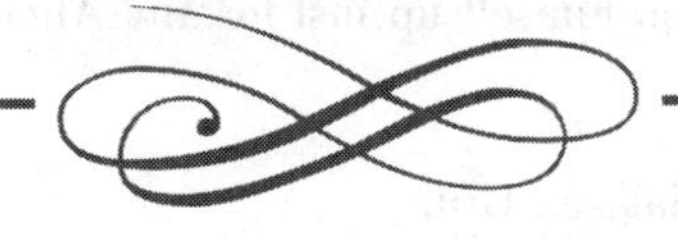

片简介：

转眼间，曾梦游仙境的爱丽丝已长大成人。在一个聚会上，傲自大的哈米什当众向19岁的爱丽丝求婚，而爱丽丝在没好准备的情形下，只得无奈地逃跑了。她跟着一只兔子来到花园，却不小心掉到了洞穴里，而那里便是旧地仙境的入口。而9年后的她却对这里的一切都感到陌生，以前的经历她丝毫没有印象。于是那里的老朋友开始帮助爱丽丝找回记，并希望爱丽丝能把他们从"红桃皇后"的暴政下解救出来……

经典对白(一)

Decision 决定

疯帽子为了让爱丽丝逃走而被红桃皇后的士兵抓走了，丽丝便决意要救它……

Alice: You were supposed to lead them away! The Hatter trusted you!

Bayard: They have my wife and pups.

Alice: What's your name?

Bayard: Bayard.

Alice: Sit!

Bayard: Would your name be Alice, by any chance?

Alice: Yes, but I'm not the one that everyone's talking about.

Bayard: The Hatter would not have given himself up just for any Alice.

Alice: Where did they take him?

Bayard: To the Red Queen's castle at Salazen Grum.

Alice: We're going to rescue him.

Bayard: That is not **foretold**[1].

Alice: I don't care. He wouldn't be there if it weren't for me.

Bayard: The Frabjous Day is almost upon us. You must prepare to meet th Jabberwocky.

Alice: From the moment I fell down that rabbit hole, I've been told what I must d and who I must be. I've been **shrunk**[2], **stretched**[3], **scratched**[4] and **stuffe into**[5] a teapot. I've been accused of being Alice and of not being Alice, bu this is my dream. I'll decide where it goes from here.

Bayard: If you diverge from the path...

Alice: I make the path. Take me to Salazen Grum, Bayard, and don't forget the hat

Bayard: There's only one way across.

Alice: Lost my muchness, have I? Bayard! The hat!

爱丽丝：你应该把他们引开。疯帽子那么信任你！

1 foretell *v*. 预言，预示

2 shrink *v*. 缩小，畏缩

3 stretch *v*. 伸展

4 scratch *v*. 抓，刮，挠

5 stuff into *v*. 把……塞进

亚德：我的妻儿在他们手上。

丽丝：你叫什么？

亚德：贝亚德。

丽丝：坐吧！

亚德：你不会是爱丽丝吧？

丽丝：我是爱丽丝，但我不是你们所说的那个爱丽丝。

亚德：疯帽子可不会随便为了一个爱丽丝而交出自己的。

丽丝：他会被带到哪儿去？

亚德：红皇后的城堡，在萨拉真格莱姆。

丽丝：我们要去救他。

亚德：预言可不是这么说的。

丽丝：我不管。要不是因为我，他也不会被抓走。

亚德：决战之日即将到来，你得做好对付炸脖龙的准备。

丽丝：从我掉进兔子洞的那一刻起，你们就不断地告诉我该做什么，该成为什么样的人。我会缩小，会放大，刮伤了胳膊，还被塞到茶壶里。你们还说我是那个爱丽丝，或者不是，但这是我的梦。从现在起一切由我说了算。

亚德：如果你走错了路……

丽丝：我会开一条出来。带我去萨拉真格莱姆，贝亚德，别忘了那顶帽子。

亚德：只有一条路通向那里。

丽丝：我不再是从前那勇敢的我了，真的吗？贝亚德！帽子！

What if something had happened to you? What if I couldn't get to you? What would I have done without you? You're my family. You're all I've got.

要是你出了事怎么办？要是我找不到你怎么办？如果没有你我该怎么办？你是我的家人，你是我的一切。

经典对白(二)

Encouragement 鼓励

爱丽丝在取回沃尔铂剑后，还是对自己能杀死炸脖龙一事到很犹豫，白皇后和阿布索伦便用不同的方式来鼓励她……

White Queen: My sister preferred to study **Dominion**[6] Over Living Things. Tell m how does she seem to you?

Alice: Perfectly **horrid**[7].

White Queen: And her head?

Alice: **Bulbous**[8].

White Queen: I think she may have some kind of growth in there, something pressir on her brain. Three coins from a dead man's pocket, two teaspoons wishful thinking.

Alice: You can't imagine the things that go on in that place.

White Queen: Oh, yes, I can. But when a **champion**[9] steps forth to slay the Jabberwock the people will rise against her. That should do it. Blow. Feel better?

Alice: Much, thank you.

White Queen: There's someone here who would like to speak with you.

Alice: Absolem?

Absolem: Who are you?

Alice: I thought we'd settled this. I'm Alice, but not that one.

Absolem: How do you know?

Alice: You said so yourself.

Absolem: I said you were not hardly Alice, but you're much more her now. I fact, you're almost Alice.

Alice: Even so, I couldn't slay the Jabberwocky if my life depended on it.

Absolem: It will. So I suggest you keep the Vorpal sword on hand when th Frabjous Day arrives.

Alice: You seem so real. Sometimes I forget that this is all a dream. Will yo stop doing that?

---

6 dominion *n*. 统治，管辖

7 horrid *adj*. 令人恐惧的，吓人的

8 bulbous *adj*. 球状的

9 champion *n*. 勇士，捍卫者

白皇后：我的姐姐喜欢研究"如何统治世界"。能告诉我你对她的印象如何吗？

爱丽丝：真是可怕极了！

白皇后：她的头呢？

爱丽丝：像个大圆球。

白皇后：我想她的脑袋里可能长了什么东西，压迫了神经。三枚硬币，取自亡魂的口袋，两勺"希望的念头"。

爱丽丝：你一定无法想象那里发生了什么。

白皇后：哦不，我能想到。不过一旦我的勇士能站出来杀了炸脖龙的话，人民就会起来反抗她。做好了。喝点儿吧。好点儿了吗？

爱丽丝：好多了，谢谢。

白皇后：这里有人想和你谈谈。

爱丽丝：阿布索伦？

阿布索伦：你是？

爱丽丝：我以为你知道我是谁呢。我是爱丽丝，但不是你们所说的那个。

阿布索伦：你怎么知道你不是呢？

爱丽丝：你就是这么说的。

阿布索伦：我是说你不完全像是那个爱丽丝，现在倒是像多了。事实上，你差不多就是那个爱丽丝了。

爱丽丝：即便如此，我也无法杀死炸脖龙，就算是我命里注定要去做。

阿布索伦：你会的。所以我建议你在决战之日来临时，手里要握着沃尔铂剑。

爱丽丝：你好像真实存在的，有时我都忘记了这只是一场梦。你可不可以不这样做？

Beautiful Sentences 妙语佳句

1. Therefore, it is high time to forgive and forget or forget and forgive, whichever comes first or is, in any case, most convenient. I'm waiting.
所以,正是时候去原谅而后遗忘,或者遗忘后再原谅。不管先做什么,总之怎么方便怎么来。我等着呢。
2. On the Frabjous Day, when the White Queen once again wears the crown, on that day, I shall Futterwacken vigorously.
等到决战之日那天,白皇后重新戴上皇冠,我会热情洋溢地跳起福特韦根舞。
3. Alice, you cannot live your life to please others. The choice must be yours, because when you step out to face that creature, you will step out alone.
爱丽丝,取悦他人可不是你生活的目的。你要自己做出决定,因为一旦你站出来面对那个怪兽,你就得独自战斗了。
4. Remember, the Vorpal sword knows what it wants. All you have to do is hold on to it.
要记住,沃尔铂剑了解它的使命。你要做的就是和它一起坚持下去。
5. I fell down a hole and hit my head. I'm sorry, Hamish. I can't marry you. You're not the right man for me. And there's that trouble with your digestion. I love you, Margaret, but this is my life. I'll decide what to do with it. You're lucky to have my sister for your wife, Lowell, and you be good to her. I'll be watching very closely. There is no prince, Aunt Imogene. You need to talk to someone about these delusions. I happen to love rabbits, especially white ones. Don't worry, Mother, I'll find something useful to do with my life. You two remind me of some funny boys I met in a dream.
我掉到洞里撞到了头。抱歉,哈米什,我不能嫁给你,你也不是我的真命天子,何况你还有些消化不良。我很爱你,玛格丽特,但这是我的人生,我要自己决定该怎么做。你能娶我姐姐作妻子,洛威尔,你很幸运了。对她好点儿,我会紧盯着你的。世上没有白马王子,伊莫金姨妈。你得找个人说说你那奇幻的想法了。我突然好喜欢兔子,尤其是白色的。别担心,妈妈,我会找到生活的方向的。你们俩让我想起了我在梦里遇到的一对儿有趣的兄弟。

Thought about Life 人生感悟

拯救人民于危难之中，这好像是只有大英雄才能做到的事儿,难怪弱小的爱丽丝会对自己产生不信任感,甚至打算退缩和放弃。其实下决定并不难,难就难在下了决心后,就要坚持做完它。也正是因为结果常常难以预料,特别是这种生死关头,所以我们才会犹豫不决。不过我想生活终归是属于每个人自己的,既然已经做出了决定,那就坚持走下去,相信未来的结果总会是好的。

You got a dream, you have got to protect it. People can't do something themselves, they want to tell you that you can't do it. If you want something, go get it. Period.

如果你有梦想的话,就要去捍卫它。那些一事无成的人想告诉你你成不了大器。如果你有理想的话,就要去努力实现。就这样。

十八、勇猛的钢铁战士
——《钢铁侠 I》

影片简介:

托尼·斯塔克生于富豪之家,他天资聪颖,喜好研究发明。在父母去世后,他独自一人撑起了家族企业的重担,并使家族事业发展得如日中天。不久,他在一处荒无人烟的地方进行新型武器实验时,遭人绑架,这伙恐怖分子要他研制出威力更强的新型武器。聪明的托尼并没有屈服,反而利用这个机会制造出了一个能自由活动并具有攻击能力的钢铁盔甲, 这就是钢铁侠的雏形。从此托尼便开始了他作为"钢铁侠"的冒险经历……

经典对白(一)

Got a Kidnap 遭遇绑架

斯塔克醒来后发现自己遭到一群恐怖分子的绑架, 他只能被迫接受对方提出的条件……

Yinsen: He wants to know what you think.

Stark: I think you got a lot of my weapons.

Yinsen: He says they have everything you need to build the Jericho missile. He wants you to make the list of materials. He says for you to start working immediately, and when you're done, he will set you free.

Stark: No, he won't.

Yinsen: No, he won't. I'm sure they're looking for you, Stark. But they will never find you in these mountains. Look, what you just saw, that is your legacy, Stark. Your life's work, in the hands of those murderers. Is that how you want to go out? Is this the last act of **defiance**[1] of the great Tony Stark? Or are you going to do something about it?

Stark: Why should I do anything? They're going to kill me, you, either way. And if they don't, I'll probably be dead in a week.

Yinsen: Well, then, this is a very important week for you, isn't it?

Stark: If this is going to be my work station, I want it well-lit. I want these up. I need **welding**[2] gear. I don't care if it's **acetylene**[3] or **propane**[4]. I need a **soldering**[5] station. I need helmets. I'm gonna need **goggles**[6]. I would like a smelting cup. I need two sets of precision tools. How many languages do you speak?

Yinsen: A lot. But apparently, not enough for this place. They speak Arabic, Urdu, Dari, Pashto, Mongolian, Farsi, Russian.

Stark: Who are these people?

Yinsen: They are your loyal customers, sir. They call themselves the Ten Rings. You know, we might be more productive if you include me in the planning

---

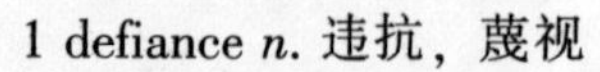

1 defiance *n*. 违抗，蔑视

2 weld *v*. 焊接

3 acetylene *n*. 乙炔

4 propane *n*. 丙烷

5 solder *v*. 焊接

6 goggle *n*. 护目镜

process.

Stark: Okay, we don't need this.

Yinsen: What is that?

Stark: That's **palladium**[7], 0.15 grams. We need at least 1.6, so why don't you go break down the other 11? Careful. Careful, we only get one shot at this.

Yinsen: Relax. I have steady hands. Why do you think you're still alive?

Stark: What do I call you?

Yinsen: My name is Yinsen.

Stark: Yinsen. Nice to meet you.

Yinsen: Nice to meet you, too. That doesn't look like a Jericho missile.

Stark: That's because it's a **miniaturized**[8] **arc**[9] reactor. I got a big one powering my factory at home. It should keep the **shrapnel**[10] out of my heart.

Yinsen: But what could it generate?

Stark: If my math is right, and it always is, three gigajoules per second.

Yinsen: That could run your heart for 50 lifetimes.

Stark: Yeah. Or something big for 15 minutes. This is our ticket out of here.

Yinsen: What is it?

Stark: **Flatten**[11] them out and look.

Yinsen: Impressive.

I'm going to make him an offer he can't refuse.

我会给他点好处，让他无法拒绝。

---

7 palladium *n*. 钯

8 miniaturize *v*. 使……微型化

9 arc *n*. 弧形，弧状物

10 shrapnel *n*. 弹片

11 flatten *v*. 把……弄平

尹　森:他想知道你的想法。

斯塔克:你有很多我制造的武器。

尹　森:他说他们有你制造耶利哥导弹所需的一切材料,他要你列个清单,现在就开工,等导弹造完后,就放你走。

斯塔克:他不会放的。

尹　森:确实不会。斯塔克,你的人肯定在找你,可在这山区里他们是永远也找不到的。你刚刚也看到了,那些军火就是你的遗产了,斯塔克。你毕生的心血却落到了这些杀人犯的手里。你就想这样一走了之吗?这就是伟大的托尼·斯塔克最后的反抗吗? 还是你得做点儿什么?

斯塔克:我还能做什么?反正他们总会杀了我们的。就算他们不杀我,我也就能活一个星期。

尹　森:那么,这个星期对你来说就非常重要了,对吗?

斯塔克:我的工作间要光线充足,把这些东西准备好。我需要焊接设备,乙炔或丙烷都可以;还需要焊接台、头盔和护目镜;还有坩埚和两套切割工具。你会说几种语言?

尹　森:很多。不过在这儿还是不够用。他们说阿拉伯语、乌尔都语、达里语、普什图语、蒙古语、波斯语和俄语。

斯塔克:他们是什么人?

尹　森:他们都是您的忠实客户,自称为"自由战士"。要是你让我给你搭把手的话,效率可能会更高的。

斯塔克:好了,不需要这个。

尹　森:这是什么?

斯塔克:金属钯,0.15 克。我们至少需要 1.6 克,你能把剩下的 11 个也拆了吗?要十分小心,我们可是孤注一掷了。

尹　森:放心,我手很稳的,要不你还能活到现在?

斯塔克:怎么称呼你?

尹　森:我叫尹森。

斯塔克:尹森,很高兴认识你。

尹　森：我也是。这可不像耶利哥导弹。

斯塔克：因为这是小型方舟反应堆啊。我家的工厂那儿还有个大的，用来供能。这个能阻止弹片进入我的心脏。

尹　森：它供能的效果怎么样？

斯塔克：如果我没算错的话，当然我一直都没错过，每秒 30 亿焦耳。

尹　森：够你活 50 次了。

斯塔克：是啊，或者够一个大家伙用一刻钟。咱们就靠这个出去。

尹　森：这是什么？

斯塔克：摊平了看。

尹　森：这太棒了！

Keep your friends close, but your enemies closer.
亲近你的朋友，但更要亲近你的敌人。

经典对白(二)

Switch the Power 更换能源

斯塔克的能量源出了问题，他让助手裴普来帮他替换……

Stark: Pepper. How big are your hands?

Pepper: What?

Stark: How big are your hands?

Pepper: I don't understand why...

Stark: Get down here. I need you. Hey, let's see them. Show me your hands. Let's see them. Oh, wow. They are small. Very **petite**[12], indeed. I just need your help for a sec.

Pepper: Oh, my God, is that the thing that's keeping you alive?

12 petite *adj*. 小巧的

Stark: It was. It is now an antique. This is what will be keeping me alive for the foreseeable future. I'm **swapping**[13] it up for an upgraded unit, and I just ran into a little speed bump.

Pepper: Speed bump, what does that mean?

Stark: It's nothing. It's just a little snag. There's an exposed wire under this device. And it's contacting the **socket wall**[14] and causing a little bit of a short. It's fine.

Pepper: What do you want me to do?

Stark: Put that on the table over there. That is **irrelevant**[15].

Pepper: Oh, my God!

Stark: I just want you to reach in, and you're just gonna gently lift the wire out.

Pepper: Is it safe?

Stark: Yeah, it should be fine. It's like Operation. You just don't let it touch the socket wall or it goes "beep".

Pepper: What's up? Sorry. What do you mean, "Operation"?

Stark: It's just a game, never mind. Just gently lift the wire. Okay?

Pepper: Okay.

Stark: Great.

Pepper: You know, I don't think that I'm qualified to do this.

Stark: No, you're fine. You're the most capable, qualified, **trustworthy**[16] person I've ever met. You're gonna do great. Is it too much of a problem to ask? 'Cause I'm...

Pepper: Okay, okay.

Stark: I really need your help here. Okay.

Pepper: Oh, there's **pus**[17]!

13 swap *v*. 交换

14 socket wall 底座

15 irrelevant *adj*. 无关的

16 trustworthy *adj*. 值得信赖的

17 pus *n*. 脓

Stark: It's not pus. It's an **inorganic**[18] **plasmic**[19] **discharge**[20] from the device, not from my body.

Pepper: It smells!

Stark: Yeah, it does. The copper wire. The copper wire, you got it?

Pepper: Okay, I got it! I got it!

Stark: Okay, you got it? Now, don't let it touch the sides when you're coming out...oh, eyes, eyes!

Pepper: I'm sorry. I'm sorry.

Stark: That's what I was trying to tell you before. Okay, now make sure that when you pull it out, you don't... There's a **magnet**[21] at the end of it! That was it. You just pulled it out.

Pepper: Oh, God! Okay, I was not expecting...

Stark: Don't put it back in! Don't put it back in!

Pepper: Okay, What's wrong?

Stark: Nothing, I'm just going into **cardiac**[22] arrest 'cause you yanked it out like a **trout**[23]...

Pepper: What? You said it was safe!

Stark: We gotta hurry. Take this. Take this. You gotta switch it out really quick.

Pepper: Okay. Okay. Tony? It's going to be okay.

From that you would get angry with your friends, we can conclude you sitll care about the friendship between you.

如果朋友让你生气，那说明你仍然在意他的友情。

---

18 inorganic *adj.* 无机的，非生物的

19 plasmic *adj.* 浆状的

20 discharge *n.* 释放、排出 (的物质)

21 magnet *n.* 磁铁

22 cardiac *adj.* 心脏的

23 trout *n.* 鳟鱼

Stark: What? Is it?

Pepper: It's gonna be okay. I'm gonna make this okay.

Stark: Let's hope. Okay, you're gonna attach that to the base plate. Make sure you... Was that so hard? That was fun, right? Here, I got it. I got it. Here. Nice.

Pepper: Are you okay?

Stark: Yeah, I feel great. You okay?

Pepper: Don't ever, ever, ever, ever ask me to do anything like that ever again.

Stark: I don't have anyone but you. Anyway...

Pepper: What do you want me to do with this?

Stark: That? Destroy it. **Incinerate**[24] it.

Pepper: You don't want to keep it?

Stark: Pepper, I've been called many things. **"Nostalgic**[25]**"** is not one of them.

Pepper: Will that be all, Mr. Stark?

Stark: That will be all, Miss Potts. Hey, Butterfingers, come here. What's all this stuff doing on top of my desk? That's my phone, that's a picture of me and my dad. Right there. In the garbage. All that stuff.

斯塔克: 裴普,你的手有多大?

裴　普: 什么?

斯塔克: 我说你的手有多大?

裴　普: 你要做什么……

斯塔克: 下来,帮我个忙。嘿,让我看看你的手。手伸出来,我看看。哦,哇哦,挺小的,非常纤细。只占用你几分钟的时间。

裴　普: 天啊,就是这个东西让你活着的?

斯塔克: 是的,不过现在这个就是古董了,我要使用这个来度过我的未来生活。我打算用这个新的来替换旧的,不过我遇到了点儿小问题。

裴　普: 小问题,什么意思?

24 incinerate *v*. 把……焚毁

25 nostalgic *adj*. 怀旧的

斯塔克：没什么，就是有个地方堵上了。这个装置下面有根裸露的电线，它跟底座接触后便会引起短路，不过没事。

裴　普：我应该怎么做？

斯塔克：先把那东西放到那张桌子上，用不着它。

裴　普：哦，天哪！

斯塔克：我要你把手伸进去，轻轻地把电线取出来。

裴　普：没危险吧？

斯塔克：嗯，应该挺安全的。就像做手术一样，只要不碰到底座，就不会有问题。

裴　普：什么？抱歉，你说"手术"是什么意思？

斯塔克：就像玩游戏一样轻松，别担心。轻轻拿出来，行吗？

裴　普：行。

斯塔克：很好。

裴　普：可是，我觉得这事儿我可干不了。

斯塔克：哦，你能行的。你是我认识的最有能力，也是我最信任的人，你能做好的。要求不太过分吧？因为我……

裴　普：好的，好的。

斯塔克：我非常需要你的帮助。好的。

裴　普：哦，这是脓吧！

斯塔克：不是脓，这是设备流出来的电解液，不是我身上的脓。

裴　普：真难闻！

斯塔克：是啊，是难闻呢。那根铜线，抓到了吗？

裴　普：是的，抓到了。

斯塔克：好，抓到了吧？现在只要拿出来时别碰到……哦，小心，小心！

裴　普：对不起，对不起！

斯塔克：正想跟你说这个呢。好了，现在，在拿出来时，一定不要把……啊！末端有块儿磁铁！就是这个，你给拽出来了。

Carpe diem. Seize the day, boys. Make your lives extraordinary.
人生就应该是快乐的，要抓住每一天，孩子们。让你们的生活变得非凡起来。

裴　普:哦,天哪！我没想到……

斯塔克:别放回去！别放回去！

裴　普:好,会出什么问题吗？

斯塔克:没事儿,也就是心脏要停了而已,因为你像钓鱼似的把它给拽出来了……

裴　普:什么？你不是说很安全吗？

斯塔克:咱们得快点儿。拿着这个,拿着。你得赶紧把它替换出来。

裴　普:好的,好的。托尼？不会有事儿的。

斯塔克:什么？是吗？

裴　普:不会有事儿的。我会弄好的。

斯塔克:希望如此。好的,你把它接到底座上,一定要……难吗？挺有意思的吧？在这儿,我找到了,在这儿呢。干得不错。

裴　普:你还好吗？

斯塔克:嗯,感觉不错。你没事儿吧？

裴　普:你千万不要……不要再让我做这种事了。

斯塔克:除了你,我找不到其他人了。不管怎样……

裴　普:这个要怎么处理？

斯塔克:那个古董吗？毁了它。烧了它。

裴　普:你不想留着吗？

斯塔克:有很多词能形容我,"怀旧"可不在其中。

裴　普:没什么事了吧,斯塔克先生？

斯塔克:没事了,波茨小姐。嘿,"笨丫头",过来。我桌上怎么这么乱？我的手机,和老爸的合影,都堆在这儿？都扔了,都给我扔了。

Beautiful Sentences 妙语佳句

1. It's an imperfect world, but it's the only one we've got. I guarantee you, the day weapons are no longer needed to keep the peace, I'll start making bricks and beams for baby hospitals.

世界并不完美，不过这是我们仅有的世界。我向你保证，如果有天不用武器来维护和平，我就转行盖儿童医院去。

2. I never got to say goodbye to Dad. I never got to say goodbye to my father. There're questions that I would have asked him. I would have asked him how he felt about what this company did, if he was conflicted, if he ever had doubts, or maybe he was every inch the man we all remember from the newsreels. I saw young Americans killed by the very weapons I created to defend them and protect them. And I saw that I had become part of a system that is comfortable with zero accountability. I had my eyes opened. I came to realize that I have more to offer this world than just making things that blow up. And that is why, effective immediately, I am shutting down the weapons manufacturing division of Stark International until such a time as I can decide what the future of the company will be.

我没机会和我的父亲道别，没能见他最后一面。我很想问他一些问题，想问他对生产军火这件事儿有什么看法，想问他是否矛盾过，动摇过，抑或是像媒体报道的那样是个硬汉。我亲眼目睹年轻的美国军人被我制造的武器杀害，而我制造这些武器的目的是为了保护他们的，我还认识到我竟对此不负任何责任。我清醒了，我意识到除了制造武器外，我还能为世界贡献更多。所以，从即刻起，我决定关闭斯塔克企业武器生产部门，直到我确定公司未来的新方向以后。

3. You know what? I was naive before, when they said, "Here's the line. We don't cross it." This is how we do business. If we're double-dealing under the table, are we?

知道吗？我以前很天真，当别人说："这就是界限，我们不能跨越。"我们真就这样做生意。我们幕后真做了双重交易吗？

What the world needs is a return to sweetness and decency in the souls of its young men...
这个世界需要的是美丽和高尚回到年轻一代的灵魂之中……

4. There is nothing except this. There's no art opening. There is no benefit. There is nothing to sign. There is the next mission and nothing else.
   这件事儿没有其他的目的。我不是为了炫耀,也没有任何利益,更没有签什么合同。我还会继续这样做,仅此而已。
5. You stood by my side all these years while I reaped the benefits of destruction. And now that I'm trying to protect the people that I put in harm's way, you're going to walk out?
   你在我身边这么多年了，当初我靠制造军火肆意破坏和平来获利时你也在我身边。现在我想保护那些因战乱而饱受痛苦的人,你却要离我而去?
6. I shouldn't be alive, unless it was for a reason. I'm not crazy, Pepper. I just finally know what I have to do. And I know in my heart that it's right. You're all I have, too, you know.
   如果不是因为这个,我早就死了。我没有疯,裴普,我只是终于发现我要做什么了。我内心深处有个声音告诉我,这是正确的。你知道,我身边只有你。

Thought about Life 人生感悟

战士通常是用来称呼为了某一信仰而勇往直前的人，我们的主人公斯塔克就是这样一位勇猛的战士。他在实现自己人生价值的同时,也发现了人生的另一层含义。他是个热爱和平的人,希望自己所做的一切能够为人们带来和平和安宁,可是现实与理想总是存在着差距。于是他决定,为这个世界,为人类做出更多的贡献,而他也坚信,自己的决定就是正确的。这也许就是战士的可敬之处吧。

十九、传奇海盗的复仇记
——《加勒比海盗1：黑珍珠号的诅咒》

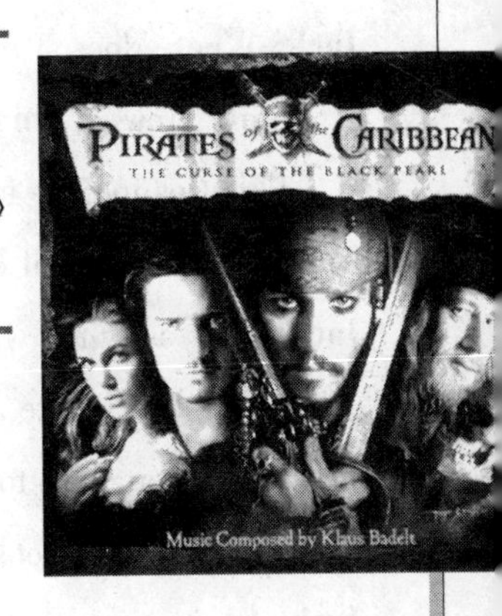

影片简介：

传奇海盗杰克·史派罗因其大副巴博萨的背叛而失去了一切，还被遗弃在了一座荒岛上。他从荒岛逃走后，无意中救了总督的女儿伊丽莎白·斯旺，此后又与爱慕斯旺小姐的威尔·特纳相识。在巴博萨袭击海港之时，斯旺小姐被他们带走并囚禁起来。威尔为了救心上人，向杰克求助，而杰克也为了夺回他的"黑珍珠"号与威尔联手……

经典对白(一)

● Ask for Help 求助

威尔的心上人斯旺小姐被海盗巴博萨带走了，威尔为了救斯旺小姐，向关押在狱中的杰克船长求助……

Will: You, Sparrow.

Jack: Eh?

Will: You are familiar with that ship, the Black Pearl.

Jack: I've heard of it.

Will: Where does it make **berth**[1]?

Jack: Where does it make berth? Have you not heard the story? Captain Barbossa and his crew of **miscreants**[2] sail from the **dreaded**[3] Island Muerta. It's an island that cannot be found except, by those who already know where it is.

Will: The ship's real enough. Its **anchorage**[4] must be a real place. Where is it?

Jack: Why ask me?

Will: Because you're a **pirate**[5].

Jack: And you want to turn pirate yourself, is that it?

Will: Never. They took Miss Swan.

Jack: Oh, so it is that you found a girl. I see. Well, if you're **intending**[6] to brave all, **hasten**[7] to her rescue, and so win fair lady's heart, you'll have to do it alone, mate. I see no profit in it for me.

Will: I can get you out of here.

Jack: How's that? The key's run off.

Will: I helped build these cells. These are half-pin barrel **hinges**[8]. With the right **leverage**[9] and the proper application of strength, the door will lift free.

1 berth n. (船只) 停泊

2 miscreant n. 恶棍，歹徒

3 dreaded adj. 可怕的

4 anchorage n. (船只的) 停泊地点

5 pirate n. 海盗

6 intending adj. 想要的，意欲的

7 hasten v. 赶紧做

8 hinge n. 铰链

9 leverage n. 杠杆装置

Jack: What's your name?

Will: Will Turner.

Jack: That would be short for William, I imagine. Good, strong name. No doubt named for your father, right?

Will: Yes.

Jack: Uh-huh. Well, Mr. Turner, I've changed my mind. If you **spring**[10] me from this cell, I swear on pain of death, I shall take you to the Black Pearl and your bonny **lass**[11]. Do we have an accord?

Will: Agreed.

Jack: Agreed. Get me out.

Will: Hurry. Someone will have heard that.

Jack: Not without my things.

威尔:嘿,史派罗!

杰克:哎!

威尔:你对那艘"黑珍珠"号很熟悉吧。

杰克:我听说过它。

威尔:它会停靠在哪儿?

杰克:它会停靠在哪儿?你没听说过吗?巴博萨船长和他那群混蛋船员来自那可怕的"死亡之岛"。除非你知道那个小岛在哪儿,否则你是找不到的。

威尔:真有那艘船的,所以它的停泊之处也一定存在。它在哪儿?

杰克:为什么要问我?

威尔:因为你是海盗。

If there's any kind of magic in this world, it must be in the attempt of understanding someone or sharing something.

如果这个世界上存在奇迹,那一定是在努力理解别人或者接受不同建议的过程中发生的。

10 spring v. 逃走

11 lass n. 姑娘

杰克:你也想成为海盗,是吗?

威尔:决不会。他们带走了斯旺小姐。

杰克:哦,你有了喜欢的女孩。我明白了。不过你想要英雄救美来赢得她的芳心,就得一个人去做,伙计。我可看不出这事儿对我有什么好处。

威尔:我能让你离开这儿。

杰克:你怎么做?钥匙都没了。

威尔:这牢房是我帮着造的。这些铁棍的铰链是半固定的,利用恰当的杠杆原理和巧劲儿,就能轻而易举地把门提起来。

杰克:你叫什么?

威尔:威尔·特纳。

杰克:我猜,那是威廉的简称吧。非常不错的名字。毫无疑问你是沿用了你父亲的名字,对吧?

威尔:没错。

杰克:嗯。好吧,特纳先生,我改变主意了。如果你能帮我逃出去的话,我发誓会不惜一切代价把你带到"黑珍珠"号那儿,见你心爱的姑娘。成交吗?

威尔:成交。

杰克:成交。把我弄出去。

威尔:快点儿,会被人听见的。

杰克:还有我的东西。

经典对白(二)

To Freedom 为了自由

杰克的计划失败了,他和斯旺小姐都被遗弃在荒岛上,万分沮丧的杰克便对复仇计划失去了信心……

Jack: That's the second time I've had to watch that man sail away with my ship.

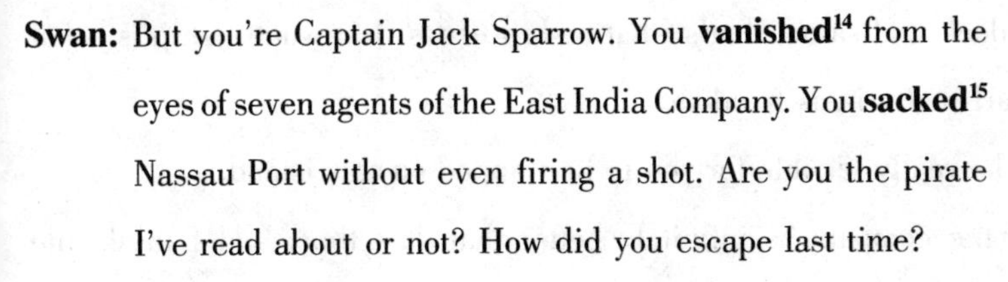

Swan: But you were **marooned**[12] on this island before, weren't you? So we can escape in the same way you did then.

Jack: To what point and purpose, young missy? The Black Pearl is gone. Unless you have a rudder and a lot of sails hidden in that **bodice**[13]. Unlikely. Young Mr. Turner will be dead long before you can reach him.

Swan: But you're Captain Jack Sparrow. You **vanished**[14] from the eyes of seven agents of the East India Company. You **sacked**[15] Nassau Port without even firing a shot. Are you the pirate I've read about or not? How did you escape last time?

Jack: Last time, I was here a grand total of three days, all right? Last time, the **rumrunners**[16] used this island as a **cache**[17], came by, and I was able to **barter** passage **off**[18]. From the looks of things, they've long been out of business. Probably have your bloody friend Norrington to thank for that.

Swan: So that's it, then? That's the secret grand adventure of the **infamous**[19] Jack Sparrow? You spent three days lying on a beach, drinking the rum?

12 maroon v. 放逐某人到孤岛上
13 bodice n. 有裙撑式连衣裙的紧身上衣
14 vanish v. 消失，突然不见
15 sack v. 洗劫
16 rumrunner n. 酒品走私者
17 cache n. 藏匿处，藏物处
18 barter off v. 交易，交换
19 infamous adj. 声名狼藉的，臭名昭著的

Jack: Welcome to the Caribbean, love.

Both: (*sing*) We're devils, we're black sheep. We're really bad eggs. Drink up, me hearties, yo ho! Yo ho, yo ho! Ouch! A pirate's life for me.

Jack: I love this song! Really bad eggs! Oh! When I get the Pearl back, I'm gonna teach it to the whole crew, and we'll sing it all the time.

Swan: And you'll be positively the most **fearsome**[20] pirate in the Spanish Main.

Jack: Not just the Spanish Main, love. The entire ocean, the entire world, wherever we want to go, we go. That's what a ship is, you know. It's not just a **keel**[21] and a hull and a deck and sails. That's what a ship needs. But what a ship is, what the Black Pearl really is, is freedom.

Swan: Jack, it must be really terrible for you to be trapped on this island.

Jack: Oh, yes. But the company is infinitely better than last time, and I think, the scenery has definitely improved.

Swan: Mr. Sparrow!

Jack: Mm-hmm.

Swan: I'm not entirely sure I've had enough rum to allow that kind of talk.

Jack: I know exactly what you mean, love.

Swan: To freedom!

Jack: To the Black Pearl!

杰克: 这是我第二次眼睁睁地看着他把我的船开走。

斯旺: 可你以前也曾被遗弃在这个岛上,对吗?所以我们还可以用同样的方法逃走的。

杰克: 那有什么用,小姐?“黑珍珠”已经走了,除非你的衣服里还藏着舵轮和帆。不可能吧。等你追上他们,特纳先生早就死了。

斯旺: 你可是杰克·史派罗船长啊。你能从东印度公司七个特工的眼皮子底下溜掉,甚至不用一枪一炮就能洗劫整个拿骚港。你真的是我所知道的那个海盗吗?

20 fearsome adj. 吓人的,可怕的

21 keel n. (船的) 龙骨

上次你是怎么逃走的？

杰克：上次，我在这儿只待了三天，懂吗？走私犯把酒藏在这座岛上，他们经过这里，我好说歹说才能搭船离开。现在看来，他们也很久没做生意了。这恐怕要归功于你那位残忍的朋友诺灵顿了。

斯旺：这就完了？这就是传奇人物杰克·史派罗那神秘而又伟大的冒险经历？在沙滩上喝着酒，躺了三天？

杰克：欢迎来到加勒比海，亲爱的。

合唱：我们是恶魔，是害群之马。我们真是大坏蛋。干了，兄弟们，哟嗬！哟嗬！哟嗬！哦，海盗生活乐逍遥！

杰克：我喜欢这首歌！真是大坏蛋！哦！夺回“黑珍珠”后，我要把它教给所有船员，要一直唱着它。

斯旺：那你一定会成为西班牙大陆上最令人畏惧的海盗。

杰克：不只是西班牙大陆，亲爱的。整个海洋，整个世界，我们想去哪儿就去哪儿。这才是船的真正意义，懂吗？并不只是龙骨、船身、甲板和风帆。那只是船的必要部件。然而船的真正意义，“黑珍珠”的真正意义，是自由。

斯旺：杰克，被困在这座岛上，你一定觉得很可怕吧。

杰克：噢，当然。但这次的伙伴可比上次好多了，而且我觉得，风景也优美多了。

斯旺：史派罗先生！

杰克：嗯。

斯旺：我想我还没醉到想听你在这儿疯言疯语。

杰克：我明白你的意思，亲爱的。

斯旺：为自由！

杰克：为“黑珍珠”！

I guess it comes down to a simple choice. Get busy living or get busy dying!

我认为是到了作个了断的时候了，要么忙着生存，要么忙着死亡。

Beautiful Sentences 妙语佳句

1. Worry about your own fortunes, gentlemen. The deepest circle of hell is reserved for betrayers and mutineers.
   顾好你们自己吧,先生们。你们这些叛徒是会下十八层地狱的。
2. First, your return to shore was not part of our negotiation, nor our agreement, so I must do nothing; and secondly, you must be a pirate for the Pirate's Code to apply, and you're not; and thirdly, the Code is more what you'd call guidelines than actual rules. Welcome aboard the Black Pearl, Miss Turner.
   第一,送你上岸可不在我们的协议之中,所以我没这个义务;第二,你必须是个海盗,法典才有效力,可你并不是;第三,法典不过是些指导性的建议,并不等同于实际规定。欢迎你登上"黑珍珠"号,特纳小姐。
3. This is either madness or brilliance. It's remarkable how often those two traits coincide.
   要么说它疯狂,要么说它绝妙。而它们常常相伴而行。
4. That's got to be the best pirate I've ever seen.
   他是我见过的最厉害的海盗。
5. The only rules that really matter are these. What a man can do and what a man can't do. For instance, you can accept that your father was a pirate and a good man or you can't. The pirate is in your blood boy, so you'll have to square with that someday. Now, me, for example, I can let you drown. But I can't bring this ship into Tortuga all by me oneself, savvy? So, can you sail under the command of a pirate or can you not?
   唯有这条规则才真正有用:人能做什么,不能做什么。比如,你可以认为你的父亲既是个海盗,又是个好人,或者你并不这样认为。但孩子,你有海盗的血统,所以你迟早都得接受它。再比如我,我可以淹死你,但我无法单靠自己航行到特图加,懂吗?所以,你要在海盗的领导下航行,能还是不能?

6. The more we gave them away, the more we came to realize, the drink would not satisfy, food turned to ash in our mouths, and all the pleasurable company in the world could not slake our lust.
我们挥霍得越多就越能意识到,美酒佳肴已无法满足我们,它们不过是我们口中的尘土,世间一切的寻欢作乐,也都无法抑制我们的欲望。

7. And last we saw of Old Bill Turner, he was sinking to the crushing, black oblivion of Davy Jones' locker. Course it was only after that we learned we needed his blood to lift the curse. That's what you call ironic.
我们最后一次看到老比尔·特纳,他沉入了那片幽暗的汪洋大海之中。当然,就在那之后,我们才发现只有他的血才能解除诅咒。很讽刺吧。

Don't cry because it is over, smile because it happened.
不要因为结束而哭泣,微笑吧,为你的曾经拥有。

8. And a dishonest man you can always trust to be dishonest. Honestly, it's the honest ones you want to watch out for, because you can never predict when they're gonna do something incredibly stupid.
像我这样不可信的人,你总是知道不该相信的。老实说,你该小心那些忠厚老实的人,因为你永远不会知道他们何时会做出些什么难以置信的蠢事来。

9. If you were waiting for the opportune moment, that was it.
如果你在等待时机的话,刚刚就是。

10. Perhaps on the rare occasion pursuing the right course demands an act of piracy, piracy itself can be the right course?
在特殊情况下,追求正当目标也可以利用海盗的行事方式,或许,海盗这种行事方式本身也是正当的?

Thought about Life 人生感悟

当被这花花世界所围绕时，我们就不可避免地会产生各种欲望。对财富的渴望,对名誉的追求,对玩乐的放纵,此时周围的一切都会成为我们贪恋的对象。然而这一切却无法令我们满足,就像是毒品,吃了便会上瘾一样。不过杰克船长的生活却完全是另外一番景象,他自有他的生存方式——崇尚自由。大概也正是因为这个原因,他才能过着如此洒脱的生活吧。

二十、人类共有的财富
——《国家宝藏 I》

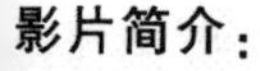

影片简介：

本·富兰克林·盖茨是一位喜爱考古的冒险家。小的时候，他的祖父就对他讲了盖茨家族的一个秘密，即独立战争时期，美国领导人将一笔宝藏埋在了某处，但至今也无人知晓这笔宝藏的藏匿之处。盖茨一直想找到这笔宝藏，不仅是为了家族的荣誉，更重要的是他想将宝藏归还国家。他最终按照一系列线索解开了这个谜题，发现了宝藏的埋藏之地。然而对这笔宝藏感兴趣的还有另一位冒险家伊恩，伊恩想独占这笔宝藏。于是盖茨便和伊恩展开了一场夺宝大战……

经典对白(一)

Warn 警告

本和瑞利得知伊恩会盗取《独立宣言》，于是二人来到切斯博士的办公室，提醒她防范盗贼……

Assistant: Dr. Chase can see you now, Mr. Brown.

Ben: Thank you.

Riley: Mr. Brown?

Ben: The family name doesn't get a lot of respect in the academic community.

Riley: Huh. Being kept down by the man. A very **cute**[1] man.

Abigail: Thank you. Good afternoon, gentlemen.

Riley: Hi.

Abigail: Abigail Chase.

Ben: Paul Brown.

Abigail: Nice to meet you.

Riley: Bill.

Abigail: Nice to meet you, Bill. How may I help you?

Ben: Your accent. Pennsylvania Dutch?

Abigail: Saxony German.

Ben: Oh!

Riley: You're not American?

Abigail: Oh, I am an American. I just wasn't born here. Please don't touch that!

Ben: Sorry. A neat collection. George Washington's campaign buttons. You're missing the 1789 inaugural, though. I found one once.

Abigail: That's very fortunate for you. Now, you told my assistant that this was an urgent matter.

Ben: Yes, ma'am. Well, I'm gonna get straight to the point. Someone's gonna steal the *Declaration of Independence*.

Riley: It's true.

1 cute adj. 漂亮的，精明的

Abigail: I think I'd better put you gentlemen in touch with the FBI.

Ben: We've been to the FBI.

Abigail: And?

Riley: They assured us that the Declaration cannot possibly be stolen.

Abigail: They're right.

Ben: My friend and I are less certain. However, if we were given the privilege of examining the document we would be able to tell you for certain if it were actually in any danger.

Abigail: What do you think you're gonna find?

Ben: We believe that there's an encryption on the back.

Abigail: An **encryption**[2], like a code?

Ben: Yes, ma'am.

Abigail: Of what?

Ben: A **cartograph**[3].

Abigail: A map.

Ben: Yes, ma'am.

Abigail: A map of what?

Ben: The location of...of hidden items of historic and **intrinsic**[4] value.

Abigail: A treasure map?

Riley: That's where we lost the FBI.

Abigail: You're treasure-hunters, aren't you?

Only a life lived for others is a life worthwhile.
只有为他人而活着，生命才有价值。

2 encryption n. 加密，加密技术，密钥

3 cartograph n. 绘制图

4 intrinsic adj. 固有的，本质的，内在的

Ben: We're more like treasure-protectors.

Abigail: Mr. Brown, I have personally seen the back of the Declaration of Independence, and I promise you, the only thing there is a **notation**[5] that reads, "Original Declaration of Independence..."

Ben: "...dated Four of July, 1776." Yes, ma'am.

Abigail: But no map.

Ben: It's invisible.

Abigail: Oh! Right.

Riley: And that's where we lost the Department of Homeland Security.

Abigail: What led you to assume there's this invisible map?

Ben: We found an **engraving**[6] on the **stem**[7] of a 200-year-old **pipe**[8].

Riley: Owned by Freemasons.

Abigail: May I see the pipe?

Riley: We don't have it.

Abigail: Did Big Foot take it?

Ben: It was nice meeting you.

Abigail: Nice to meet you, too.

Ben: And, you know, that really is a nice collection. Must have taken you a long time to hunt down all that history.

助理:布朗先生,切斯博士现在可以见你了。

本:谢谢。

瑞利:布朗先生?

本:我的姓在学术界可不怎么受欢迎。

瑞利:嗯,真是多亏了你的老祖宗。好漂亮的博士啊。

艾比嘉尔:谢谢。下午好,先生们。

5 notation n. 记号,注释

6 engrave v. 雕刻

7 stem n. 茎部,干

8 pipe n. 烟斗

瑞利:嗨!

艾比嘉尔:艾比嘉尔·切斯。

本:保罗·布朗。

艾比嘉尔:很高兴见到你。

瑞利:比尔。

艾比嘉尔:很高兴见到你,比尔。有什么要帮忙的吗?

本:听你的口音,是宾夕法尼亚州的荷兰后裔?

艾比嘉尔:是德国萨克森人。

本:噢!

瑞利:你不是美国人?

艾比嘉尔:哦,我是美国人,只是不在美国出生。请别碰那个!

本:哦,抱歉。不错的收藏品,乔治·华盛顿的纪念章。不过你好像没有1789年他在就职典礼上戴的那一枚。我倒是有。

艾比嘉尔:那你真幸运。你跟我的助理说有要紧事儿吧。

本:啊,是的,女士。呃,我们长话短说好了,有人想偷走《独立宣言》。

瑞利:是真的。

艾比嘉尔:我想我最好帮你们和联邦调查局联系。

本:我们已经去过联邦调查局。

艾比嘉尔:他们怎么说?

瑞利:他们向我们保证说《独立宣言》不可能被偷。

艾比嘉尔:他们是对的。

本:我们可不这么看。但是,如果可以给予我们特权让我们检查一下这份文物的话,我们便可以证明是否存在这种危险。

艾比嘉尔:你觉得你们能找到什么?

本:我们认为在它背面有……一组密码。

艾比嘉尔:密码?你是说编码吧?

本:是的,女士。

艾比嘉尔:关于什么的?

本:呃……一幅图。

艾比嘉尔:地图?

本:是的,女士。

艾比嘉尔:什么地图?

本:是一张绘有具体位置的地图,那里埋藏着一些具有很高历史价值的东西。

艾比嘉尔:一张藏宝图?

瑞利:联邦调查局听到这个就把我们赶走了。

艾比嘉尔:你们是来寻宝的,对吧?

本:确切地说,我们是来护宝的。

艾比嘉尔:布朗先生,我亲眼见过《独立宣言》原件的背面,我向你保证,那里唯一的字样是“《独立宣言》原件,签署于……”

本:“……签署于1776年7月4日”。我知道,女士。

艾比嘉尔:但没什么地图。

本:那张地图是隐形的。

艾比嘉尔:噢!是这样。

瑞利:国土安全部的人听到这个,也不肯相信。

艾比嘉尔:你们凭什么相信,那有幅隐形的地图呢?

本:我们在一根二百年前的烟斗底部,发现了一些雕刻字样。

瑞利:是“共济会”的烟斗。

艾比嘉尔:我能看看那根烟斗吗?

瑞利:现在不在我们手里。

艾比嘉尔:被“大脚怪”偷走了吗?

本:很高兴见到你。

艾比嘉尔:我也是。

本:哦,要知道,您的收藏确实很精美。收集这么多,您一定花了很多时间吧。

经典对白(二)

National Treasure 国家宝藏

伊恩撇下盖茨一行人独自去波士顿寻宝，不过盖茨他们在原处找到了宝藏并安全逃脱了。逃脱后的盖茨告诉塞德斯基警长，他决定把宝藏上交给国家……

We talk about fate as if it were something visited upon us, we forget that we create our fate every day we live.

我们谈论命运，似乎它是某种惩罚我们的东西，然而却忘记了我们活着的时候每日都在创造命运。

Sadusky: Just like that?

Ben: Just like that.

Sadusky: You do know you just handed me your biggest bargaining chip?

Ben: *The Declaration of Independence* is not a bargaining chip. Not to me.

Sadusky: Have a seat. So what's your offer?

Ben: How about a **bribe**[9]? Say...ten billion dollars?

Sadusky: I take it you found the treasure?

Ben: It's about five stories beneath your shoes.

Sadusky: You know, the Templars and the Freemasons believed that the treasure was too great for any one man to have, not even a king. That's why they went to such lengths to keep it hidden.

Ben: That's right. The Founding Fathers believed the same thing about government. I figure their solution will work for the treasure too.

9 bribe v. 贿赂

Sadusky: Give it to the people.

Ben: Divide it amongst the Smithsonian, the Louvre, the Cairo museum...There's thousands of years of world history down there. And it belongs to the world, and everybody in it.

Sadusky: You really don't understand the concept of a bargaining chip.

Ben: OK, here's what I want. Dr. Chase gets off completely clean, not even a little Post-it on her service record.

Sadusky: OK.

Ben: I want the credit for the find to go to the entire Gates family, with the assistance of Mr. Riley Poole.

Sadusky: And what about you?

Ben: I'd really love not to go to prison. I can't even begin to describe how much I would love not to go to prison.

Sadusky: Someone's got to go to prison, Ben.

Ben: Well, if you've got a **helicopter**[10], I think I can help with that.

塞德斯基: 你就这么给我了?

本: 对,就这样。

塞德斯基: 你知道你已经把最大的谈判筹码给了我吧?

本: 《独立宣言》不是谈判的筹码,对我而言不是。

塞德斯基: 请坐。你有什么要求吗?

本: 收买你怎么样?我出呃……一百亿美元怎么样?

塞德斯基: 看来你已经找到宝藏了?

本: 它大约在你脚下五层的地方。

塞德斯基: 你知道共济会和圣殿骑士认为,如此巨额的财富不应归属于个人,即便是国王。所以他们才会找这么深的地方把它埋藏起来。

本: 没错。我相信那些开国元勋们一样也认为政府不该得到这笔财宝。他们

10 helicopter n. 直升机

的决定最适合这笔财宝了。

塞德斯基:把财富交给人民。

本:把它分给史密森尼博物馆、卢浮宫、开罗博物馆……这地底下有上千年的世界历史。宝藏属于全世界,属于每一个人。

塞德斯基:你真是不理解筹码的真正含义啊。

本:好吧,我的要求如下,切斯博士完全是无辜的,别在她的档案里记上一笔。

塞德斯基:好的。

本:我想把找到宝藏的荣誉归于整个盖茨家族和瑞利·波尔先生的协助。

塞德斯基:那你本人呢?

本:我真的不想坐牢。我实在无法形容我有多么地不想坐牢。

塞德斯基:总得有人进去的,本。

本:好吧,如果你有直升机的话,我想我能帮上你的忙。

Life is rather like a tin of sardines, we're all of us looking for the key.
人生就像一罐沙丁鱼,我们大家都在找开启的起子。

Beautiful Sentences 妙语佳句

1. We don't need someone crazy, but one step short of crazy, what do you get?
   我们不需要疯狂的人,我们自己离疯狂仅一步之遥,懂吗?
2. 180 years of searching, and I'm three feet away. Of all the words written here about freedom, there's a line here that's at the heart of all the others. "But when a long train of abuses and usurpations, pursuing invariably the same object, evinces a design to reduce them under absolute despotism, it is their right, it is their duty to throw off such government and

provide new guards for their future security." People don't talk that way any more.
找了180年,我离它仅一步之遥了。《独立宣言》关于自由的文字中,只有一句话最能打动人心。"然而,当一系列熟视无睹、强取豪夺的行为,表明它们企图把人民置于水深火热之中时,人民就有权利,也有义务去改变这样的状况,并为其未来的安全提供保障。"现在人们再也不会这么说了。

3. It means, if there's something wrong, those who have the ability to take action have the responsibility to take action. I'm gonna steal it.
这句话是说,如果情况恶化,那些有能力采取行动的人就有责任去采取行动。我要把它偷走。

4. A toast, yeah? To high treason. That's what these men were committing when they signed the Declaration. Had we lost the war, they would have been hanged, beheaded, drawn and quartered, and—Oh! Oh, my personal favorite and had their entrails cut out and burned! So, here's to the men who did what was considered wrong in order to do what they knew was right. What they knew was right. Well, good night.
干杯吧!为了革命者。就是当年那些签署《独立宣言》的人们,当时他们签署宣言时被定犯有叛国罪。当时如果战争失败了,他们就会被砍头、绞死、淹死、五马分尸,哦,还有我最喜欢的一项,开膛破肚。所以,让我们为那些被人误解,却仍旧坚持自己信念的人干杯!为那些坚持信念的人。好了,晚安!

5. No, I wasn't right. This room is real, Ben. And that means the treasure is real. We're in the company of some of the most brilliant minds in history, because you found what they left behind for us to find and understood the meaning of it. You did it, Ben. For all of us. Your grandfather, and all of us. And I've never been so happy to be proven wrong.
不,我是错的。这间房真的存在,本,那说明宝藏也是真的。我们和历史上的伟人们一同做伴,因为你找到了他们留给我们让我们去寻找的答案,并理解了其中的内涵。你做到了,本,为了我们的家族,为了你祖父,和我们的全家人。我是错了,但是我从心底里感到高兴。

Thought about Life 人生感悟

一个惊人的秘密联系着一份巨大的宝藏，可人们能够追寻的却只有无穷无尽的线索。多亏了主人公本是个博学多才，又很有毅力的人，才能不断地追寻着前人遗留下来的秘密，进而找到属于全人类的宝藏。故事总是虚构的，但是在寻宝的过程中，我们看到了人性的贪婪，也看到了团结的力量，看到了相互信任与支持，看到了坚持不懈的努力。人生总会有属于自己的宝藏，就看你能否挖掘出来了。

Snatch at today and trust as little as you can in tomorrow.
不要放过今天，尽可能少相信明天。

二十一、魔法少年历险记
——《哈利·波特与魔法石》

影片简介：

从小就是孤儿的哈利·波特一直和他的姨夫姨妈一起生活，但是他并没有快乐的童年。就在哈利11岁生日的那天，一只猫头鹰送来了一份录取通知书，邀请哈利到一所名叫霍格沃茨的魔法学校去上学。于是哈利便在学校开始了他快乐的学习生活，他结识了好友罗恩和赫敏，老校长邓布利多，严厉的副校长麦格，以及对他关怀备至的海格。然而哈利却总觉得有种神秘的力量围绕在他周围，并且接二连三地遇见一些古怪的事件。哈利下定决心要查明真相，然而这个真相却和他的亲生父母息息相关……

经典对白(一)

Acquaintance 相识

在乘车去往魔法学校的路上，哈利认识了好友罗恩和赫敏……

Ron: Excuse me. Do you mind? Everywhere else is full.

Harry: Not at all.

Ron: I'm Ron, by the way. Ron Weasley.

Harry: I'm Harry. Harry Potter.

Ron: So it's true! I mean, do you really have the…?

Harry: The what?

Ron: The scar?

Harry: Oh!

Ron: Wicked!

Seller: Anything off the **trolley**[1], dears?

Ron: No, thanks. I'm all set.

Harry: We'll take the lot. Bertie Bott's Every Flavor Beans?

Ron: They mean every flavor. There's chocolate and **peppermint**[2] and also **spinach**[3], liver and **tripe**[4]. George sweared he got a **booger-flavored**[5] one once.

Harry: These are real frogs, are they?

Ron: It's just a spell. Besides, it's the cards you want. Each pack's got a famous witch or wizard. I've got about 500 meself. Watch it! That's rotten luck. They've only got one good jump in them to begin with.

Harry: I've got Dumbledore!

Ron: I've got about six of him.

Harry: Hey, he's gone!

Ron: Well, you can't expect him to hang around all day, can you? This is Scabbers by the way. Pathetic, isn't he?

1 trolley *n.* 手推车

2 peppermint *n.* 薄荷

3 spinach *n.* 菠菜

4 tripe *n.* 牛肚

5 booger-flavored *adj.* 鼻屎味道的，-flavored表示"……味道的"

Harry: Just a little bit.

Ron: Fred gave me a spell to turn him yellow. Want to see?

Harry: Yeah.

Ron: Ahem. Sun...

Hermione: Has anyone seen a **toad**[6]? A boy named Neville's lost one.

Ron: No.

Hermione: Oh, are you doing magic? Let's see, then.

Ron: Ahem. Sunshine, **daisies**[7], butter mellow turn this stupid, fat rat yellow.

Hermione: Are you sure that's a real spell? Well, it's not very good, is it? Of course, I've only tried a few simple ones myself but they've all worked for me. For example, Oculus Reparo. That's better, isn't it? Holy cricket! You're Harry Potter! I'm Hermione Granger. And you are?

Ron: I'm Ron Weasley.

Hermione: Pleasure. You two better change into **robes**[8]. I expect we'll be arriving soon. You've got dirt on your nose by the way. Did you know? Just there.

Life is a progress from want to want, not from enjoyment to enjoyment.
生活是从需要到需要，而不是从享受到享受发展。

罗恩:打扰了,我可以坐吗?其他车厢都满了。

哈利:当然可以。

罗恩:我叫罗恩,罗恩·韦斯利。

哈利:我叫哈利,哈利·波特。

罗恩:这么说,那是真的啦!我是说,你真的有……?

6 toad *n.* 蟾蜍，癞蛤蟆

7 daisy *n.* 雏菊

8 robe *n.* 长袍

哈利:有什么?

罗恩:那道疤?

哈利:哦!

罗恩:真炫!

售货员:买点儿吃的吗,孩子们?

罗恩:不,谢了。我带了吃的。

哈利:我都要了。"柏蒂博特"多种口味豆?

罗恩:有各种口味的。巧克力和薄荷的,菠菜、肝脏和牛肚的,乔治还发誓说有次他吃到了鼻屎味的呢。

哈利:这该不会是真的青蛙吧?

罗恩:只是施了个咒语。再说,你要的是卡片。每张卡片上都有个有名的巫师。我已经收集差不多500张了。小心!哦,运气真背!它们就只有最开始那下跳得最好。

哈利:我的是邓布利多!

罗恩:我已经有6张邓布利多了。

哈利:嘿,他不见了!

罗恩:对啊,你总不能要他一整天都待在那儿吧。对了,这是斑斑。他很可怜,对吗?

哈利:还好吧。

罗恩:弗莱德教了我一个咒语可以把它变成黄色。想看看吗?

哈利:好啊。

罗恩:啊哼!阳……

赫敏:你们看到过一只蛤蟆吗?有个叫纳威的,丢了一只蛤蟆。

罗恩:没有。

赫敏:哦,你在施魔法吗?让我们瞧一瞧吧。

罗恩:啊哼!阳光,雏菊,黄油飘香,将这只又胖又蠢的老鼠变成黄色。

赫敏:你确定这真的是咒语吗?它可不是很管用,对吧?当然,我也只试过几个简单的咒语,但每次都非常成功。比方说,"欧卡拉斯雷培洛"。这个不错吧?我的天哪,你是哈利·波特!我叫赫敏·格兰杰。你是……?

罗恩:我叫罗恩·韦斯利。

赫敏:幸会。你们两个最好赶快换上长袍,我们就快到了。你鼻子上有点儿脏,知道吗?就在这儿。

经典对白(二)

For man is man and master of his fate.
人就是人，是自己命运的主人。

Face Voldemort 面对伏地魔

哈利拜托赫敏照顾好罗恩后，一个人只身前行，他来到伏地魔的所在地，却见到了奇洛教授……

Harry: You? No it can't be. Snape, he was...he was the one...

Quirrell: Yes! He does seem the type, doesn't he? Next to him who would suspect p–p–poor st–st–**stuttering**[9] Professor Quirrell?

Harry: But that day, during the Quidditch match, Snape tried to kill me.

Quirrell: Oh no, dear boy! I tried to kill you! And trust me if Snape's cloak hadn't caught on fire and broken my eye contact, I would have succeeded. Even with Snape **muttering**[10] his little counter–curse.

Harry: Snape was trying to save me?

Quirrell: I knew you were a danger to me right from the off. Especially after Halloween.

Harry: Then, then you let the **troll**[11] in!

9 stutter *v*. 结巴

10 mutter *v*. 小声嘟囔

11 troll *n*. 巨人，巨怪

Quirrell: Very good Potter, yes. Snape unfortunately wasn't fooled, when every one else was running about the **dungeon**[12], he went to the third floor to head me of. He of course never trusted me again. He rarely left me alone. But he doesn't understand, I'm never alone. Never. Now what does this mirror do? I see what I desire. I see myself holding the Stone. But how do I get it?

Voldemort: Use the boy.

Quirrell: Come here, Potter! Now! Tell me, what do you see? What is it? What do you see?

Harry: I'm shaking hands with Dumbledore. I've won the House Cup.

Voldemort: He lies.

Quirrell: Tell the truth! What do you see?

Voldemort: Let me speak to him.

Quirrell: Master, you are not strong enough.

Voldemort: I have strength enough for this. Harry Potter, we meet again.

Harry: Voldemort?

Voldemort: Yes, you see what I have become? See what I must do to survive? Live off another. A mere **parasite**[13]. Unicorn blood can sustain me, but it cannot give me a body of my own. But there is something that can. Something that conveniently enough lies in your pocket. Stop him! Don't be a fool! Why suffer a horrific death when you can join with me and live?

Harry: Never!

Voldemort: Bravery, your parents had it, too. Tell me, Harry, would you like to see your mother and father again? Together we can bring them back. All I ask is for something in return. That's it, Harry. There is no good and evil, there is only power and those too weak to seek it. Together we'll do extraordinary things. Just give me the Stone!

12 dungeon *n.* 地牢

13 parasite *n.* 寄生虫

Harry: You liar!

Voldemort: Kill him!

Quirrell: What is this magic?

Voldemort: Fool, get the Stone!

哈　利:是你?不!不可能!斯内普,他才是……

奇　洛:对,没错!他的确给你这样的印象。有他在身边的话,还有谁会怀疑可……可怜的,结……结……结巴教授奇洛呢?

哈　利:可是魁地奇比赛的那天,斯内普想要杀我!

奇　洛:不,孩子,是我想要杀你!知道吗,要不是斯内普的斗篷着火,遮挡了我的视线,我早就成功了!而斯内普就算再怎么念解咒也没有用。

哈　利:斯内普是想救我?

奇　洛:我早就知道你一定会来妨碍我,尤其是万圣节之后。

哈　利:这么说,山怪是你放进来的!

奇　洛:说得好,波特,没错。不过很不幸,被斯内普发现了。当所有人都跑去地牢时,他却跑到三楼来堵我!当然啦,从此他再也不信任我了,他再也不放心让我独处。可是他不知道,我不是一个人,从来都不是。好了,这面镜子到底是做什么用的?我看得到我想要的东西,我看到我拿着石头,但我要怎样才能拿到它?

伏地魔:让他来拿!

奇　洛:过来!波特。快!告诉我,你看到了什么?是什么?你到底看到了什么?

哈　利:我在和邓布利多握手,我赢得了学院杯!

伏地魔:他说谎。

奇　洛:说实话!你看到了什么?

伏地魔:让我跟他说。

It is far more important that one's life should be perceived than it should be transformed, for no sooner has it been perceived, than it transforms itself of its own accord.

理解生活比改变生活重要的多,因为生活一旦被理解,它就会自愿地改变。

奇　洛:主人,你还很虚弱。

伏地魔:我还有力气跟他说话。哈利·波特,咱们又见面了。

哈　利:伏地魔?

伏地魔:没错!你看到我现在的样子了?看到我为了生存必须要做什么?依附别人维生,像个寄生虫一样。独角兽的血只能维持我的生命,但却不能帮我重建身体。但是有个东西可以,那小东西够神奇,它就在你的口袋里!抓住他!别傻了,你可以和我一起,好好活下去,别自寻死路!

哈　利:别想!

伏地魔:很勇敢呢,你的父母也是这样。告诉我,哈利,你想不想再见到你的父母?跟我一起,我们可以把他们带回来。你只需要做点儿事来回报我!没错,哈利!世上没有善与恶,只有掌权者和无能的弱者。我们一起,就能成就一番事业,只要你先把石头给我!

哈　利:你这个骗子!

伏地魔:杀了他!

奇　洛:这是什么魔法?

伏地魔:蠢货,快去拿石头!

Beautiful Sentences 妙语佳句

1. Back again, Harry? I see that you, like many before you...have discovered the delights of the Mirror of Erised. I trust by now you realize what it does. Let me give you a clue. The happiest man on earth would look in the mirror and see only himself.
又回来了吗,哈利?我知道你和以前那些人一样,都发现了"意若思"镜的乐趣。我想你已经知道镜子的作用了。给你一点儿暗示吧,只有世上最幸福的人,才能在镜中看到一个人,那就是他自己。

2. It shows us nothing more or less than the deepest and most desperate desires of our hearts. Now you, Harry, who have never known your family, you see them standing beside you. But remember this, Harry. This mirror gives us neither knowledge or

truth. Men have wasted away in front of it. Even gone mad. That is why tomorrow, it will be moved to a new home. And I must ask you not to go looking for it again. It does not do to dwell on dreams and forget to live.

镜子反映出的正是我们内心深处最渴望的事。哈利,你从没见过家人,所以你才会看到他们站在你身边。但你要记住,哈利,这面镜子既不能带给我们学识,也不能告诉我们真相。人们在这面镜子前虚掷光阴,甚至因此而发疯。所以明天,我就要把镜子移到别的地方去。请你千万别再来找这面镜子了。人不能总是活在梦里而因此遗忘了现实生活。

The poorest way to face life is to face it with a sneer.
对待生活最拙劣的办法是用轻蔑的态度去对待它。

3. Do you wanna stop Snape from getting that Stone or not? Harry, it's you that has to go on. I know it. Not me. Not Hermione. You.

   你到底想不想阻止斯内普偷走魔法石?哈利,你必须继续前行。我知道的。该前行的人,不是我,不是赫敏,而是你。

4. You see, only a person who wanted to find the Stone, find it, but not use it, would be able to get it. That is one of my more brilliant ideas. And between you and me, that is saying something.

   你知道吗?只有真心想找到魔法石,而不是存心要利用它的人,才能得到它。这是我想出来的好方法。咱们俩一直很默契,自始至终都很默契。

5. Finally, it takes a great deal of bravery to stand up to your enemies, but a great deal more to stand up to your friends.

   最后,对敌人坚持原则奋力抵抗,的确需要很大的勇气。但要对朋友坚持原则,更是需要很大的勇气。

Thought about Life 人生感悟

小主人公波特是个勇敢正直的男孩儿,他不畏强敌,和邪恶势力斗争到底。而他也是个孤独的男孩儿,从小便失去了父母,没有感受过家庭的温暖。好在他还算幸运,在他身边,总会有一群能为他挺身而出的好朋友,也有关爱他的师长。在他的世界里,友爱、正直和勇敢一直伴随着他,这也是小波特最终能成长为一名优秀的魔法师所必备的优点。

二十二、弱者的呼喊
——《沉默的羔羊》

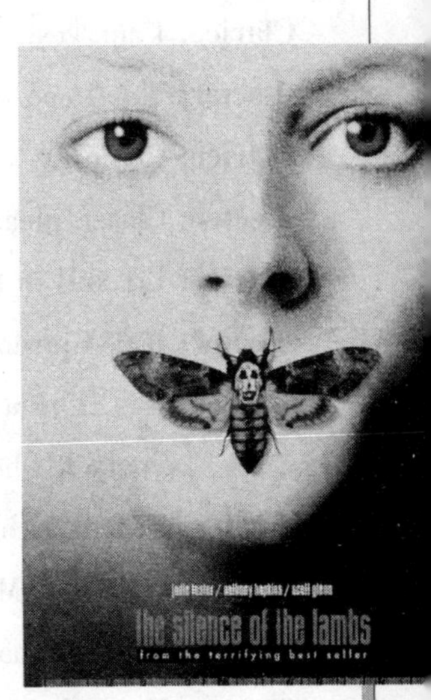

影片简介：

见习警员克拉莉丝受命调查一起系列凶杀案，凶手是一名变态杀人狂，人称“水牛比尔”。为了追查凶手的下落，克拉莉丝去访问了在狱中服刑的精神病学专家汉尼拔·莱克特医生。汉尼拔医生是一位智商极高的人，他答应帮助克拉莉丝，但却要求她提供个人经历来换取。最后，在汉尼拔医生的指引下，克拉莉丝终于找到了“水牛比尔”的下落，然而孤身一人面对“水牛比尔”的她自己也是身陷险境……

经典对白(一)

Talk to Dr. Lecter 对话“吃人医生”

为了查找“水牛比尔”的下落，克拉莉丝前往汉尼拔医生所在的监狱与之谈话……

Lecter: Good morning.

Clarice: Dr. Lecter. My name is Clarice Starling. May I speak with you?

Lecter: You're one of Jack Crawford's, aren't you?

Clarice: I am, yes.

Lecter: May I see your **credentials**[1]?

Clarice: Certainly.

Lecter: Closer, please. Closer. That **expires**[2] in one week. You're not real FBI, are you?

Clarice: I'm still in training at the academy.

Lecter: Jack Crawford sent a trainee to me?

Clarice: Yes, I'm a student. I'm here to learn from you. Maybe you can decide for yourself whether or not I'm **qualified**[3] enough to do that.

Lecter: That is rather slippery of you, Agent Starling. Sit, please. Now then, tell me. What did Miggs say to you? "Multiple Miggs" in the next cell. He **hissed**[4] at you. What did he say?

Clarice: He said, "I can smell your cunt."

Lecter: I see. I myself cannot. You use Evyan skin cream. And sometimes you wear L'Air du Temps. But not today.

Clarice: Did you do all these drawings, doctor?

Lecter: That is the Duomo, seen from the Belvedere. Do you know Florence?

Clarice: All that detail just from memory, sir?

Lecter: Memory, Agent Starling, is what I have instead of a view.

Clarice: Well, perhaps you'd care to lend us your view on this **questionnaire**[5], sir.

Lecter: No, no, no. You were doing fine. You had been **courteous**[6] and **receptive**[7] to

1 credential *n.* 身份证明

2 expire *v.* 期满终止

3 qualified *adj.* 有资格的

4 hiss *v.* 发嘶嘶声，向某人发嘘声

5 questionnaire *n.* 调查问卷

6 courteous *adj.* 有礼貌的

7 receptive *adj.* 接受能力强的，能迅速接受的

courtesy[8]. You had established trust with the embarrassing truth about Miggs. And now this ham handed **segue**[9] into your questionnaire. It won't do.

Clarice: I'm only asking you to look at this, doctor. Either you will or you won't.

Lecter: Yeah. Jack Crawford must be very busy indeed if he's **recruiting**[10] help from the student body. Busy hunting that new one, Buffalo Bill, what a naughty boy he is. Do you know why he's called "Buffalo Bill"? Please tell me. The newspapers won't say.

Maybe the biggest problem in life is how to spend it.
也许人生最大的问题是如何度过。

Clarice: Well, it started as a joke in Kansas City Homicide. They said, "This one likes to skin his humps."

Lecter: Why do you think he removes their skins, Agent Starling? Thrill me with your **acumen**[11].

Clarice: It excites him. Most serial killers keep **trophies**[12] from their victims.

Lecter: I didn't.

Clarice: No. No, you ate yours.

Lecter: You send that through now. Oh, Agent Starling, you think you can **dissect**[13] me with this **blunt**[14] little tool?

Clarice: No! I thought that your knowledge...

Lecter: You're so **ambitious**[15], aren't you? You know what you

8 courtesy *n*. 礼貌
9 segue *v*. 继续不断
10 recruit *v*. 招募，吸收
11 acumen *n*. 敏锐，机敏
12 trophy *n*. 战利品
13 dissect *v*. 剖析，分析
14 blunt *adj*. 钝的
15 ambitious *adj*. 有野心的

look like, with your good bag and your cheap shoes? You look like a **rube**[16], a well-scrubbed, **hustling**[17] rube with a little taste. Nutrition has given you some length of bone. But you're not more than one generation from poor white trash, are you, Agent Starling? And the accent you've tried so desperately to **shed**[18] Pure West Virginia. Is your father a coal miner? Does he stink of the lamp? I know how quickly the boys found you all those **tedious**[19], sticky **fumblings**[20] in the back seats of cars while you could've dreamed of getting out, getting anywhere, getting all the way to the FBI.

Clarice: You see a lot, doctor. But are you strong enough to point that high-powered **perception**[21] at yourself? What about it? Why don't you look at yourself and write down what you see? Or maybe you're afraid to.

Lecter: A **census**[22] taker once tried to test me. I ate his **liver**[23] with some **fava**[24] beans and a nice Chianti. You fly back to school now little Starling. Fly, fly, fly!

莱 克 特:早安!

克拉莉丝:莱克特医生,我是克拉莉丝·史达琳。可以和你谈谈吗?

莱 克 特:你是克劳福的人,是吗?

克拉莉丝:是的。

莱 克 特:可以看看你的证件吗?

克拉莉丝:当然。

莱 克 特:请拿近一点儿,近一点儿。一周后到期,你还不是联邦调查局探员吧?

16 rube *n.* 乡下人

17 hustle *v.* 奔忙

18 shed *v.* 摆脱

19 tedious *adj.* 乏味的, 单调的, 冗长的

20 fumble *v.* 乱摸, 摸索

21 perception *n.* 洞察力

22 census *n.* 人口普查

23 liver *n.* 肝脏

24 fava *n.* 蚕豆

克拉莉丝:我还在学校受训。

莱 克 特:克劳福派个见习生来见我?

克拉莉丝:是的,我是学生。我来是向你学习的,或许你可以判断出我是否有资格做个联邦探员呢。

莱 克 特:你谈话很有技巧,史达琳探员。请坐。请你告诉我,米格斯对你说了什么?我是说隔壁房间里那位“多重人格的米格斯”。他对你发出嘘声,他说了什么?

克拉莉丝:他说,“我能嗅到你淫荡的气息”。

莱 克 特:我知道了,我连自己都闻不到了。你用爱肤恩牌的润肤霜,有时还会擦点儿劳莱德香水。今天倒是没有。

克拉莉丝:医生,这些画是你画的吗?

莱 克 特:那是意大利大教堂,从观景楼望去,就是这样。知道佛罗伦萨吗?

克拉莉丝:那些细节之处你都能记得?

莱 克 特:史达琳探员,我只能回忆,却无法眺望。

克拉莉丝:那或许你能在这份问卷上帮我们眺望一些事情呢。莱克特:不,不,不,你做得很好。你一直很有礼貌,而且也能做出很有礼貌的回应,对于米格斯的羞辱也处理得很好。可现在你却要把这么顺利的谈话转移到问卷上来,这就不行了。

克拉莉丝:我只是想请你看看,医生,做不做都取决于你。

莱 克 特:当然。克劳福竟要找学生来帮忙,那他一定很忙了。在忙于追捕那个新手“水牛比尔”吧,他可真是个坏孩子。你知道他为什么被称为“水牛比尔”吗?请告诉我,报纸上可没有提到。

克拉莉丝:好吧,这来源于堪萨斯城凶案组开的一个玩笑。他们说,“这个人喜欢剥他猎物的皮”。

Life can only be understood backwords, but it must be lived forwards.

只有向后看才能理解生活,但是要生活好必须向前看。

莱　克　特:史达琳探员,你们为什么会认为是他剥了她们的皮呢?用你的敏锐来刺激我吧。

克拉莉丝:这样做令他兴奋。大多数连环杀手都会保留受害人身上的某些东西作为战利品。

莱　克　特:我就不会。

克拉莉丝:是的,你没有。你吃了他们。

莱　克　特:把那个递过来吧。哦,史达琳探员,你以为凭这份拙劣的东西就可以剖析我吗?

克拉莉丝:不!我相信你的学识……

莱　克　特:你很有野心,对吧?可你知道你拿着高级皮包,穿着廉价鞋子像什么样子吗?像个乡巴佬,一个精心打扮过的,略带品味的乡巴佬。足够的营养让你长得还可以,但你的上一辈儿也就不过是个贫穷的下层白人,是吗,史达琳探员?你极力地想掩饰你那纯正的西弗吉尼亚口音。你父亲是个矿工吗?他身上散发着羊骚味儿吧?我知道很快那些男孩儿就能找到你,还在汽车后座里对你动手动脚,而你却想拼命地逃出去,逃到联邦调查局去。

克拉莉丝:真是观察入微啊,医生。但你能用你那敏锐的洞察力来分析一下你自己吗?怎么样?为什么不探究一下你自己再把观察所得写下来呢?还是你害怕这样做呢?

莱　克　特:曾有一个人口调查员想测试我,我把他的肝脏给吃了,还配上了些蚕豆和美味儿的红酒。小史达琳,你该回学校了。飞吧,飞吧……

经典对白(二)

Information Exchange 交换信息

汉尼拔医生答应帮助克拉莉丝分析“水牛比尔”的信息,但是却要用克拉莉丝的经历来交换……

Clarice: If your profile helps us catch Buffalo Bill in time to save Catherine Martin, the senator promises you a transfer to the VA Hospital at Oneida Park, New York with a view of the woods nearby, Maximum security still applies, of course. You'd have reasonable access to books, best of all, though, one week of the year, you get to leave the hospital, and go here, Plum Island. Every day of that week you may walk on the beach. You may swim in the ocean for up to one hour under SWAT team **surveillance**[25], of course. And there you have it, a copy of the Buffalo Bill case file, a copy of the senator's offer. This offer is **non-negotiable**[26] and final. Catherine Martin dies you get nothing.

Lecter: Plum Island Animal Disease Research Center. Sounds charming.

Clarice: That's only part of the island. There's a very nice beach, **terns**[27] nest there. There's beautiful...

Lecter: Terns? If I help you, Clarice, it will be "turns" with us too. Quid pro quo. I tell you things, you tell me things. Not about this case, though. About yourself. Quid pro quo. Yes or no? Yes or no, Clarice? Poor little Catherine is waiting.

Clarice: Go, doctor.

Lecter: What is your worst memory of childhood?

Clarice: The death of my father.

This life of yours is just an empty field. Your mind doesn't care what you plant in it... but whatever you plant.you fertilize it, and that is what grows.

你的生命就像一块空旷的土地。你心里并不介意你在这块土地上种什么……但无论种什么，你都要给它施肥，使之成长。

25 surveillance *n.* 监视，监管

26 non-negotiable *adj.* 无商量余地的

27 tern *n.* 燕鸥

Lecter: Tell me about it. And don't lie, or I'll know.

Clarice: He was a town marshal and one night he surprised two burglars coming out of a drugstore. They shot him.

Lecter: Was he killed **outright**[28]?

Clarice: No, he was very strong. He lasted more than a month. My mother died when I was very young, so my father had become the whole world to me and when he left me, I had nothing. I was 10 years old.

Lecter: You're very frank, Clarice. I think it would be quite something to know you in private life.

Clarice: Quid pro quo, doctor.

Lecter: So tell me about Miss West Virginia. Was she a large girl?

Clarice: Yes.

Lecter: Big through the hips, **roomy**[29]?

Clarice: They all were.

Lecter: What else?

Clarice: She had an object **deliberately**[30] inserted into her throat. Now, that hasn't been made public yet. We don't know what it means.

Lecter: Was it a butterfly?

Clarice: Yes, a **moth**[31]. Just like the one we found in Benjamin Raspail's head an hour ago. Why does he place them there, doctor?

Lecter: The significance of the moth is change. **Caterpillar**[32] into **chrysalis**[33], or **pupa**[34] and from **thence**[35] into beauty. Our Billy wants to change too.

28 outright *adv*. 立刻，立即

29 roomy *adj*. 宽大的

30 deliberately *adv*. 故意地

31 moth *n*. 飞蛾

32 caterpillar *n*. 蝴蝶的幼虫，毛虫

33 chrysalis *n*. 蛹，茧

34 pupa *n*. 蛹

35 thence *adv*. 因此

Clarice: There's no **correlation**[36] between **transsexualism**[37] and violence. Transsexuals are very passive.

Lecter: Clever girl. You're so close to the way you're gonna catch him. Do you realize that?

Clarice: No. Tell me why.

Lecter: After your father's murder you were **orphaned**[38]. What happened next? I don't imagine the answer is on those second-rate shoes, Clarice.

Clarice: I went to live with my mother's cousin and her husband in Montana. They had a **ranch**[39].

Lecter: Was it a cattle ranch?

Clarice: Sheep and horses.

Lecter: How long did you live there?

Clarice: Two months.

Lecter: Why so briefly?

Clarice: I ran away.

Lecter: Why, Clarice? Did the rancher make you perform fellatio? Did he **sodomize**[40] you?

Clarice: No. He was a very **decent**[41] man. Quid pro quo, doctor.

Lecter: Billy is not a real transsexual. But he thinks he is. He tries to be. He's tried to be a lot of things, I expect.

Clarice: You said I was very close to the way we'd catch him.

Living without an aim is like sailing without a compass.

生活没有目标，犹如航海没有罗盘。

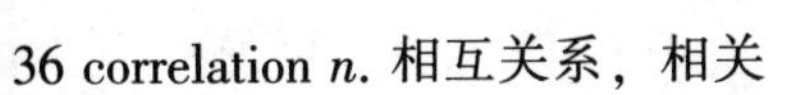

36 correlation *n*. 相互关系，相关

37 transsexualism *n*. 易性癖

38 orphan *v*. 使成为孤儿

39 ranch *n*. 大牧场，饲养场

40 sodomize *v*. 奸污

41 decent *adj*. 正派的

What did you mean, doctor?

Lecter: There are three major centers for transsexual surgery, Johns Hopkins, the University of Minnesota, and Columbus Medical Center. I wouldn't be surprised if Billy had applied for sex **reassignment**[42] at one or all of them and been rejected.

Clarice: On what basis would they reject him?

Lecter: Look for severe childhood **disturbances**[43] associated with violence. Our Billy wasn't born a criminal, Clarice. He was made one through years of systematic abuse. Billy hates his own identity, you see. And he thinks that makes him a transsexual. But his **pathology**[44] is a thousand times more **savage**[45] and more terrifying.

克拉莉丝: 如果你的分析能帮助我们抓到水牛比尔，并及时地救出凯瑟琳·马丁，参议员答应把你转送到纽约奥尼达公园的一个医院。在那儿你可以看到附近的园林景色，当然仍是有警卫的。但你会有书看，而且最好的是，每年有一周时间，你可以离开医院到普拉姆岛去。在那一周里，你每天都可以在沙滩上漫步，也可以在海中畅泳，不过最多就一小时，当然还是在特种部队的监视下。这是给你的，水牛比尔的档案副本，还有参议员的提议书副本。这些提议无商讨余地，一旦凯瑟琳·马丁死了，你就一无所得。

莱 克 特: 普拉姆岛动物病症研究中心。听来很诱人。

克拉莉丝: 那只是岛上的一部分。岛上还有迷人的海滩，燕鸥巢，还有漂亮的……

莱 克 特: 燕鸥？如果我帮你，克拉莉丝，我们也会有些"转变"的。交换信息吧。我告诉你我知道的，你也告诉我你的。不过不是关于这案子的，是关于你的。交换信息，怎么样？怎么样，克拉莉丝？可怜的小凯瑟琳还在等着呢。

克拉莉丝: 请说，医生。

莱 克 特: 你最糟的童年记忆是什么？

42 reassignment *n.* 再次转变

43 disturbance *n.* 扰乱，打扰，烦恼

44 pathology *n.* 病理学

45 savage *adj.* 凶残的，野蛮的

克拉莉丝:家父去世。

莱 克 特:和我说说。若是说谎,我可是看得出来的。

克拉莉丝:他是镇上的警长,有一晚他遇上两个窃贼从药房跑出来。窃贼向他开了枪。

莱 克 特:他当场死亡?

克拉莉丝:不,他很坚强,撑了一个多月。我母亲在我年幼时去世,所以父亲就是我的一切。在他辞世后,我便一无所有,那时我才十岁。

莱 克 特:你很诚实,克拉莉丝。我相信私底下结识你会很有好处。

克拉莉丝:交换信息,医生。

莱 克 特:谈谈西弗吉尼亚小姐吧。她很丰满吧?

克拉莉丝:是的。

莱 克 特:臀部肥大,很丰满的?

克拉莉丝:死者都是这样的。

莱 克 特:还有什么线索?

克拉莉丝:凶手在她的喉咙里塞了些东西,这件事儿还没有让公众知晓,我们还不知道他有何用意。

莱 克 特:是蝴蝶吗?

克拉莉丝:是的,是飞蛾。一小时前,我们在本杰明·赖斯佩尔的口中也发现了这个东西。医生,他为何要放飞蛾进去?

莱 克 特:飞蛾意为改变。幼虫变成蝶蛹,进而再变成美丽的蝴蝶。我们的比尔也想改变。

克拉莉丝:易性癖和暴力之间没有任何关联。具有易性癖的人是很被动的。

莱 克 特:聪明。你就快抓住他了,知道吗?

克拉莉丝:不知道,为什么?

Something is out of our control, so we have to command ourselves.

有些事情本身我们无法控制,只好控制自己。

莱　克　特:父亲被杀后你成了孤儿,后来呢?我可不希望你给我个像你鞋子那样廉价的回答,克拉莉丝。

克拉莉丝:我去了蒙大拿州,跟我姨妈姨夫同住。他们有个农场。

莱　克　特:养牛的农场?

克拉莉丝:饲养马和羊。

莱　克　特:你在那儿住了多久?

克拉莉丝:两个月。

莱　克　特:为什么住了那么短的时间?

克拉莉丝:我跑掉了。

莱　克　特:为什么?牧场主逼着你做些淫乱的事儿?他欺负你了?

克拉莉丝:不,他是个很正派的人。交换信息,医生。

莱　克　特:比尔不是真正的易性癖者,但他以为自己是。他试图去做,我相信他试图去做很多事情。

克拉莉丝:你说我们快要抓住他了,是什么意思?

莱　克　特:有三处主要做变性手术的中心,约翰霍普金斯、明尼苏达州大学和哥伦布医疗中心。比尔可能向这三个地方都提交过做变性手术的申请,但都被拒绝。

克拉莉丝:他们根据什么来拒绝他?

莱　克　特:想想吧,童年的生活凄惨,见惯了暴力,比尔并非天生是个罪犯,克拉莉丝,多年来的虐待使他变成了罪犯。他讨厌自己的性别,他以为那是令他成为易性癖的原因。但他的病征是极为严重,极为可怕的。

Beautiful Sentences 妙语佳句

1. I've been in this room for eight years now, Clarice. I know they will never ever let me out while I'm alive. What I want is a view. I want a window where I can see a tree or even water. I want to be in a federal institution far away from Dr. Chilton.
克拉莉丝,我在这个房间里已经呆了八年了。我知道在我有生之年,他们都不会让我出去的。我只想看看风景,想要个有窗子的房间,从那儿我可以看到树木,甚至河流。我想去一个能远离奇顿医生的联邦监狱。

2. I'm offering you a psychological profile on Buffalo Bill based on the case evidence. I'll help you catch him, Clarice
我会依照证据,向你提供对水牛比尔所做的心理分析。我会帮你抓住他的,克拉莉丝。

3. Well, he's a white male. Serial killers tend to hunt within their own ethnic groups. He's not a drifter. He's got his own house, not an apartment. Why? What he does with them takes privacy. He's in his 30s or 40s. He's got real physical strength. Combined with an older man's self-control. He's cautious, precise. And he's never impulsive. He'll never stop. He's got a real taste for it now, and he's getting better at his work.
男性白人,连环杀手喜欢猎杀同种族的人。他不是流浪汉,有自己的房子,但不是公寓。为什么呢?因为他下毒手时,总得有个私人的地方。他年约三、四十岁,很有一把子力气,还有年长者的自我控制能力。他做事儿很谨慎,很精细,不轻易冲动,但也不会罢休。他正得意着,因为他越干越熟练了。

4. Oh, Clarice, your problem is, you need to get more fun out of life.
哦,克拉莉丝,你的毛病是,你要从生活中多找些乐趣。

5. No, we begin by coveting what we see every day. Don't you feel eyes moving over your body, Clarice? And don't your eyes seek out the things you want?
不,我们是从每天看到的事物上开始渴求的。你难道没有在打量着你的身体吗?难道你的眼睛没在寻找你想要的东西吗?

Only till my natural death could I tell which of what I have been doing is right or wrong, so now I have to try to do well in everything, and then wait to die a natural death.

我不知道我现在做的哪些是对的,哪些是错的,而当我终于老死的时候我才知道这些。所以我现在所能做的就是尽力做好每一件事,然后等待着老死。

Thought about Life 人生感悟

沉默的羔羊意味“弱者”，正如影片中的受害者那样，在遇害之时，却只能沉默。主人公克拉莉丝小时候就看到了那些可怜的待宰羔羊，所以她便认为弱者绝不能任人宰割，只有通过自身的努力，才能自我救赎，这也是她敢于面对吃人医生的深层原因。然而更具讽刺意味的是水牛比尔这个变态杀人狂，他悲剧的一生不正是他懦弱的体现吗？

二十三、对人性的审判
——《七宗罪》

影片简介：

老探员萨默塞特还有 7 天就要退休了，此时却发生了一系列离奇的杀人案。萨默塞特和年轻的探员米尔斯共同侦查此案，将看似毫无联系的案件理出了头绪，原来凶手是按照天主教教义中的七宗罪来作案的。可就在 5 桩命案后，凶手却自首了，并且还宣称他一定会完成这项“惊世的杰作”……

经典对白(一)

Doubt 疑惑

萨默塞特和米尔斯的调查陷入了僵局，萨默塞特在不停地思索突破案件的新方法……

Somerset: Victor's landlord said there was an envelope of cash in the office mailbox the first of every month. Quote, "I never heard a single complaint from the tenant in apartment 306, and nobody ever complained about him. He's the best **tenant**[1] I've ever had", end quote.

Mills: Yeah, a landlord's dream, a **paralyzed**[2] tenant with no tongue.

Somerset: Who pays the rent on time.

Mills: I'm sick of all this waiting!

Somerset: This is the job.

Mills: Why aren't we out there, huh? Why we gotta sit here, **rotting**[3], waiting until the **lunatic**[4] does it again?

Somerset: It's **dismissive**[5] to call him a lunatic. Don't make that mistake.

Mills: Come on, he's **insane**[6] Look, right now, he's probably dancing around in his grandma's panties, yeah, rubbing himself in peanut butter. Ooh, how's that?

Somerset: I don't think so.

Mills: His luck will run out.

Somerset: He's not depending on luck. We walked into that apartment exactly one year after he tied Victor to the bed. One year to the date. He wanted us to.

Mills: Don't know that for sure.

Somerset: Oh, yes, we do. This note he left, his first words to us, "Long is the way, and hard, that out of Hell leads up to light."

Mills: Fuck him. So what?

Somerset: He's right so far. Imagine the will it takes to keep a man bound for a full year, to sever his hand, use it to plant fingerprints, to insert tubes into his

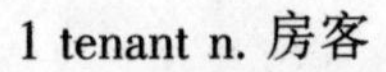

1 tenant n. 房客

2 paralyzed adj. 瘫痪的

3 rot v. 腐烂，腐朽

4 lunatic adj. 疯狂的

5 dismissive adj. 轻视的

6 insane adj. 疯狂的，精神失常的

genitals[7]. This guy's **methodical**[8], exacting, and worst of all, patient.

Mills: He's a **nut-bag**[9]! Just because the fucker's got a library card doesn't make him Yoda.

Somerset: How much money you got?

Mills: I got fifty, fifty bucks.

Somerset: I propose a field trip. Come on. We'll make a list. At the top, we'll put *Purgatory, Canterbury Tales*... anything relating to the Seven Deadly Sins. Ask yourself...

Mills: Hey, wait, wait.

Somerset: What would he study to do the things he's done? What are his interests now? Jack the Ripper for instance?

Mills: Where are we going?

Somerset: The library.

萨默塞特: 维克多的房东说,每月的1号,他都会把房租装在信封里,放在他办公室的信箱里。他说:"我从没听过306的房客有过一句抱怨,也从没听过别人抱怨他。他是我遇到过的最好的房客了。"

米 尔 斯: 是嘛,房东的理想房客,就是个没舌头的瘫痪。

萨默塞特: 而且还是个会准时付房租的人。

米 尔 斯: 我已经等得不耐烦了!

萨默塞特: 这就是警察的工作。

米 尔 斯: 我们为什么不出去呢?为什么我们要坐在这儿等着,

7 genital n. (pl.) 生殖器,外阴部

8 methodical adj. 办事有条不紊的,有条理的

9 nut-bag n. 疯子

是在等那个疯子再一次杀人吗?

萨默塞特:称他为疯子,可太小看他了。千万不能对他掉以轻心。

米 尔 斯:拜托,他就是个疯子。看吧,他现在很可能正穿着他祖母的内裤在跳舞,对,全身还涂满了花生酱。嘿,你觉得呢?

萨默塞特:我可不这么认为。

米 尔 斯:他不会总是那么走运的。

萨默塞特:他可不是靠运气的。我们进到那所公寓的时间刚好是他把维克多绑在床上后的一年。刚好是满一年的那天。是他想让我们去的。

米 尔 斯:那可不一定呢。

萨默塞特:不,是一定的。这是他留下的字条,他第一次对我们说话,"路途漫长而艰苦,一出地狱即光明。"

米 尔 斯:是,那又怎么样?

萨默塞特:目前为止他都是对的。想想看他的意志力吧,他能把一个人整整绑了一年,砍下这个人的手用来制造指纹,还给这个人插尿管。凶手做事儿有章可循,并且能严格执行,更主要的是,他很有耐心。

米 尔 斯:他根本就是个疯子!会去图书馆可不意味着他就是个天才。

萨默塞特:你有多少钱?

米 尔 斯:我有50块。

萨默塞特:那我们出去吧。走吧。先列张单子,先是《炼狱》、《坎特伯雷故事集》等一切和七宗罪有关的书。先想想看……

米 尔 斯:嘿,等等。

萨默塞特:他会看什么书来犯这些案吗?他目前对什么感兴趣呢?也许是开膛手杰克?

米 尔 斯:我们要去哪儿?

萨默塞特:图书馆。

经典对白(二)

The Truth 真相

约翰在萨默塞特和米尔斯的看守下来到了一片高压电线下，这时邮差送来了一个包裹，那包裹里究竟是什么？约翰还剩下最后两桩命案才能完成他所谓的“杰作”……

Fear not that the life shall come to an end, but rather fear that it shall never have a beginning.

不要害怕你的生活将要结束,应该担心你的生活永远不会真正开始。

Somerset: I'm sending the driver out on foot. He's headed north along the road. Have him picked up. Well, I don't know. I'm gonna open it.

John: When I said I admired you, I meant what I said.

Somerset: There's blood.

John: You've made quite a life for yourself, Detective. You should be very proud.

Mills: Shut the fuck up, you piece of shit.

Somerset: California, stay away from here! Stay away from here. Don't come in here. Whatever you hear, stay away! John Doe has the upper hand! Mills!

John: Here he comes.

Somerset: Throw your gun down!

Mills: What?

John: I wish I could've lived like you did.

Mills: Shut up! What the fuck you talking about?

John: Do you hear me, Detective? I'm trying to tell you how much I admire you and your pretty wife.

Mills: What?

John: Tracy.

Mills: What did you fuckin' say?

John: It's **disturbing**[10] how easily a member of the press can purchase information from the men in your **precinct**[11].

Somerset: Throw your gun down!

John: I visited your home this morning after you'd left. I tried to play husband. I tried to taste the life of a simple man.

Somerset: Throw it away!

John: It didn't work out, so I took a **souvenir**[12], her pretty head.

Somerset: Mills!

Mills: What the fuck's he talking about?

Somerset: Give me the gun!

Mills: What's going on over there?

Somerset: Put the gun down.

Mills: I saw you with the box. What's in the box?

John: Because I envy your normal life.

Somerset: Put the gun down, David.

John: It seems that envy is my sin.

Mills: No, what's in the box?

Somerset: I'm not telling you...

Mills: What's in the fucking box?

Somerset: Give me the gun!

John: He just told you.

Mills: You lie! You're a fucking liar! Shut up!

Somerset: That's what he wants. He wants you to shoot him.

10 disturbing adj. 令人不安的

11 precinct n. 管辖区

12 souvenir n. 纪念品，纪念

Mills: No, no. You tell me, tell me that that's not true. That's untrue.

John: Become **vengeance**[13], David.

Mills: No, she's all right. Tell me.

John: Become **wrath**[14].

Mills: Tell me she's all right!

Somerset: If you murder a suspect, David...

Mills: No!

Somerset: You blow off all the way, you know.

Mills: No!

John: She begged for her life, Detective.

Somerset: Shut up!

John: She begged for her life, and for the life of the baby inside of her.

Somerset: Shut up!

John: Oh, he didn't know.

Somerset: Give me the gun, David. David, if you kill him, he will win.

Mills: Oh, God! Oh, God! Oh!

(*Mills fires, John dead.*)

Life is a test and this world a place of trial. Always the problems – or it may be the same problem will be presented to every generation in different forms.

人生是一种考验，而这个世界就是考场。每一代都要面对一些问题：可能是相同的问题，只不过问题的形式不同。

萨默塞特：我已经让司机步行离开了。他沿着路向北走了。叫辆车来接他。现在我也不知道怎么办了。我要打开它。

约　　翰：我说过我敬佩你，我是真心的。

萨默塞特：有血迹。

约　　翰：你的生活过得很幸福了，探长。你应该引以为傲的。

米 尔 斯：闭上你的臭嘴，混蛋。

13 vengeance n. 复仇，报仇

14 wrath n. 愤怒，暴怒

萨默塞特:加州警方,你们不要过来!不要过来!别靠近这里。无论听到什么,都不要过来!约翰已经占了上风!米尔斯!

约　　翰:他过来了。

萨默塞特:把枪丢掉!

米 尔 斯:什么?

约　　翰:我真希望能过上你那样的生活。

米 尔 斯:闭嘴!你到底在说什么?

约　　翰:你听到我说的了吗,探长?我在告诉你我有多羡慕你,还有你那漂亮的妻子。

米 尔 斯:你说什么?

约　　翰:翠西。

米 尔 斯:你在说什么?

约　　翰:记者都能轻易地从你所在的分局买到一些资料,真让人不安啊。

萨默塞特:把枪丢掉!

约　　翰:今早在你走后,我去了你家。我想扮演老公的角色,也想试着去过平常人的生活。

萨默塞特:扔掉它!

约　　翰:但没能成功,所以我就拿了样纪念品,她美丽的头。

萨默塞特:米尔斯!

米 尔 斯:他到底在说什么?

萨默塞特:把枪给我!

米 尔 斯:那边儿出什么事儿了?

萨默塞特:把枪放下!

米 尔 斯:我看见你动那个盒子了。里面装的什么?

约　　翰:因为我嫉妒你的平常生活。

萨默塞特:把枪放下,大卫!

约　　翰:看来我犯了嫉妒之罪。

米 尔 斯:不,盒子里装的什么?

萨默塞特:我不能告诉你……

尔 斯:盒子里到底装的是什么?
默塞特:把枪给我!
翰:他刚刚告诉你了。
尔 斯:你撒谎!你这个该死的骗子!给我闭嘴!
默塞特:这正是他想要的。他想要你开枪打死他。
翰:复仇吧,大卫。
尔 斯:不,她没事儿的。告诉我她没事儿。
翰:愤怒吧。
尔 斯:告诉我她没事儿!
默塞特:如果你杀了嫌疑犯,大卫……
尔 斯:不!
默塞特:一切就都前功尽弃了,知道吧。
尔 斯:不!
翰:她求我饶她性命,探长。
默塞特:闭嘴!
翰:她求我饶她性命,还有她腹中的胎儿。
默塞特:闭嘴!
翰:哦,他还不知道呢。
默塞特:把枪给我,大卫。大卫,如果你杀了他,他就赢了。
尔 斯:哦,天啊!哦,天啊!哦!

(米尔斯开了枪,约翰死了。)

You don't have to suffer to be a poet. Adolescence is enough suffering for anyone.

你不必为当诗人而品尝痛苦。青春期足以使每个人饱受折磨。

Beautiful Sentences 妙语佳句

Gentlemen, gentlemen. I'll never understand. All these books, a world of knowledge at your fingertips. What do you do? Play poker all night.

先生们,我真是不明白。这里有这么多书,那可是一片知识的海洋。你们又做什么呢？通宵玩扑克。

2. Picking up diamonds on a deserted island...saving them in case we get rescued.

就像在荒岛上捡钻石……留着它们,获救后会有用的。

3. Even the most promising clues usually only lead to others. So many corpses ro away unrevenged.

即便是最有力的线索,通常也只会指向另一个线索。所以有那么多人含冤入土

4. Ernest Hemingway once wrote, "The world is a fine place and worth fighting for." I agree with the second part.

海明威曾写道,"这个世界如此美好,值得人们为它奋斗。"我只同意后半句。

Thought about Life 人生感悟

影片中的七宗罪来源于天主教的教义，它们分别是"饕餮、贪婪、懒惰、淫欲、傲慢、嫉妒和暴怒"。影片中的凶手通过道德标准对人性进行审判，最终达到他"传道"的目的。然而令我们震撼的并不是凶手对信仰的执着，而是对人性理解的偏差。也正因为如此，我们才更要为这个也许并不完美的世界去奋斗。

二十四、理智与偏见的激烈冲撞
——《十二怒汉》(1953)

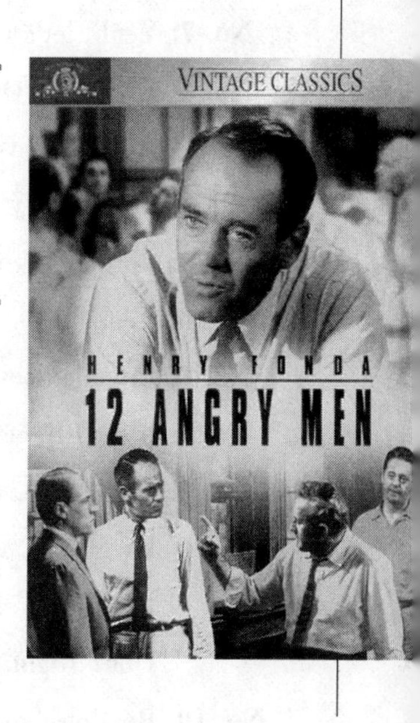

影片简介：

一名刚刚年满18周岁的男孩儿被控杀害了自己的父亲。在法院做出宣判前,先由陪审团对案件进行裁定。这个陪审团由12名身份各异的成员组成，但由于先前对被告的偏见,所以除了8号陪审员外,其他成员均认定被告有罪。8号陪审员为了维护法律的公正,力排众议,将自己认为存在的疑点抛出,最终被告将会……

经典对白(一)

A Different Opinion 不同意见

陪审团团长（下称1号陪审员）开始主持会议，有人提议先投票，如果一致通过的话，就可以直接提交裁决了……

No. 1: OK, gentlemen. If I can have your attention. You fellows can handle this an
way you want. I'm not going to make any rules. We can discuss it first an
then vote on it. Of course, that's one way. And, well, we can vote on it right now.

No. 4: I think it's customary to take a **preliminary**[1] vote.

No. 7: Yeah, let's vote. Maybe we can all get out of here.

No. 1: OK, then. Of course we know that we have a first-degree murder charge her
And if we vote the accused guilty, we've got to send him to the chair. That'
mandatory[2].

No. 4: think we know that.

No. 10: Yeah. Let's see who's where.

No. 1: Anyone doesn't want to vote?

No. 7: It's all right with me.

No. 1: Well, then, remember that this has to be 12 to nothing, either way. That's th
law. Okay, are we ready? Now, all those voting guilty, please raise your hands.
nine, ten, eleven. OK. Okay, that's eleven guilty. Who's voting not guilty
One? Right, eleven guilty, one not guilty. Well, now we know where we are.

No. 10: Boy, oh, boy, there's always one.

No. 7: So, what do we do now?

No. 8: I guess we talk.

No. 3: Boy, oh, boy. You really think he's **innocent**[3]?

No. 8: I don't know.

No. 3: Well, you sat in court with the rest of us. You heard what we did. The kid is
dangerous killer.

No. 8: He's 18 years old.

No. 3: Well, that's old enough. He **stabbed**[4] his own father. Four inches into the ches

---

1 preliminary *adj*. 初步的，预备的

2 mandatory *adj*. 命令的

3 innocent *adj*. 无辜的

4 stab *v*. 戳，刺

They proved it in a dozen different ways in court. Would you like me to list them for you?

No. 8: No.

No. 10: Then what do you want?

No. 8: I just want to talk.

No. 7: What do we talk about what? Eleven say, "guilty". Nobody has to think twice about it except you.

No. 10: I want to ask you. Do you believe his story?

No. 8: I don't know if I do. Maybe I don't.

No. 7: So how come you vote not guilty?

No. 8: There were eleven votes for guilty. It's not easy for me to raise my hand and send the boy off to die without talking about it first.

No. 7: Who says it's easy?

No. 8: No one.

No. 7: What? Just because I voted fast? I honestly think the guy's guilty. Couldn't change my mind if you talked for a hundred years.

No. 8: I don't want to change your mind. It's just that we're talking about somebody's life here. Who can decide it if I'm supposing we're wrong!

No. 7: Supposing we're wrong! Supposing this building should fall. You could suppose anything.

No. 8: That's right.

No. 7: What's the difference how long? Suppose we do it in 5 minutes? So what?

No. 8: Let's take an hour. The ball game doesn't start until 8:00.

No. 1: Who's got something to say?

No. 9: I'll sit for an hour.

No. 10: Great. I heard a pretty good story.

No. 8: That's not why we're sitting here.

No. 10: All right, then you tell me. What are we sitting here for?

No. 8: I don't know, maybe no reason. Look, this kid's been kicked around all hi life. You know, born in a slum, his mother dead since he was 9, lived for year and a half in an **orphanage**[5] when his father was serving a jail term fo **forgery**[6]. That's not a very happy beginning. He is a wild angry kid. Yo know why? Because he's been hit on the head by somebody once a day ever day. He's had a pretty miserable 18 years. I just think we owe him a fe words That's all.

No. 10: I don't mind telling you this, mister. We don't owe him a thing. He got a fai trial, didn't he? What do you think that trial cost? He's lucky he got it. Kno what I mean? Look, we are all gown-ups here. We heard the facts, didn't we You're not going to tell me that we're supposed to believe this kid, knowin what he is. Listen, I've lived among them all. I know you can't believe wha they say. You know that. I mean they're born liars.

No. 9: Only an ignorant man can believe that.

1号：请安静，先生们。请注意。现在我们可以用我们想用的方法来解决这个问 了。我不会指定规则。我们可以先讨论再投票。当然这只是一种方法，我 也可以现在就投票。

4号：按照惯例应该进行预先投票吧。

7号：对，投票吧。没准儿投完了我们就能离开了呢。

1号：好吧。当然我们要知道，我们现在定的是一级谋杀罪。如果我们裁定被告 罪，他就将被执行死刑，无条件的。

4号：我们知道的。

5 orphanage *n.* 孤儿院

6 forgery *n.* 伪造，伪造的物品

)号:投吧,也好知道大家都是什么意见。

1号:有人要弃权吗?

7号:没有。

1号:好吧,只有全数投票通过才能通过,否则就要再投,法律就这样规定的。好吧,准备好了吗?认为有罪的,请举手……9、10、11。11个人认为有罪。无罪的呢?1人。好吧,有罪11人,无罪1人,情况就是这样了。

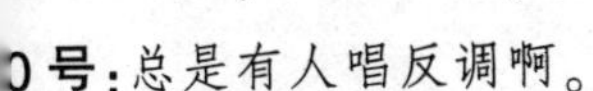

0号:总是有人唱反调啊。

7号:我们现在要做什么?

8号:讨论啊。

3号:嘿,伙计,你真的认为他无罪?

8号:我不知道。

3号:好吧,你也和我们一样坐在庭上的,你也听到他做了些什么吧。这个孩子是个危险的凶手。

8号:他只有18岁。

3号:那就够大的了。他刺死了他的父亲,匕首刺进胸膛有4英寸。他们在庭上用了很多种方法来证实了。你还要我们再给你一一列举吗?

8号:不用。

0号:那你想要怎样呢?

8号:我只想谈谈。

7号:我们要谈什么?11人认为有罪,除了你以外,大家意见都一致了。

0号:我能问问你,你相信他说的话吗?

8号:我不知道。或许不信吧。

7号:那你为什么会投无罪?

8号:已经有11个人投了有罪,我想在没讨论过之前,不能这么轻率地就将一个孩子送上刑台。

7号:谁说这轻率了?

8号:没人说。

7号:什么?就因为投票太快了吗?我确实是觉得被告有罪,就算你说到天黑也不会改变我的看法。

8号:我没想改变你的看法。只是因为我们现在是在讨论他人的生死问题。假设我们错了呢?谁能替他做主?

7号:假设我们错了,还假设这座大楼会倒塌呢,你能举出很多个假设来。

8号:没错。

7号:那我们呆在这儿有什么意义呢?还不如5分钟就解决呢。怎么样?

8号:咱们用1个小时来讨论吧。球赛8点钟才开始呢。

1号:还有谁有意见的?

9号:我得坐上1小时了。

10号:好吧,就当听故事了。

8号:那不是我们坐在这儿的目的。

10号:好,那你说,我们坐在这儿干什么?

8号:我也不知道,或许没有原因。听着,这个孩子的人生已经被毁掉了。他生于贫民窟,9岁时母亲去世,父亲又因造假而进了监狱,在孤儿院生活了1年半。这可不是个好的开始。说他是个愤怒的孩子,知道为什么吗?就是因为他每天都要挨打。他已经过了18年的悲惨生活了,我只是觉得我们欠他些什么。仅此而已。

10号:先生,你还是听我说吧。我们什么都不欠他的。他的审判很公平的,不是吗?难道你觉得审判不要花钱吗?他能受审就已经是幸事了。知道我是什么意思吗?听着,我们都是成年人,在庭上也都听了事实的陈述,对吧?用不着你来教我们去相信这个孩子,因为我们太清楚他是什么人了。听着,我一直和这样的人生活在一起。我太清楚不该相信他们所说的话了。知道吗?他们就是天生的骗子。

9号:只有无知的人才会相信那些。

经典对白(二)

A New Doubt 新的疑点

再次投票过后，赞成无罪的人又多了一些，此时细心的9号陪审员又发现了一个新的疑点……

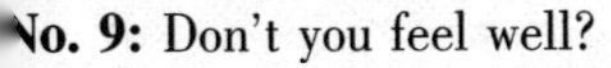

No. 9: Don't you feel well?

No. 4: I feel perfectly well, thank you. I was saying that 7:00 would be a reasonable time…

No. 9: The reason I asked about that was because you rubbed your nose like that. I'm sorry for interrupting. But you made a gesture that reminded me of something.

No. 4: I'm trying to settle something. Do you mind?

No. 9: But I think it is important. Thank you. Now then, I'm sure you'll pardon me for this, but I was wondering why you rubbed your nose like this?

No. 3: Oh, come on!

No. 9: I happen to be talking to the gentleman sitting next to you! Now, why were you rubbing your nose like that?

No. 4: If it's any of your business, I was rubbing it because it bothered me a little.

No. 9: I'm sorry. Is it because of your eyeglasses?

No. 4: It is. Now, can we get on to something else?

No. 9: Your eyeglasses made two deep impressions beside your nose. I haven't noticed it before. It must be very annoying.

No. 4: Very annoying.

Few things are more satisfying than seeing your children have teenagers of their own.

很少有比看见你的孩子们拥有自己的小伙伴更让你心满意足了。

No. 9: I wouldn't know about that. I've never worn glasses. Twenty-twenty vision.

No. 7: Will you come on already with the **optometrist**[7] bit?

No. 9: The woman who testified that she saw the killing had those same marks on th sides of her nose.

No. 5: Yes, right!

No. 9: Please just give me a minutes. Let me finish. I don't know if anyone els noticed that. I didn't think of it then, but I've been going over her face in m mind. She had those same marks. She kept rubbing them in court.

No. 5: He's right. She did do that a lot.

No. 9: This woman was about 45 years old. But she was making a tremendous effort t look 35 for her public appearance. Heavy makeup. **Dyed**[8] hair. Brand-ne clothes that should be worn by a younger woman. No glasses. Women do tha See if you can get the mental picture.

No. 3: What do you mean, no glasses? How do you know? Because she was rubbin her nose?

No. 5: She had those marks, I saw

No. 3: What do you think that means?

No. 6: I'm getting so sick of your yelling...

No. 5: Come on, forget it.

No. 1: Listen. He's right. I saw them too. I was the closest one to her. She had thes things on her nose. What do you call those?

No. 3: What point are you making? She had dyed hair and marks on her nose. Wha does that mean?

No. 9: Could these marks be made by anything other than eyeglasses?

No. 4: No, they couldn't.

No. 3: I didn't see any marks.

7 optometrist *n*. 验光师，配镜师

8 dye *v*. 染发

No. 4: I did. Strange I didn't think about it before.

No. 3: What about the lawyer? Why didn't he say something?

No. 8: There are 12 people in here. Eleven of us didn't think of it either.

No. 3: OK. She had marks on her nose, from glasses, right? She didn't want to wear them out of the house so people would think that she was gorgeous. But when she saw the kid kill his father, she was in the house, alone!

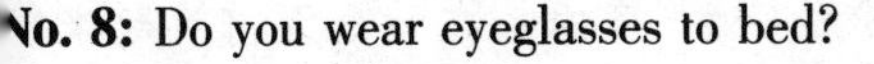

No. 8: Do you wear eyeglasses to bed?

No. 4: No, I don't. No one wears eyeglasses to bed.

No. 8: So, it's logical to assume that she wasn't wearing them when she was in bed, tossing and turning, trying to fall asleep.

The world is a book, and those who do not travel, read only a page.
世界是一本书，不出门旅行的人只读了书中的一页。

9号：你不舒服吗？

4号：没有，我很好，谢谢。我是说7点钟这个时间是可以的……

9号：我之所以这样问，是因为你像这样搓了搓鼻子。抱歉打断你，但是你的这个动作让我想起了一件事儿。

4号：如果您不介意的话，我想快点儿解决这个问题。

9号：我觉得这件事儿挺重要的。谢谢。冒昧地问一下，你为什么要这样搓鼻子吗？

3号：得了吧！

9号：我在跟坐在你隔壁的先生谈话呢。我能问为什么吗？

4号：如果您想知道的话，我这样搓是因为我觉得有点儿不舒服。

9号：抱歉，是因为戴眼镜的缘故吗？

4号：是的。现在我们能谈别的事儿了吗？

9号：你的眼镜在你的鼻翼两侧留下了印记，以前我还没注意到呢，这一定很烦吧。

4号：是的，很烦。

9号:我是不会了解了,我从没戴过眼镜,我两眼的视力都是2.0。

7号:能不能别总说验光师才会关心的事儿?

9号:那个作证说她看到了凶杀过程的女人,鼻翼两侧也有这样的印记。

5号:是啊,她有!

9号:请安静,让我说完。我不知道其他人是不是注意到了,我那会儿还没注意到,但是我不断地回想她的样子,她的确也有同样的印记。在法庭上她也不停地搓鼻子。

5号:他说得对,她的确总是搓鼻子。

9号:这个女人有45岁左右,但她却精心打扮了一番,目的是在公众面前看起来能像35岁那样年轻。她浓妆艳抹,染发,穿着新衣服,打扮得很年轻。但她没戴眼镜。女人都会这么做的。在头脑中想想看吧。

3号:你说不戴眼镜是什么意思?你怎么知道的?因为她搓鼻子?

5号:我看到她鼻翼两侧的印记了。

3号:你觉得那是什么意思?

6号:我实在受不了你大喊大叫了……

5号:算了,算了。

1号:听着,他是对的。我也看见了。我坐的位置离她很近,她的鼻子上的确有这样的印记,这个应该叫……

3号:你想表达什么?她染了发,鼻子上有个印,这能说明什么?

9号:除了戴眼镜以外,还有什么能留下这样的印记吗?

4号:没有了。

3号:我可没看到印记。

4号:我看到了。奇怪,我以前怎么没想到?

3号:律师呢?律师怎么不说这个呢?

8号:我们有12个人坐在这儿,11个人都没想到呢。

3号:好吧,她鼻子上有印记,眼镜压的,对吧?她在公众面前没有戴眼镜,好给别人留下一个好印象。不过她目睹凶案的时候,她可是一个人在家的!

8号:你会戴着眼镜睡觉吗?

4号：当然不会。没人会戴眼镜睡的。

8号：那么我们可以推断，她也不会戴眼镜躺在床上翻来覆去地想睡觉了。

Beautiful Sentences 妙语佳句

1. One man is dead. Another man's life is at stake. If there's a reasonable doubt as to the guilt of the accused a reasonable doubt, then you must bring me a verdict of not guilty.
在本案中已有一人身亡。另一个人的生死则掌握在你们手中。如果你们能提出合理的疑点，无法确定被告有罪，基于这个合理的疑点，你们必须做出无罪的判决。

2. I kept putting myself in the kid's place. I'd have asked for another lawyer. I mean, if I was on trial for my life, I'd want my lawyer to tear their witnesses to shreds, or try to.
我一直让自己站在那个孩子的立场上，或许我会再请个律师来的。我是说，如果这次审判关乎我的生死，我会希望我的律师竭尽所能地去反驳目击者的证词，至少他该试试看。

3. A guy talks like that to an old man ought to get stepped on. You ought to have more respect, mister. You say stuff like that to him again, I'm gonna lay you out.
那样子跟老人说话应该要受到谴责的。你得学着去尊敬别人，先生。你敢再那样子跟他说话，我一定会要你好看。

4. That we are notified by mail to come down to this place to decide on the guilt or innocence of a man we have never heard of before. We have nothing to gain or lose by our verdict. This is one of the reasons why we are strong. We should not make it a personal thing.

An optimist sees an opportunity in every calamity; a pessimist sees a calamity in every opportunity.
乐观者于一个灾难中看到一个希望，悲观者于一个希望中看到一个灾难。

我们收到信件通知来到这里，是为了裁定一个跟我们素昧谋面的人是否有罪不论做出什么样的裁决,都与我们个人的得失无关。这也说明了我们的国家是优于其他国家的。所以我们不应该把它看作是个人的事儿。

5. It's always difficult to keep personal prejudice out of a thing like this. Whenever you run into it, it always obscures the truth. I don't really know what the truth is. I don't suppose anybody will ever really know. Now nine of us feel that the defendant is innocent. We are just gambling on probabilities. We may be wrong. We may be trying to let a guilty man go free. I don't know. Nobody really can. But we have a reasonable doubt. That's something very valuable in our system. No jury can declare a man guilty unless it's sure. We nine can't understand why you three are still so sure. Maybe you can tell us.

要摆脱个人偏见去看待某事真的是很难。无论何时碰到件事儿,偏见总会遮掩真相。我也不知道真相是什么。我想也没谁会知道。不过我们之中有9个人都认为被告无罪,我们就是在赌,在赌这个可能性。我们可能是错的,我们现在可能正在帮一个杀人犯逃之夭夭。我也不知道。也没谁知道。但是我们有合理的疑点,这就是司法制度优势的体现。除非证据确凿,否则没有哪个法官能宣判某人有罪。我们9个人想知道为什么你们3个会这么确定他有罪呢？说说吧。

Thought about Life 人生感悟

我们在评判或认定某事时,往往会受主观偏见的影响,而做出错误的决断。就像影片中这12名陪审团成员一样,对被告存有偏见,所以在做出裁决时,就会被偏见所愚弄,对事实真相视而不见了。很欣赏8号陪审员的冷静与睿智,正是他的冷静思考挽救了被告的性命,维护了法律的公正。冷静思考的确是决断之时最有力的帮手。

二十五、改变过去
——《蝴蝶效应 I》

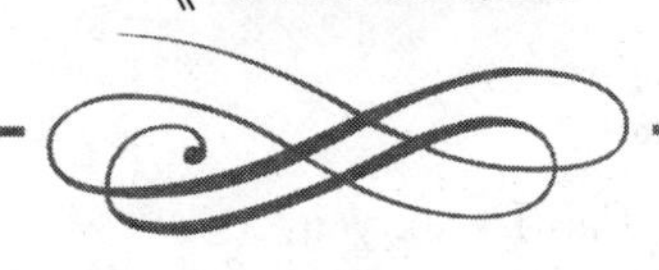

影片简介：

“蝴蝶效应”是指事物的结果会受到最初条件的影响，而变得千差万别。主人公埃文从小便患有“间歇性失忆症”，他的行为举止显得很怪异，于是心理医生建议他用记日记的方法来治疗他的疾病。虽然埃文有着灰暗的童年，但是他却并不记得多少。后来，埃文考上了大学。一天，他拿出了以前的日记本翻看，还渐渐回忆起了童年所发生的不堪回首的经历。最不可思议的是，他发现在他阅读日记的过程中，自己能够回到过去。于是埃文为了改变自己以及好友的生活现状，决定改变过去……

经典对白(一)

Reencounter 重逢

埃文在读了日记后，又隐约记起了小时候发生的某些事情，为了证实这些事情是真实存在的，埃文找到了小时候的玩伴凯莉……

Evan: Hi!

Kayleigh: Evan? Oh, my God, it's been a long time. How've you been?

Evan: Same old same old, you know.

Kayleigh: No, I don't know. Fill me in.

Evan: Well, I'm going to State now. It's going good. My mom's good.

Kayleigh: Want a smoke?

Evan: No. Not since we were kids.

Kayleigh: I've quit, like, a hundred times.

Evan: Are you walking home, or...? Can I walk you?

Kayleigh: Sure. My God.

Evan: So...how's Tommy?

Kayleigh: Well, they kept him in **juvy**[1] for a few years. Now he's working over at Dale's Auto Body.

Evan: That's good. Still living with your dad?

Kayleigh: No. I **emancipated**[2] myself at 15.

Evan: Must've taken a lot of courage.

Kayleigh: Not if you remember my dad.

Evan: Why can't you just have moved in with your mom?

Kayleigh: Nah, she had a new family. Wasn't enough room. Whatever.

Evan: Well, look, the reason I came back to town was to talk to you.

Kayleigh: To me? Why?

Evan: Well...remember when we were kids and I used to have those **blackouts**[3]?

Kayleigh: Yeah, of course.

Evan: Well, some of those memories have been coming back to me. And I jus

1 juvy *n.* 少管所

2 emancipate *v.* 解放

3 blackout *n.* 一时的眩晕 (这里是说埃文眩晕后，不记得一些事情)

wanted to talk to you about one of them in particular.

Kayleigh: Well, I'll try to remember.

Evan: When we were kids, your dad was making a movie about Robin Hood or something.

Kayleigh: What do you want to know, Evan?

Evan: Did he...? What happened in the basement?

Kayleigh: Look, it was a long time ago.

Evan: I know.

Kayleigh: Is that why you came all the way back here? To ask a lot of stupid questions about Robin Hood?

Evan: No. I just think that something really bad might've happened.

Kayleigh: Is there a point to any of this?

Evan: Whatever happened, it wasn't our fault. We were kids. There was nothing that we could do to deserve...

Kayleigh: Just shut up, Evan! You're wasting your breath.

Evan: You can't hate yourself because your dad's a **twisted**[4] **freak**[5].

Kayleigh: Who are you trying to convince, Evan? You come all the way back to stir up my shit because you have a bad memory? What do you want me to do? Just cry on your shoulder and tell you everything's all better now? Fuck you, Evan. Nothing's all better, okay? Nothing ever gets better. You know, if I was so wonderful, Evan, why didn't you call me? Why did you leave me here to rot?

We have no right to consume happiness without producing it than to consume wealth without producing it.

我们如果不能创造快乐，我们便没有权利去享受快乐，正如我们如果不能创造财富，便没有权利去享用财富一样。

4 twisted *adj*. 扭曲的

5 freak *n*. 怪胎，怪物

埃文:嘿!

凯莉:埃文?我的天啊,好久不见了!你好吗?

埃文:还是老样子,你知道的。

凯莉:不,我不知道。说给我听听?

埃文:嗯,我现在在读州立大学。一切都不错,我妈妈也很好。

凯莉:抽烟吗?

埃文:不了,我们还是小孩子的时候,我就已经不抽了。

凯莉:我好像已经戒了上百次了。

埃文:你走回去吗,还是……?我能送你一程吗?

凯莉:当然。真难以相信。

埃文:呃……汤米还好吗?

凯莉:他在劳教所里关了几年,现在他在一家车行工作呢。

埃文:那还不错。还跟你爸爸一起住呢?

凯莉:没有,我十五岁就离开家了。

埃文:这需要很多勇气。

凯莉:换作是你,也会离开的。

埃文:那你为什么不搬去与你妈妈同住呢?

凯莉:不,她再婚了,地方不够。算了吧。

埃文:呃,我这次回到小镇上就是想与你谈一谈。

凯莉:与我谈?为什么?

埃文:你还记得小时候,我偶尔会不记得一些事情吗?

凯莉:是的,当然。

埃文:现在,我正在回忆起那些事情,其中有些事情我想和你谈谈。

凯莉:我会试着想想的。

埃文:我们小时候,你爸爸在拍电影,好像是关于罗宾汉什么的。

凯莉:你想知道什么?埃文。

埃文:他,是不是……?到底发生什么了?

凯莉:听着,那是很久以前的事了。

埃文:我知道。

凯莉:这就是你大老远跑回来的原因?问一些关于罗宾汉的愚蠢问题?

埃文:不,我只是觉得可能发生了一些非常糟糕的事情。

凯莉:有什么关系吗?

埃文:不管发生了什么事情,都不是我们的错。我们只是孩子,我们也无需为所做过的事情背负什么。

凯莉:闭嘴,埃文!你只是在浪费唇舌。

埃文:你不能因为你父亲的扭曲变态而怨恨你自己。

凯莉:你想说服谁呢?埃文?你大老远跑回来,扰乱我的生活,就是因为你没能记住那些事情?你想要我怎样呢?靠在你的肩上哭泣,然后对你说现在一切都很好?见你的鬼去吧,埃文。所有的事都不会好,你满意了吗?所有的事情永远都不会好。要知道,如果我真的那么完美,埃文,你为什么不打电话给我?为什么把我丢在这里,让我自生自灭?

Hearts are not had as a gift but hearts are earned.
人心只能赢得,不能靠别人馈赠。

经典对白(二)

A Bad Ending 糟糕的结局

埃文再次回到了过去,他又一次地改变了过去,但是这次凯莉却变成了一个妓女……

Kayleigh: Oh, I thought you were someone else. Make it fast, I'm expecting someone.

Evan: It's good to see you. Can I come in?

Kayleigh: If I knew you were coming, I would have cleaned the sheets. What do you want?

Evan: Just to see a friendly face.

Kayleigh: Time is money, Evan.

Evan: Money.

Kayleigh: Guess I can spare 10 minutes for an old friend, right? So how's tricks? Sorry. **Occupational**[6] humor.

Evan: I got it. You can stop now.

Kayleigh: Sorry. Does my line of work make you uncomfortable, precious?

Evan: No. Just that you felt like you had to use it to hurt me. I've been where you've been.

Kayleigh: Where is that?

Evan: You wouldn't believe if I told you. I know people always say that, in this case it's not even worth trying. I knew I needed to find you. So I went over to your dad's and made him tell me where you were. Then I came here, the rest you know.

Kayleigh: You're right. I don't believe you.

Evan: I never thought you would. That's why I never told a soul until now and I never will again.

Kayleigh: I'm the only person you've told? That's a great line. Does that make other girls wet? Do they actually eat up that bullshit?

Evan: You know, I could give a shit whether you believe me or not. Frankly, I'm too tired to prove it to you.

Kayleigh: Oh, there's proof now, huh?

Evan: How else would I know that you have twin **moles**[7] on your inner **thigh**[8]?

Kayleigh: Anyone with $50 bucks could tell you that.

6 occupational *adj.* 职业的，与职业相关的

7 mole *n.* 痣

8 thigh *n.* 大腿

Evan: Okay. Forget that. How about the fact that you prefer the smell of **skunk**[9] to flowers? Or that you hate **cilantro**[10]? For some reason unknown to you, it reminds you of your stepsister. Or that when you have an **orgasm**[11] your toes go numb? I'm sure all your **clientele**[12] know that. Look, I just thought you should know.

Kayleigh: Know what?

Evan: That you were happy once. With me.

Kayleigh: You know, there's one major hole in your story. There's no way on this planet I'd ever be in a fucking **sorority**[13]!

Evan: You were happy then.

Kayleigh: You crying? Sure you don't want your wallet?

Evan: No. I don't need it where I'm going.

Kayleigh: Are you off to change everyone else's life again? Maybe next you'll pop up in a mansion while I end up in Tijuana doing a donkey act.

Evan: You know what? I'm over it. Every time I try to help someone, everything just goes to shit.

Kayleigh: Well, don't give up now, slick. You've already done so much for me! Why don't you go back in time and save Mrs. Halpern and her baby? And then maybe Lenny wouldn't freak out and ruin my family! No! Go back to when I was 7 and fuck me in front of my daddy's video camera. Straighten me out a bit.

In the mountain of truth you never climb in vain.
在真理的高山上，你永远不会徒然攀登。

9 skunk *n.* 黄色狼

10 cilantro *n.* 香菜

11 orgasm *n.* 性爱高潮

12 clientele *n.* 客户，常客

13 sorority *n.* 女生联谊会

凯莉：噢，还以为是别人呢！快说吧，我在等人。

埃文：嘿，见到你真好。能进来吗？

凯莉：早知道你要来的话，我就该铺下床单的。你有何贵干啊？

埃文：就是想来看看你。

凯莉：我会计时收费的，埃文。

埃文：钱在这儿。

凯莉：我想我能和老朋友共度十分钟的，是吧？你的活怎么样？抱歉，职业幽默。

埃文：我明白。你别干了。

凯莉：噢，对不起。是不是我的职业让你觉得不舒服了，宝贝儿？

埃文：不是。除非你想拿这个来伤害我。我去了你过去呆过的地方。

凯莉：哈？哪儿啊？

埃文：就算我告诉你，你也不会信的。人们不是常说，有些事情根本不值得一试。我必须要找到你，所以我去了你父亲那儿，向他问了你的住处，然后我就找到这儿了。

凯莉：你说对了，我不相信你。

埃文：我从没指望你会相信。正因为这样，我从没和其他人提过，而且也不会再提了。

凯莉：你只告诉过我一个人？我是不是该感到庆幸？听过这些她们是不是都哭了？还是根本就没理会过这些废话？

埃文：知道吗？不管你信不信，我都可以说这些废话。老实说，我真的很累，懒得去证明这一切了。

凯莉：哦，你还能证明啊？

埃文：那你说我是怎么知道你大腿根部有两颗痣呢？

凯莉：谁给我 50 元钱，我就告诉谁。

埃文：好吧。不提这个。这个怎么样？比起花香，你更喜欢黄鼠狼的臭味？还有你讨厌香菜，因为它会让你莫名地想起你同父异母的姐妹。还有当你高潮时，你的脚趾会发麻。我想你所有的顾客应该都知道的吧。听着，我只是觉得这些事儿你应该知道。

凯莉:知道什么?

埃文:你和我曾幸福地生活在一起。

凯莉:知道吗?你的故事里有个严重的漏洞。在这个星球上,根本就没有可以改变过去的方法。

埃文:你那时真的很幸福。

凯莉:噢,你哭了。你确定你真的不要钱包了吗?

埃文:是的,我不需要带着它。

凯莉:你又要去改变他人的生活是吗?或许下次你会住进高级公馆,而我会在提华纳扮驴呢。

埃文:知道吗,我已经厌倦了。每次我想帮助别人的时候,事情总会变得更糟。

凯莉:别放弃啊,小机灵鬼儿。你都为我做这么多了!你为什么不赶回去救哈尔波恩夫人和她的孩子呢?那样的话,或许兰尼也不会发狂而毁了我的家!不!回到我7岁那年吧,在我爸爸的摄影机前跟我做爱吧。让我的生活走上正规吧!

He most lives who thinks most, feels the noblest and acts the best.

思想深刻,感情高尚,行为优良者乃是能过最佳生活之人。

Beautiful Sentences 妙语佳句

1. "If anyone finds this, it means that my plan didn't work and I'm already dead. But, if I can somehow go back to the beginning of all of this, I might be able to save her."
   "如果有人找到这个的话,那就意味着我的计划并没起作用,而我也早已经死了。如果我能以某种方式回到最初的那一刻,或许我能够挽救她。"
2. If the scar on my stomach didn't just come out of nowhere, maybe my father wasn't as crazy as everyone thought. If I can make scars, do I have the power to heal them?

如果我腹部的伤疤不是凭空出现的，或许我的父亲并不像大家所说的那样疯狂。我若是能制造伤疤，那我是否能治愈它呢？

3. There is no "right"! You can't change who people are without destroying who they were.

根本就没有什么"正确"可言！你不可能改变别人的同时而又不去破坏他们。

Thought about Life 人生感悟

如果我有一种超能力的话，我绝不会选择去改变过去的。在我看来，改变过去真的是个很疯狂的想法，甚至是种可怕的想法。正如埃文的父亲所说，你不可能在不改变他人生活的情形下去改变过去，因为改变了其中一个条件，结果就会有相当大的差别。生活就是复杂在这里，因为人们都是相互联系的。所以在改变过去时，改变的不是某一个人的过去，而是一群人的过去。恐怕没人能承担这么大的风险吧。

二十六、沉重的负担
——《赎罪》

影片简介：

一日，13岁的布里奥妮·泰丽思无意间看到了管家的儿子罗比正和姐姐塞西莉亚亲热着。年幼无知的她误以为罗比要欺负姐姐，可事实上，罗比和塞西莉亚却是一对热恋的情侣。由于布里奥妮对罗比的误解，使得罗比蒙冤入狱。在战乱时期，罗比和塞西莉亚也相继死去，这对有情人因为种种原因，最终也没能在一起。多年后，布里奥妮一直无法释怀当年犯下的错误，于是她将姐姐和罗比的故事写成了一本书……

经典对白(一)

● A Talk Between Sisters 姐妹谈话

13岁的布里奥妮刚刚完成她的剧本，在公演之前，她和姐姐塞西莉娅在草地上聊天……

Briony: Cee.

Cecilia: Yes?

Briony: What do you think it would feel like to be someone else?

Cecilia: Cooler, I should hope.

Briony: I'm worried about the play.

Cecilia: I'm sure it's a **masterpiece**[1].

Briony: But we only have the afternoon to **rehearse**[2]. What if the twins can't act?

Cecilia: You have to be nice to them. I wonder how'd you feel if your mother had run off with Mr. What's-his-name who reads the news on the wireless?

Briony: Perhaps I should have written Leon a story. If you write a story, you only have to say the word "castle", and you could see the towers and the woods and the village below, but...in a play, it's...it all depends on other people. Cee?

Cecilia: Yes?

Briony: Why don't you talk to Robbie any more?

Cecilia: I do. We just move in different circles, that's all.

布里奥妮: 西。

塞西莉亚: 怎么了?

布里奥妮: 如果你变成了另一个人,你觉得那会是什么样的?

塞西莉亚: 我想会变得更酷吧。

布里奥妮: 我挺担心那部剧的。

塞西莉亚: 我确信它会是部杰作的。

布里奥妮: 可我们只有一个下午的排练时间,要是那对双胞胎不会演该怎么办呢?

塞西莉亚: 你得对他们好点儿。你想想如果你妈妈跟个只会从无线电上收听新闻的某某先生私奔了,你会怎么想?

布里奥妮: 或许我应该给里昂写个故事。在故事里,只需说"城堡"这个词,你就能想

1 masterpiece *n.* 杰作

2 rehearse *v.* 彩排, 排演

象出高塔、树林，还有下面的村庄，但在话剧本中，这一切都要靠人来表现。西？

塞西莉亚：又怎么了？

布里奥妮：你为什么不跟罗比说话了？

塞西莉亚：我们说啊，只是我们所处的圈子不同，仅此而已。

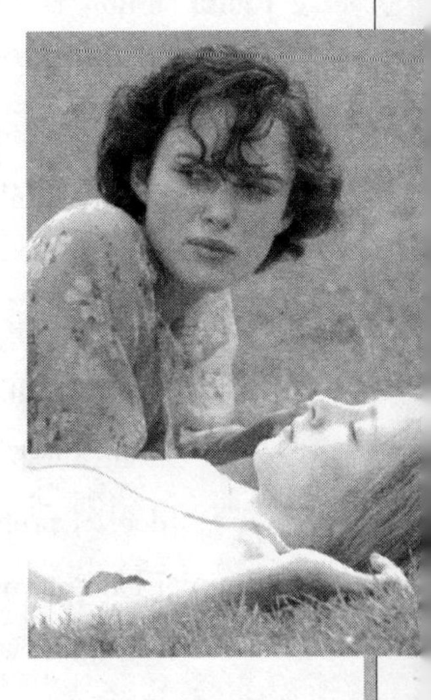

For many, life's longest mile is the stretch from dependence to independence.

对于大都数人来说，生命中最长的一英里是从依赖他人到独立自主的那一段。

经典对白(二)

The New Book 新书

布里奥妮长大后，当了一名护士，但同时她也一直在写书。一晚，她的一个朋友发现了这个秘密……

Fiona: Don't panic! It's only me.

Briony: Fiona, I almost jumped out of my skin.

Fiona: So this is where you duck to after lights out. I thought you might be in the middle of some **tempestuous**[3] romance. Don't you freeze to death up here?

Briony: I love London.

Fiona: Do you think all of this will be bombed and just disappear?

Briony: No. I don't know.

Fiona: Do you write about Sister Drummond? Do you write about me?

Briony: Sometimes.

Fiona: Can I look?

Briony: I'd rather you didn't. It's private.

3 tempestuous *adj*. 狂暴的

Fiona: I don't see any point in writing a story if you're not going to let anyone read it.

Briony: It's not ready yet. It's unfinished.

Fiona: What's it about?

Briony: It's complicated.

Fiona: Yes?

Briony: It's just...It's about a young girl, a young and foolish girl, who sees something from her bedroom window which she doesn't understand, but she thinks she does. I probably won't ever finish it.

Fiona: I look at you, Tallis, and you're so mysterious. I've never been mysterious. Do you know what I decided tonight?

Briony: What?

Fiona: I could never marry a man who wasn't in the Royal Navy.

费 欧 娜: 别慌！是我。

布里奥妮: 费欧娜,你吓死我了。

费 欧 娜: 原来熄灯后你就窝在这儿啊。我还以为你在寻欢作乐呢。在这儿你不怕被冻死吗?

布里奥妮: 我喜欢伦敦。

费 欧 娜: 你不觉得炸弹会将这儿夷为平地吗?

布里奥妮: 不,我不知道。

费 欧 娜: 你在写德鲁蒙德护士长的故事吗?你有写到我吗?

布里奥妮: 有时会写。

费 欧 娜: 我能看看吗?

布里奥妮: 最好不要,这是隐私。

费 欧 娜: 要是你不让别人看,那你写它就没什么意义了。

布里奥妮: 还没到时候呢,我还没写完。

费 欧 娜: 是讲什么的?

布里奥妮: 很复杂的。

费 欧 娜：是吗？

布里奥妮：就是……是关于一个年轻无知的女孩，她从房间的窗子那儿看到了一件她并不理解但却自以为很了解的事。我大概永远都写不完它。

费 欧 娜：在我看来，泰丽思，你是如此的神秘，而我却一点儿都不神秘。你知道我今晚做了什么决定吗？

布里奥妮：什么决定？

费 欧 娜：没当过皇家海军的人，我就不嫁。

We only live once, but if we work it right once is enough.

我们的生命只有一次，但我们如能正确地运用它。一次已足矣。

Beautiful Sentences 妙语佳句

1. I have to get back. I promised her to put things right. And she loves me. She's waiting for me.

   我必须得回去。我答应她了，要去澄清一切。她爱我，她在等我。

2. I'm dying. My doctor tells me I have something called vascular dementia, which is essentially a continuous series of tiny strokes. Your brain closes down, gradually you lose words, you lose your memory, which for a writer is pretty much the point. So that's why I could finally write the book, I think. I had to. And why, of course, it's my last novel. Strangely enough, it would be just as accurate to call it my first novel.

   我要死了。医生告诉我，我患了血管性失智症，就是一连串的轻微中风。脑部停止运作，逐渐丧失语言能力和记忆力，这些对于作家来说都是极为重要的。我想这是我终于能完成这本书的原因，因为我必须写完，所以这将是我最后一本书。不过奇怪的是，它也可以说是我的第一本小说。

Thought about Life 人生感悟

这是一部让人难以忘怀的悲剧。年幼的布里奥妮亲手葬送了姐姐的幸福，当她得知时已经追悔莫及了。所以她用她的一生来赎罪，并在书中为姐姐和罗比安排了幸福的结局。但那终究不是事实，最终布里奥妮还是无法逃脱自己的罪责。人们总会去设法弥补自己所犯下的过错，然而赎罪最终仍只是一种自我安慰，我们永远都无法弥补自己曾犯下的过错。